PROPHECY'S DAUGHTER

ALSO BY RICHARD PHILLIPS

The Endarian Prophecy

Mark of Fire
Prophecy's Daughter
Curse of the Chosen (forthcoming)

The Rho Agenda

The Second Ship
Immune
Wormhole

The Rho Agenda Inception

Once Dead
Dead Wrong
Dead Shift

The Rho Agenda Assimilation

The Kasari Nexus
The Altreian Enigma
The Meridian Ascent

PROPHECY'S DAUGHTER

THE ENDARIAN PROPHECY

RICHARD PHILLIPS

This is a work of fiction. Names, characters, organizations, places, events, and incidents are either products of the author's imagination or are used fictitiously. Any resemblance to actual persons, living or dead, or actual events is purely coincidental.

Published by 47North, Seattle

www.apub.com

ISBN-13: 9781542047234
ISBN-10: 1542047234

Cover design by Shasti O'Leary Soudant

Printed in the United States of America

I dedicate this novel to my wife and lifelong best friend, Carol.

Endarian Continent
Brinje Ocean
KINGDOM OF ENDAR
Lika River
Northeastern Plains
Erzen River
Endar Pass
Gauga River
Northern Plains
Lagoth
Banjee River
GLACIER MOUNTAINS
Mo'Lier
Val'Dep
Coastal Range
Endless Valley
Areana's Vale
MOGEV DESERT
Borderland Range
Rork
Sul River
Hannington
Rafel's Keep
Far Castle
Rake River
KINGDOM OF TAL
Coldain's Keep
N

PART I

The daughter of Endarian queen and human lord shall seek out the wielder of last hope.

And Death shall ride alongside her.

—From the *Scroll of Landrel*

1

Hannington Castle
Year of Record (YOR) 413, Late Winter

Blalock was gone. In his place stood Kragan, clothed in the mighty flesh of Kaleal. Young King Gilbert had needed weeks to adjust to the transformation from the horribly scarred Blalock into this seven-foot-tall body with the bronze skin, golden eyes, slitted pupils, and fanged mouth of the strangely seductive primordial. In truth, Gilbert still quailed in terror at the sight of Kragan. But of all who dwelled within Hannington Castle, only the king was allowed by Kragan to see his true form. All others still beheld the magic wielder with the left side of his face melted off, a mind trick hardly worthy of being called a spell.

Now King Gilbert stood atop Hannington Castle's battlements at Kragan's side, staring in horror at the army of vorgs and brigands that rampaged through the city beyond.

When Gilbert spoke, Kragan heard a tremor in his voice.

"The vorgs have their siege engines ready. Why have they not yet attacked my castle? Do they not know how few soldiers we have within?"

"They are waiting for me to act."

King Gilbert turned to look up at Kragan, his face a mask of wonder and hope. "Do they fear you that much? Will it be enough to turn away this horde?"

Kragan felt his lips curl to reveal the large canines within his mouth. "Turn away?" Kragan said, feeling the anticipation that arose within the mind of the primordial whose body he shared. "Now why, my king, would I want to do that, when they have marched all the way from Lagoth in answer to my summons?"

For several seconds, confusion clouded the pale eyes of the nineteen-year-old monarch until a spreading panic wiped the look from his face. Turning back toward the battlements, Kragan leapt atop the nearest parapet, reaching downward toward the castle's barred gate, and spoke the name of an earth elemental he favored, grabbing control of it with his mind. "Dalg."

With a rumble, the ground beneath the fortifications that supported the heavy gateway acquired the consistency of quicksand. A shudder ran along the wall as a section of the battlements collapsed upon itself, crushing soldiers and sending forth a great plume of flying dirt and debris. As if on command, Kragan's army surged across the detritus into Hannington Castle's stunned defenders.

When Kragan turned back toward the king, he saw that Gilbert had fled. That was just fine. Soon there would be no place for Tal's ruler to hide.

Kragan strode through the smoldering castle's ruins and up the steps leading to the top of the breached outer wall, pausing there to gaze out over the inferno below Hannington Castle. Smoke rose from fires that raged through Hannington, whipping the superheated air over the wall in a whirling tussle with the cold of the fading winter. Faint screams mingled with the moan of the wind and the yells of the vorgs and brigands who rampaged through the city.

"If I may interrupt, my lord?"

The she-vorg commander's voice brought Kragan to attention.

"Yes, Charna?"

"We found King Gilbert. He was hiding in a closet beneath the stairs as the palace burned around him. He awaits your arrival."

"Good."

Kragan glanced out over the city once more. "He hasn't got much of a kingdom anymore, has he?"

"We still have the estates of his lordlings to deal with," she said, "and their holds are scattered across the kingdom."

Kragan accompanied Charna down the stairs to where two vorgs held the terrified monarch. Seeing his royal blue tunic torn and blackened, tears tracing sooty trails down his face, Kragan thought Gilbert more closely resembled a chimney sweep than a king.

"Spare my life, and I'll grant you anything."

Kragan snorted in disgust. "Witless fool. Look around you. Everything you had, I've already taken."

He reached out and placed a hand on the king's pale face. "Still, I suppose I owe you some favor. Had it not been for your foolishness in agreeing to send the bulk of your army in pursuit of one rebel lord, victory would have been more troublesome."

Relief washed Gilbert's face as he breathed out a sigh of relief. "Thank you. I will not forget this."

"I'm sure you won't," Kragan said.

As he turned to walk away, he signaled to the she-vorg commander. "Charna, King Gilbert is yours to do with as you will."

Charna's snarls mingled with Gilbert's screams. Both sounds were cut off as Kragan once again called on Dalg, stepping through the solid rock of the palace wall.

2

Endless Valley
YOR 414, Early Spring

At five-foot-eight, with her long brown hair swirling around her suntanned face, Carol sat atop her horse and gazed out through her brown eyes over the rolling hills to the east, which climbed toward the mountains the caravan had left behind. She stood in her stirrups to stretch her slender body, thankful for the warmth her buckskin pants, wool shirt, and riding boots provided. She was happy for the arrival of the spring equinox and, with it, the start of a new year. The year that had just ended had filled her with heartache. This being the season of her birth in year of record 390, it held special meaning for her.

The early-morning breeze that swept down from the mountains was cool, but not the cold, biting breeze that had been a hallmark of the high mountain pass to the east, where High Lord Rafel and his legion had been forced to stop for the winter. She breathed in deeply. Her sensitive nose detected the faint twang of evergreen trees, a smell she had grown to love. The crunching of wagon wheels on rocky ground and the snorts of horses mingled with the yells of drivers and the crack of whips.

Carol was happy to be leaving their winter camp at Mud Flats and the high pass that had left her with such bitter memories. In the months since Hawthorne had died, she had tried to throw off her depression and get on with her life, but there seemed to be holes in her very being. And she no longer had access to her magic.

She realized that the physical scar inflicted when the fire elemental Jaa'dra had branded her left shoulder was the least of the damage done to her. The battle between herself and the combined wills of Blalock and Jaa'dra had inflicted far deeper mental wounds. Hawthorne had said that an elemental only placed its personal mark on a wielder at the moment of possession. As far as her mentor had known, only she alone had ever been branded thus and yet retained control of her mind. Nonetheless, the mental trauma had taken its toll.

She felt as if she were a soldier who, upon returning from the battlefield, suffered the lingering side effects of war. The memory of the event invaded her dreams and her attempts at deep meditation; it was something she had not yet been able to drive from her head.

Her brother Alan had tried to rejuvenate her spirits, but even his devilish grin and sharp wit provided only temporary relief. Worse, she knew what she needed to do to work through the problem, but could not force herself to act.

Carol felt that if she could bring herself to face her fears and break through the mental barrier that blocked her from her magical studies, she could set about achieving the potential that Hawthorne had worked so hard to bring to fruition. He had said that her true talent lay in her strength of will and ability to channel the psychic power necessary to control the most powerful of elementals, as evidenced by her encounter with the Lord of the Third Deep. She had contested with Kaleal and emerged from the Ritual of Terrors victorious. Yet despite this knowledge, she could not take the desired action. No amount of cursing and self-criticism helped.

She looked back down the long line of wagons that stretched behind her to the south. A week ago, the caravan had entered a wide valley and turned north to follow the trail. The length of the wagon train as seen from her current vantage point caused Carol to catch her breath. Of the hundreds of wagons that had started the journey, they had only lost thirty-two, the result of accidents along the way. The most serious had been an avalanche that had destroyed eight wagons. Counting Hawthorne, of the four-thousand-plus people who had started this journey, they had lost 223 along the way, including their only surgeon. Sixteen of these had perished from illness as the caravan wintered in Mud Flats.

A flood of memories assailed her.

Tal's paranoid young king, Gilbert, had feared her father's popularity among the kingdom's people and ordered Rafel's assassination. Learning of this and knowing that even if the assassin failed, the king would gather an army capable of defeating his legion, her father had marched his soldiers, along with civilians who volunteered to accompany them, out of Tal. Their flight had taken them across the Borderland Range through the Mogev Desert and into the Glacier Mountains, where the might of the winter had trapped them. Along the way, she had received word of the death of the man she loved, Arn Tomas Ericson, who had come to be known as Blade.

Carol had worked through her depression and sorrow by immersing herself in her magical training. She had enjoyed such success that Hawthorne had been surprised and impressed with her ability to command multiple elementals simultaneously. But a winter storm called forth by Blalock had claimed Hawthorne's life, leaving her with one more hole in her heart.

Her thoughts shifted to the only home she had ever known. Once again she stood at her window in her father's castle, looking out over the scenic town below Rafel's Keep. Carol wondered what had become of the town the fortress had protected. She hoped that those who had chosen to remain behind had managed to survive. A sudden urge to reach out with her mind to see her old home swept over her, followed immediately by a wave of fear that left her shaking.

"Are you all right?" Alan's voice caused her to glance around.

Carol jumped. "Gods! You startled me."

"You look a little pale," Alan said as he pulled his chestnut warhorse up beside her dapple-gray mare. "You sure you're okay?"

"I'm fine. I was just wondering how those we left behind are faring."

"They made their choice. Anyway, I rode over to tell you that the rangers have found a location that they think would be ideal to make our new home. Derek and Jaradin rode in raving about a hidden valley they found a week's ride northeast of here. Derek swears it's the loveliest spot he's ever seen."

"Gods! What did Father say?"

"That's what I came to tell you. I talked him into sending an advance party to the valley to verify it suits our needs. Father won't leave the wagons, and he doesn't trust my judgment. That's why I proposed you go along."

Carol almost yelled for joy. Finally something she could do to contribute. "Who's going with us?"

"Derek Scot is leading five rangers, and we'll have a platoon of thirty soldiers. And Derek's bear, of course."

"Nothing new about that. He takes the little fellow everywhere he goes," Carol said.

"Little? That thing's as big as a horse. I've never seen anything grow so quickly. Derek swears it can follow a trail better than any dog. And I thought bears hibernated through the winter."

"Not if they're getting the kind of stimulation that Lonesome is getting," said Carol.

"Guess which platoon is going."

"No idea."

"Gaar is sending Hanibal's unit to escort us."

"Sounds like Father and Gaar are betting that we'll like what we see," Carol said. "For Gaar to be sending the platoon his son commands sure says something."

Alan scowled. "Yeah. It says he doesn't trust either one of us."

"Can't you let go of your rivalry with Captain Hanibal and just accept the good in this?"

"I'm not the one with the problem," said Alan.

Carol knew that was not the whole truth even if Alan believed it. Since he had been sixteen, Alan had beaten Hanibal in contests of physical prowess even though the battle master's son was four years Alan's senior. But Alan resented that Hanibal had risen through the ranks to a position of leadership that High Lord Rafel denied his only son.

Alan trained and worked with an unmatched ferocity that had given him his imposing form and the coordination to match. Unfortunately, his wildness in battle worked against him getting a significant leadership role, an area where the more strategic Hanibal excelled.

Carol knew that Rafel was disappointed in Alan, hating to admit this reality to herself. And every time Alan lost control of himself and succumbed to battle rage, his behavior only heightened their father's disapproval.

Alan pointed toward the north end of the caravan, where a group of riders was assembling. "We'll be forming up by the lead wagon in an hour. Better get started packing your bag," he said, then wheeled his horse around and galloped off down the line of wagons.

She stood up in the stirrups to get a better view of the group of horsemen toward which Alan rode. They were distant enough that seeing smaller details was difficult, but it was impossible to miss the large black bear that stayed very close to one of the horsemen.

Returning to her wagon, she packed her things, tied the pack behind her saddle, and leapt astride. She nudged Storm with her heels, and the mare moved smoothly into a gallop that swept Carol along the line of wagons. The wind whipped through her hair and made her eyes water. She pulled to a stop beside Derek.

The ranger glanced over at her. "Glad to see that you're getting your spunk back."

"Was I that bad?"

"You've been pretty mopey."

"I think I just needed something to look forward to."

Derek turned toward Hanibal. "Sir, we're ready to move."

The captain rose up in his stirrups, speaking the command in a booming voice. "Standard formation! Scouts out!"

The soldiers formed in a double file, with Hanibal out to one side. Derek raised both arms, pointing forward and out, sending his rangers well ahead and to the sides of the column. Carol and Alan fell in beside Derek, forward of the main group of soldiers.

Carol felt wonderful doing something of importance again. She had not realized how much she had wanted to find a new home. And even though she knew better than to allow her hopes to sweep her away, their long journey appeared to be nearing its end.

For two days, the small band had moved rapidly up through the foothills to the northeast, toward the same mountain range they had crossed to get here. As they traveled, the vegetation changed with the elevation, juniper yielding to pine. But none of this prepared Carol for the sight she now beheld. Evergreen trees with trunks as thick as a wagon's width rose upward to brush the sky. She stared up through the branches that shaded the ground, an early twilight descending. As she moved deeper into the grove, Carol was struck by the feeling that some god had shrunk the entire group down to the size of ants. Looking back, she saw some of the soldiers craning their necks as if trying to etch the magnificent sight into their minds forever.

Only Lonesome seemed unaffected. The bear cub loped ahead to claw open a rotten limb and fish out grubs before Derek's horse passed him by. Then he moved on once again.

"I had no idea that it would be this gorgeous," Carol exclaimed.

Derek turned his head. "True magnificence is yet to come."

Carol tried and failed to keep the eagerness out of her voice. "How much farther?"

"Another day's ride," Derek said, "but well worth the wait."

Derek then shut his mouth, and no amount of cajoling from Carol could coax him to expound on the matter further.

The following morning, the riders climbed up into a steep, narrow canyon. A raging mountain stream roared over and around boulders that had tumbled down from the high slopes. Here the trees were few and gnarled, bent by their struggle against harsh winters and rocky ground. The way led ever upward. Patches of snow still lay in the shadows, and the air was brisk enough that Carol wrapped herself in her heavy coat.

Evening fell as the group climbed out of the canyon through a saddle in the southwest ridgeline. Carol was pleased to see that the ground here was once again fertile and covered with tall pines. They were not as big as their giant cousins in the Great Forest, but they were pleasing nonetheless.

The rangers returned from scouting with word that it would be okay to light fires. Hanibal's men soon had three large campfires blazing and enough wood piled so that the flames could be maintained all night. Excitement erupted from the soldiers when two of the rangers arrived at camp packing a huge wild boar and a turkey. The night's feast left Carol with a longing for sleep that she was unable to resist.

Dawn found her sitting astride Storm beside Derek.

"We'll be there by noon," Derek said. His face acquired a faraway look. "Once you see the vale, you won't ever want to leave."

"I can't wait," Carol said.

The news lifted the spirits of the entire contingent, all save Hanibal. She caught him looking at Alan, a slight sneer giving his lips an unflattering turn. The captain was of average height, with a shock of red hair and beard to match, his green eyes shining with intelligence and ambition. Carol did not think him particularly handsome, nor did she regard him as ugly. But he certainly carried the charismatic aura of a leader.

By midmorning the company was well on its way down into another deep valley. Carol found the descent exhilarating. The trees again grew tall around her, and the trail was steep enough that Storm's hooves occasionally slipped on the thick layer of pine needles that covered the ground. A deer bounded out of a thicket, startling Lonesome and causing him to give out a sound somewhere between a bellow and a squeal.

"You're real ferocious," Derek said, snorting in disgust. "And don't give me that look."

Carol heard Alan laugh and shared his sentiment. It looked for all the world as if the bear were scowling up at Derek.

"Watch the trail up ahead," Derek called back to her. "We have to go down between a set of rock walls."

"I'm ready."

They burst out of the trees as they reached the floor of the canyon. Directly to the east, a swift-moving stream roared through a narrow opening between granite walls that rose straight upward to touch the sky, blocking Carol's view of what might lie beyond the constricted opening. Toward this gap in the cliffs, Derek headed at a trot, followed closely by the rest of the company.

As she approached the spot where the stream swept out from between the cliffs, Carol noted that the distance between the rock walls was greater than she had originally thought, perhaps a hundred paces. Pines closed in on the stream, but the path remained clear of underbrush.

The floor of the canyon wound its way between the magnificent cliffs for several leagues, the rushing mountain water switching back and forth across its width in a series of rapids broken only briefly by stretches of relative calm. Several times the way narrowed, leaving barely enough room for wagons to pass.

As she rounded a bend in the trail, the way opened. A small cry of wonder escaped from Carol's lips as she gazed forward. A verdant valley widened out before her, grassy meadows amidst groves where deer and elk grazed in abundance. What brought the cry to her lips, however, was her view of the sheer cliffs that formed the sides of the lowland. Those walls rose thousands of paces, turning the wide valley into an unassailable fortress for as far as her eyes could see.

The mountain walls looked as if they had been hewn by a god bored with the normal order of things. And from high up on these walls, streams leapt outward to plunge toward the grassland below, spreading like the train of a bridal gown. All of the streams flowed into the watercourse that cut its path through the valley's center, exiting through the narrow canyon from which Carol and company had just emerged.

One particularly spectacular waterfall cascaded from the summit before smashing onto the rocks below, only to plunge over another ledge farther down. A misty plume obscured large portions of the canyon.

"Wow!" Alan said as he pulled his mount to a stop beside hers.

"It's the most wonderful view I've ever seen," Carol said.

"No words can do such a sight justice," said Derek.

Carol trotted Storm closer to the riverbank and looked out into the clear water. Dark shapes hung suspended beneath the surface, facing upstream, slowly waving their tails back and forth to maintain their positions. As she moved along the bank, she spotted more and more of the fish.

She turned Storm away from the brook, spurring her horse into a gentle gallop. Alan fell in beside Carol on his warhorse. They swept past the column of soldiers and pulled up beside Derek. "Alan and I are going to ride on ahead. We'll link up with you before nightfall."

Derek nodded. "That'll be fine. The other rangers have already swept the area, and it's clear. The gap we just passed through is the only way in and out of the valley."

With that, Carol urged Storm after Alan. As the siblings moved up the valley, Carol discovered that it was wider than she had first thought. Again her senses had been fooled by the contrast between the meadow and the surrounding rock faces.

Carol and Alan continued eastward well into the afternoon. Two leagues in, the valley split, one side running to the northeast and the other heading southeast. The two riders kept to the wider branch to the southeast and continued on.

In one side canyon, a waterfall rushed over the edge of a cliff and onto a sloping rock wall to slide downward along the face. She had the urge to climb up the wall and slide down with the current, but another look at the great height and velocity of the water changed her mind.

The siblings made their way back the way they had come, reaching the campsite Hanibal had selected close to a stream just as darkness fell over the valley. As the light of the setting sun crawled up the eastern peaks, it painted dark cracks and striations bright orange.

Carol unsaddled and hobbled Storm, then walked around until she found the perfect location to make her bed. She rolled her blankets out on a cushion of pine needles beneath a majestic old king of the forest.

As she made her way back to the campfires and dinner that awaited, a new realization dawned on her. She was going to love this wild place that was to become their new home.

Being the children of High Lord Rafel, the kingdom's top military thinker, both Carol and Alan had been educated in the details of planning from an early age. Perhaps even more important than strategy and tactics, the study of the logistics of moving large units and the organization required to establish functional encampments had formed a core part of their learning. The lord wanted his children prepared to lead an army into battle, which required moving soldiers over long distances.

Unlike Alan, who found logistics an incredible bore, the subject had fascinated Carol. Now she put that knowledge to good use.

As the days passed in Areana's Vale, the wondrous area that Carol had named after the mountain goddess, Areana, a clear vision of the community structure and organization Carol desired began to coalesce. Several terrain factors, not the least of which was the winding nature of the creek, argued for small villages surrounded by farmland. These would be separated in the valley by at least a league, and each village would be self-sufficient. The organization into communities where farmers lived on the outskirts of their land enabled those who were not farmers to establish other businesses. Breaking Rafel's caravan into small settlements had the additional benefits of trade among the communities and an inherent improvement in sanitation. Having confirmed that the valley was an exceptional place to build their new home, Carol had instructed Hanibal to send word back to the caravan.

By the end of the week, Hanibal and Alan had presented Carol with a fortification plan that fit well with her small-village living arrangements. They wanted to establish a series of three forts in the eastern third of the high-walled canyon leading into the vale. The two cliffs that formed the bottleneck in the canyon, which Carol had named Areana's Gorge, stayed within a hundred paces of each other for almost two leagues and thus were a perfect location to set up fortifications, with each subsequent fort accessible by a single drawbridge across the raging waters. This initial plan solidified when Derek confirmed the results of his earlier reconnaissance. There was only one way in and out of the valley.

The first wagon came into view just before noon the following day and soon rolled by, following its soldier escort toward the primary campsite. A little girl sat beside her father and mother on the front seat and stood and waved when she saw Carol. Streaks of tears wound their way down the woman's dirty face, her arms wrapped tightly around her husband's shoulders.

Throughout the afternoon, wagons made their way into the valley. By the time the last of the several hundred wagons rolled in, they had carved a road.

One of the mess wagons brought up the rear, wobbling along on a broken wheel that had been patched with a tree branch. As it leaned from side to side, pots and pans clanged against the wagon and against each other, raising such a racket that a flock of ducks rose from one of the ponds, quacking loudly.

Rafel arrived with the ranger commander, Broderick, and Battle Master Gaar, to be met by Carol, Hanibal, Derek, and Alan. They were soon joined by the priest, Jason. The entire group settled down in a meadow adjacent to the camp where Carol and company had lived for the last few days.

Twilight fell before the meeting ended. Derek started a campfire, and the leaders of the settlement moved around the glow as darkness blanketed the valley. Carol, using the map that Derek had made, spelled out her plans for community organization. When she finished, she sat down to await her father's comments.

"I have some concerns with the idea of spreading all of our people out in villages," Gaar said. "We couldn't gather quickly enough if trouble arose."

"And why use just the south fork?" Jason added. "From what I understand, the north fork is even lovelier."

Gaar turned his iron gaze on Carol. "I agree with the priest," he said. "I see no valid reason not to use both sides of the valley and to congregate our people closer to the mouth of the canyon, near the upper of the three fortresses."

Several moments of silence followed in which all eyes turned toward Carol. She locked Gaar's gaze with her own. The lorness, a title given to human women of noble birth, felt the old surge of will flow through her, eliminating any sign of nerves and keeping her voice rock steady. "I realize that I have not yet had the opportunity to prove myself to your satisfaction, Gaar. I anticipated that you would doubt my judgments in matters concerning the military. That's why I did not make any recommendations concerning our fortifications. I left that entirely to Captain Hanibal, who worked out the defensive plan in conjunction with Alan. Hanibal will explain all to you."

For the next two hours, Hanibal briefed the assembled leaders on the details of his plan and how he had integrated Carol's ideas for community structure. The key to their overall strategy was the narrowness and length of the ravine that was the only entrance to the vale. The lowest of the forts would be positioned a third of the way down the two-league canyon, the midfort a little farther east, and the main fort would block the entrance.

To make its way into the vale, an enemy force would first have to traverse more than a league up the main gorge before reaching the westernmost of the forts. There was no way to do so without being seen by Broderick's rangers, thus making a surprise attack virtually impossible. Then, with the lowest fort always fully manned, Rafel's forces would have plenty of time to bring the upper two forts to full combat capacity, even if the rangers somehow failed to detect an attacking army.

Throughout the briefing, Gaar thrust pointed questions at Hanibal, but the captain parried them with ease.

At long last, Gaar rose to his feet. "Hmmm. It just might work after all."

"I'd say my daughter was ready for you this time, my old friend," said Rafel. "Carol met your challenge with someone whose military judgments you respect."

"But, Lord," the high priest interrupted, "think of the waste of not using the north fork."

"From what I've heard and seen, there's plenty of room in the south fork. Besides, I like the idea of preserving the natural beauty of this glen."

"At least let me establish a place of worship there," Jason said.

Rafel paused. "Do you see anything wrong with that, Carol?"

Carol looked at Jason. She liked the old priest, and the people depended on him to fulfill their spiritual needs. He and his subordinates were also healers of considerable ability. She recalled how, as traumatized citizens fled from Rafel's Keep, Jason and his three bishops had provided comfort to help the common folk maintain hope during their long journey.

"I have no problem with such a request," Carol replied. "There are a number of delightful canyons off the main valley, any one of which would make a fine center of worship. So long as the temple does not occupy the main vale of the north fork, I have no objection."

"Good," Rafel said. "It is settled."

And with that, the meeting ended. Carol placed her hand on Hanibal's shoulder. "You did a great job with your father," she said.

"And you with yours," Hanibal said, nodding slightly.

Long after the meeting had adjourned, Carol strolled among the trees and watched the stars, thinking about the work that lay ahead, reveling in the thought. Here they would build a new and better order, making the vale a peaceful and safe home in which to live. Carol slipped into her bedroll and fell fast asleep.

Sometime after midnight she awakened to the sound of distant thunder. Sitting up, she struggled to remember the dream that had fled with her waking. The burn of the brand on her left shoulder and the pounding of her heart told her it had not been a good one.

3

Endar, Southwestern Border
YOR 414, Early Spring

Arn sat astride Ax, the ugly brute of a warhorse he had grown to love, and watched Kim hug her brother Galad as they said their goodbyes. Although Galad and a company of a hundred of his Endarian scouts had accompanied Kim down the west side of Endar Pass, Queen Elan's orders had been clear. At Endar's southwestern border, Galad was to allow his sister and her three human companions to depart on their mission to find High Lord Rafel.

To her credit, Queen Elan hadn't ordered Arn killed, despite the Endarian High Council's disagreement about whether his place in Landrel's prophecy boded good or ill. And she had determined, come spring, to have Arn and his friends, the master archer, John, and the bare-chested Kanjari horse warrior, Ty, escort Kim on Kim's search for Rafel. In truth, it was not Rafel himself who was the target of their quest, but his twenty-four-year-old daughter, Carol. The thought of the woman Arn secretly loved brought a dryness to his mouth that made it difficult to swallow. It was a love destined to be unrequited. Seven years ago, Arn had spurned her, unwilling to allow his dark side to infect her life. She could not forgive him for that.

But during Arn's stay in Endar Pass, Queen Elan had shown him the ancient prophecy contained in the *Scroll of Landrel.* The prophecy had included a drawing of the woman Landrel predicted would brandish arcane powers that would threaten the wielder who called himself Kragan. That drawing had been a perfect depiction of Carol Rafel. And, just like on the huge statue of Carol that Arn had seen beneath the foul city of Lagoth, the image of a fire elemental had been branded on her left shoulder.

Centuries ago, Kragan had killed Landrel and taken a copy of that same scroll. Since that day, the evil wielder had searched for the woman he knew only by sight. And when he found her, he would seek to eliminate the threat she represented.

Thus, despite his heartache, Arn's mission was to find Rafel to alert him and Carol to their danger so that they could not be taken unaware.

Arn had known that Carol studied under Rafel's gray-bearded wielder, Hawthorne. But he also knew that the high lord had forbidden Hawthorne from putting Carol through the Ritual of Terrors, which would give her access to the elementals within the planes of fire, air, water, and earth. Without that, she could not defend herself against Kragan, even if Landrel's prophecy about her potential was correct. Hopefully, Rafel had rescinded that edict after he and Arn had parted ways.

Movement drew Arn's gaze, pulling his mind to the present.

Galad, resplendent in the Endarian uniform that shifted patterns and colors to blend into the background, turned away and signaled to his scouts. Then they jogged back the way they had come, their tall bodies disappearing into the pine forest, waist-length black hair blowing out behind them in the gentle breeze.

Arn's thoughts followed Galad back toward Endar Pass.

Though their winter stay had been long, it had been instructive. He had learned much about Endarian culture and history. Most interesting to Arn was the story of Landrel, the ancient Endarian master of time-shaping and life-shifting magic. The Endarians both revered and reviled him. Landrel had been the greatest of the Endarian scholars but had rejected the high council's decision to appoint him king, so that he could continue to focus on his research. But when his son, Vorgen, had contracted a rare and incurable disease, Landrel had funneled the life energies of two wolves and their five pups into the young man.

Although Vorgen fully recovered, his twin son and daughter were born disfigured, with a distended mouth and facial features that were a blend of Endarian and wolf. When the high council decided that the two babies must be euthanized to prevent the spread of the mutation, Landrel took his family and fled into the windswept northeastern plains. And as the Endarians had surmised, the mutation continued through subsequent generations, creating the race known as the vorg. The revelation had stunned Arn.

The other subject that fascinated him was Queen Elan's description of the two forms of exchange magic that many practiced but only a few mastered. To perform great feats of time-shaping or life-shifting required considerable natural ability to channel the energies involved. Mastery also required years of study and practice.

But what kept many Endarians who possessed the innate talent from putting the magic to use was fear of the danger involved. A single mistake in life-shifting could rob the wielder of his health or take his life. An error in time-shaping could leave the wielder trapped in a time-mist while the outside world sped forward or slowed to a halt. The prospect of rapidly aging or having all whom you knew age and die in what, to you, seemed like moments was a terrifying thought. Arn had no difficulty understanding Endarians who wanted no part of that.

He paused, considering the phrase that had just popped into his mind.

Wanted no part of that.

The words triggered a memory that Arn had not recalled since King Rodan's chief wielder had performed the blood ceremony delivering Slaken into his hand. He remembered the haunted look in old Gregor's eyes as he delivered his warning, as if he were giving Arn one last chance to reject the prize that the magical blade represented.

"I know of your past," Gregor had said. "But you need to know of this thing that I have created."

The way Gregor said *thing* resonated in Arn's mind, as if the wielder would be glad to be rid of it yet dreaded what the weapon would do to the one with whom it mated.

Gregor continued. "The boon you requested of King Rodan for saving his son's life required me to bind a powerful denizen from each of the four elemental planes to the runes on the haft of this knife: Vatra of fire, Voda of water, Zemlja of earth, and Zrak of air.

"Should you complete the blood-bond, these four elementals shall be trapped within those runes until the moment of your death, unable to be called upon by any wielder of magic. Only the combined abilities of these four can deflect the magics from all elemental planes. Thus, this blade shall stand alone, unique in all the world. It cannot be replicated. It cannot be unmade. And only the one who supplied the blood-bond can hold it.

"But beware. Such imprisonment enrages the beings trapped within the runes. And their thirst for revenge will amplify the lust for vengeance that already infects you."

Arn had not hesitated in his response. "I'm fine with that."

Now, as Arn looked down at the black blade sheathed at his side, he wondered if he would still give such a reply.

Shaking off the memory, Arn shifted his gaze to his companions. Companions? Was that how he saw the trio? Over the months of their shared journey and stay in Endar, they had worked their way into his heart. These were friends he would die to protect and who would each do the same for him.

Kim stood looking northeast toward her mountainous homeland. At six feet tall, the princess stood a head shorter than most of her people. That, along with the lighter color of her mocha skin, were indicators of a heritage not fully Endarian. John, a couple of inches shorter, stood beside her, clearly wanting to take his love's hand but allowing her the personal space the moment demanded. Yet the coal-black eyes within his hawkish face watched her intently. Queen Elan had performed their wedding ceremony within her white palace in the center of the lake. Arn was not surprised that the queen, who had loved a human herself, had blessed the pairing.

Kim had worn an emerald-green gown, while John's shimmering Endarian tunic had been the turquoise of the lake that surrounded the island. Galad had presented Kim's hand to John and, to Arn's surprise, had shown no distaste in doing so. Perhaps the unwavering tenderness with which John treated Kim had gradually softened Galad's objections to the relationship.

Arn turned toward Ty, who sat astride the palomino stallion that he had recently named Regoran. He faced away to the south, clearly ready to be off. Having been snowbound for several months, the Kanjari warrior had grown impatient. Now, as he sat bare-chested atop the big horse, his golden hair falling across the crescent-bladed ax strapped to his back, that restlessness for the trail was barely contained. Ty had held his notoriously sharp tongue, a testament to his high regard for the Endarian princess.

But even that had its limits.

"John," said Ty, "if Princess Kimber is done pining for home, perhaps you two could mount up so we can be off."

Kim ignored Ty for a moment, but then turned and walked back to the tree where she had tied her horse. As he mounted his own horse, John shot Ty a dark glance but said nothing.

Together, they rode out of Endar into the northernmost part of the Endless Valley, headed south.

4

Southeast of Endar
YOR 414, Early Spring

Earl Coldain stood in his stirrups surveying his troops. The line of soldiers, cavalry, and wagons stretched backward for miles down the valley, thirty thousand strong. How many months had it been since King Gilbert had ordered him to contact the other lords and tell them to serve up their armies under his command? And the lords had complied, some of them reluctantly, but they had all followed. What idiocy. The young king had stripped the kingdom bare of its defenses, and for what reason? To chase down Jared Rafel, the finest commander to ever grace the title of high lord in the kingdom of Tal.

So Coldain had formed the troops at a war camp outside of Hannington Castle. It had taken most of a season to gather the soldiers from the far corners of the kingdom, an interval that was double what could have been expected in response to a request from King Rodan. But then, this was at a summons from his feebleminded progeny, Gilbert. Gilbert and his crazy wielder, Blalock. So Coldain had dutifully raised the army and then marched out beyond the Sul River, across the Borderland Range. They had been on the march for more than a year.

Along the Banjee River, Coldain encountered a band of desert nomads he paid to guide the army across the Mogev Desert. When the nomadic leader had tried to drive a hard bargain, Coldain's threat of force had brought the man around.

Winter had seen the army of Tal working its way northward through the foothills that formed the eastern side of the Glacier Mountains as he searched for signs of High Lord Rafel's passage. His forces had failed to find the place where Rafel had crossed the mountains. And when the first snows blocked the passes that gave access to the lands west of the Glacier Mountains, Coldain had made his winter camp here in the lowlands. Nevertheless, ever the man of duty, he would continue in his relentless pursuit of his old friend.

Duty—a strange word, that. What did it really mean? Did it mean that friendship and mutual respect were to be sacrificed on the sword of madness? Was it his destiny to snuff out the life of a man who had served Tal so valiantly? Was it his responsibility to ensure the continued monarchy of a village idiot? Duty. Honor. Words to live by. And despite the lunacy of this quest, Coldain would see his duty done.

Coldain spurred his black warhorse forward, followed by his aide and a flag bearer. They swept down the hill from which he had been surveying his troops, joining the lines of fighting men. These men, many of them severely footsore, strode along stoically, bearing their pain as they bore the sacrifices of being so long away from their families. They were good men, one and all. They were the pride of Tal, as were those who served under Jared Rafel.

Before he cared to think about it, those good men, brothers all, would meet in mutual slaughter. And rivers would run red. For there was no doubt whatsoever in Coldain's mind that his old friend and mentor, Rafel, would extract a terrible price in that final battle. Outnumbered ten to one, the high lord would extract his pound of flesh. Coldain could almost hear the clash of steel, smell the odor of blood in the air, feel the sweat burning his eyes as it dripped from under his iron helmet, hear the screams of the dying. Almost.

Not for the last time, a great sadness settled upon the earl's shoulders as he gazed out across the men who marched under his command. How many of those young lads would never feel the embrace of their lovers' arms again? How many wives and families would be denied the comfort of a husband and father? And for what great and mighty purpose did these people offer themselves to the gods of war? For the whim of an insane child-king. For the desire of Gilbert's lunatic wielder.

Coldain removed a flask from his saddlebag, one that he saved for special occasions. Pausing, he held it high to the southeast. "Well, your royal high ass, here's to you, King Gilbert."

The earl brought the flask to his lips, tilted his head back, and took a long, slow swallow.

5

Areana's Vale
YOR 414, Early Summer

Spring gave way to summer, time passing with such speed that Carol lost track of the weeks. Every day was filled with supervising the building of the villages, training teachers, and organizing classroom instruction for the children. Each night she fell asleep as if she did not have a worldly care. The same could not be said of her awakenings. Her troubled dreams continued, and yet she had been unable to recall even one of them. Carol had considered consulting Jason about her worries, but threw off the idea in disgust. Was she such a child that she needed to be reassured over some dimly remembered nightmare?

Rafel kept every able-bodied person in his contingent efficiently employed. With Gaar in charge of the soldiers tasked with building the fortifications and Carol directing the workers, both men and women, in the layout and construction of the villages, their new fiefdom came together with remarkable rapidity. The growing satisfaction she felt with her performance of these duties partially filled the hole of her failure to wield magic. And her father's willingness to place her in a role traditionally reserved for men gave her hope that she would lead other women in changing the culture.

Workers cleared trees to make room for the settlements and surrounding farmland and provide the logs used to build houses and community facilities. For the construction of the forts, the soldiers cut trees in the forest west of the vale and snaked them up the narrow ravine using teams of oxen.

By the end of spring, the westernmost of the forts in the ravine leading into the vale was functional, and the villages of Colindale and Fernwood were almost complete. But Longsford Watch, the most easterly of the villages, had been delayed by a series of accidents that resulted in injuries. Some of its residents proposed renaming the town Ill Fortune.

On the positive side, the farmers had rounded up wild pigs, goats, turkeys, and guinea hens to replace the livestock they had been unable to bring with them on their flight from Tal. The animals roamed the long valley in such abundance that food shortages would not be a problem.

With overall construction nearing completion, Carol found that she had more free time. She began ranging farther out in her explorations of the valley, passing outward through the lower fortress on the west end to explore lands beyond the vale.

There was no great danger. The scouts and rangers patrolled well beyond where she rode, with no reports of anything moving within the area besides seemingly peaceful cliff dwellers and abundant wildlife.

Carol traveled several leagues to the southwest. The day was unusually hot, with no breeze other than that generated by her passage through the pines.

As she left the trees and topped a small rise, Carol rose in her stirrups to study the stream that ran through the valley to her south.

She thought about the long months since her people had fled Tal and made their way westward through the lawless borderlands, across the Mogev, over the jagged range of western mountains into the great valley that had brought them northward to the vale. It had been pure good fortune, although some would say destiny, that had led them to find Areana's Vale on the west side of the Glacier Mountains. Carol intended to take full advantage of that luck by getting to know these lands thoroughly.

Nudging Storm lightly with her heels, she sent the mare trotting down the gradual slope. Suddenly a high-pitched scream rent the air, pulling Carol's gaze. A woman in a multicolored dress ran full speed along the edge of the churning stream, her hands extended outward as if trying to grab something. Her clothing matched the description Jaradin Scot had given when he had reported the presence of a village of cliff dwellers inside a box canyon several leagues south of the vale. At first, Carol could not tell what the woman was chasing, but then she saw the focus of her concern. A brown-haired little girl was being swept along in the swift current, moving downstream more rapidly than the woman could run.

At Carol's urging, Storm whirled around and stretched her body into full stride. The lorness leaned forward, exhorting the mare to even greater speed. The woman was up ahead, with the little girl just beyond her. As Storm closed the distance, Carol saw that the child was being carried away by big rapids, sometimes disappearing beneath the surface. The girl was no longer trying to swim, her limp body tossed about by the fast-moving water.

Carol flashed past the woman, making for a spot ahead of the child, where a fallen tree lay across the roiling water. She swung down from Storm's back and scrambled out onto the log. As she reached the midpoint of the stream, she saw to her dismay that the bottom of the log was a full pace above the water. The child was almost to her. The sight pulled a curse from her lips. "Deep spawn!"

Wrapping her legs tightly around the trunk of the fallen tree, Carol let herself slide, upside down, beneath it. Water sprayed into her face, causing her to gasp for breath. She looked around, but could no longer see the girl, who had once again been sucked beneath the surface.

Carol thrust her arms down into the water, moving limbs back and forth in a frantic attempt to keep the child from getting by. The water tugged, splashing off her arms directly into her face, trying to pull her from the log. All at once, she felt a cold hand brush her own.

She lunged sideways, extending her right hand to grab the small wrist. As she did, the water swung her outward. "Come on!"

The little hand was so slippery that Carol was losing her grip.

She swung her left arm out farther, trying to bring her hand up under the girl's arm. Feeling her fingertips snag the girl's shirt, she pulled with all her strength, lifting the limp body and hugging it to her chest. Just then, the woman's hands reached downward, plucking the girl from Carol's grasp and lifting her up onto the log.

Carol struggled to right herself, but the log was too slippery. She was forced to make her way along the bottom of the log toward the shore, squirming forward until she found a place where she could safely lower herself to the rocks.

The child lay on her back as the woman leaned over her, weeping. Carol placed a hand on the woman's shoulder and moved her firmly to one side, then rolled the girl onto her stomach. She straddled the child's back and pressed downward, rocking back and forth with a steady rhythm. As she did, water dribbled from the girl's mouth.

Sudden spasms rocked the child's body. She coughed, then vomited onto the bank. Carol moved off her back as the coughs gave way to sobs. The woman swept the child up in her arms, hugging her as if there would be no tomorrow. And as Carol watched, wiping the water from her own face, she understood just how close mother and daughter had come to losing all their tomorrows together.

"Oh, my baby," the woman said. "I feared I had lost you."

It did not surprise Carol that the woman spoke the common tongue. Although there were still people who spoke different languages, such as the Endarians when among their own people, common had long been the language of trade. And over the course of centuries, its usage had replaced most of the original tongues.

Carol watched as the mother rocked her child back and forth, smothering her with kisses. Finally the woman lifted her tear-streaked face to consider Carol's eyes. "Thank you for saving my daughter's life," she said.

"I was afraid that I would be too late."

The woman rose to her feet. She was towering and lean, with bronze skin and raven hair, her dark brown eyes flecked with gold. She wore a cotton skirt and blouse, decorated with colorful, intricate patterns and beadwork.

"You must come with us," the woman said. "I want to show my husband the face of the one who saved our child."

She turned and began carrying the little girl back up the valley.

"Please, wait a moment," Carol called out, bringing her to a stop. "I don't even know your name."

The woman turned back toward Carol. A slow smile spread across her face, bathing it in radiant joy. "My name is Kira of the Kanjou Tribe. My husband, Dan, is our chief."

With that, Kira motioned once more for Carol to follow and again began walking.

Carol stood for several seconds, debating the wisdom of following the woman. Then she turned and whistled for Storm, who trotted over. Carol leapt lightly into the saddle and moved up beside Kira. "May I ask your little girl's name?"

"She is called Katya," Kira replied. "Please do not think that I am unfriendly or abrupt, but it is not my place to speak with you first. After you have met my husband, I will be able to talk more freely."

This comment raised Carol's ire. Yet another society dominated by men. But she forced herself to relax. It would not do to attack these people's customs.

Kira's eyes lingered momentarily on Carol's bare left shoulder. Then she turned her gaze forward once again.

Realizing that the sleeve of her shirt had been pulled upward to reveal the elemental brand, Carol hurriedly adjusted the garment, hoping that Kira did not know the significance of what she had seen.

After several minutes of being carried, Katya asked to be let down. As soon as the buckskin-clad child's feet touched the grass, it was as if the near-drowning had never happened. She ran off to the side to pick a puff-weed and stopped to blow the fuzz up into the air. Then she trotted over beside Storm to gaze wonderingly up at Carol. "Are you a witch?" she asked.

"Katya!" Kira said.

Carol smiled. "I certainly hope not."

"Then why do you have a picture on your arm, and why do you dress so strangely?"

"Katya! Be quiet and come here," Kira said.

"It's okay," Carol said, turning to look down at the little girl. "My clothes seem strange to you because I come from the far-off kingdom of Tal, where people dress as I do. As for my arm, I was burned by an evil man who drew that picture on me with fire."

"Ow," said Katya.

"Yes," Carol said. "May I ask you a question?"

"Okay."

"Will you be my friend, even though I have a big, ugly picture on my shoulder?"

"Yes, I will." Katya stared up at her.

"And will you do something else for me?"

"Anything."

"Could you keep the secret of the picture on my shoulder? It could be our special something, that only you, me, and your mom know about. Could you do that for me?"

Katya's face grew serious at the idea of sharing a confidence with Carol. "I promise."

Carol shifted her expectant gaze to Kira and was rewarded with the woman's nod of agreement.

Katya trotted along beside Carol's horse as they made their way into a steep canyon at the valley's westerly end. There Carol turned south into a crack in the canyon wall, and the way tapered to an opening just wide enough for horse and rider to pass. She paused momentarily just before the crevice. Kira motioned for her to follow, so she urged Storm into the narrow passage. The mare snorted nervously, but moved forward along the trail.

Then, as suddenly as the narrow passage had begun, a nearly circular, cliff-walled glen swept into view in front of her. Neat furrows between broad irrigation ditches crisscrossed the farmland. She smelled the spicy aroma given off by the fruit and vegetable plants that extended off into the distance, row after row.

High up on the cliff walls, an abundance of caves pocked the area. Rope ladders and bridges connected one to the other as if some gargantuan spider had been at work. Some of these ladders dangled several hundred paces down to the floor of the valley. Dozens of the cliff dwellers moved along the ropes.

At Kira's direction, Carol led Storm to a grassy meadow, removed the saddle, and hobbled the mare near a gurgling stream.

Katya ran to a nearby ladder and scrambled up, followed by Kira, who climbed at a more dignified pace. Carol stopped at the bottom of the ladder and gazed upward. The cave from which the rope ladder dangled was a hundred rungs above her. She caught her breath. The thought of Far Castle flashed through her mind. An eternity had passed since she and Alan had made their hazardous climb down that wall.

Taking the ladder in her right hand, she started up. It swayed back and forth as she climbed, taking on a small twisting motion as she moved higher and the weight of the ropes below her increased.

Suddenly Carol stopped. Above her, the cliff face hollowed inward several paces so that the ladder hung suspended in the air. Fifty rungs above that gap, Kira continued climbing. Katya had already disappeared over a ledge higher up.

Inhaling deeply, Carol resumed her climb.

Just don't look down, she told herself, glancing downward as she did so. A wave of vertigo shook her, then slowly passed as she forced her gaze upward once more. She focused on her task, grasping one rung at a time, stepping upward. Weakness spread from her chest into her arms, as if some force from below were leaching her strength away, willing her to let go and take the plunge.

Then she was past the open space, and solid rock once again supported the rope ladder. Ten paces farther up the cliff, Katya leaned outward to peer down at her.

When Carol reached the top, she stood on an expansive ledge, a short distance from where the walls of several interconnected buildings rose. The lowest level was dotted with doorways and windows. Farther along the wall, wooden ladders led up to the next level. The stone dwellings were stacked one above the other, each successive level retracting.

She took in the monstrous yet shallow cave. Carol could see more dwellings within other clefts in the cliffs. Ladders were everywhere, some of rope, some of wood, some spanning gaping chasms.

She followed Kira until they passed through a doorway into a large room. Two small lamps provided lighting. As Carol's eyes adjusted to the dimness, she saw that the lamps consisted of a hemp wick floating in a bowl filled with some type of oil. Except for several colorful pads that lay in a circle around the hearth, the room was empty.

"Please wait here," Kira said. "I will bring Dan."

As Kira departed, Carol seated herself on one of the comfortable pallets, rubbing her fingers across the cloth, seams, and woven patterns. The covering was made from a type of refined plant fiber, although its texture was different from that of cotton. The weave felt full and rich.

As she pondered this, three shadows darkened the doorway. A statuesque man wearing green breeches and a yellow shirt stepped forward, followed by Kira and a grandly plump man in a bright red robe. From what Carol had observed of the other members of the tribe, these brilliant colors were the primary dyes the cliff dwellers used.

The heavyset man leaned heavily on a gnarled staff.

"I am Dan," the taller chief uttered in a deep, soothing voice, extending his hand as he did so.

Carol stood to take the outstretched hand. Dan's eyes were the same brown, flecked with gold, as Kira's and Katya's, but far more penetrating. His face was etched and weathered by wind and sun, making his age difficult to judge. She guessed that he must be in the midst of his fourth decade.

Dan motioned for her to resume her seat and then sat down on one of the cushions beside her, as the larger stranger plopped down on another. When Carol looked up, she saw that Kira had departed.

"Let me introduce my chief adviser, Darlag," Dan said.

The crimson-clad man nodded his head. Carol studied him. His face was as round as his body, his hands large and puffy. His eyes sparkled with curiosity.

"I am pleased to meet you," Darlag said.

"Thank you."

"Darl manages to help me keep things in perspective," said Dan. "Despite his intellect, which I daresay is even more massive than his bulk, he refuses to see the darker side of life."

"Bah," said Darl, waving a hand dismissively. "Dan only uses me to test the strength of new ladders or rope bridges. If I can make it up or across them, then Dan figures they can handle any number of others."

"Then I shall feel much safer when next I climb out on them," said Carol.

"Kira tells me that I have you to thank for my daughter's life," Dan said. "I am forever in your debt."

"Nonsense," she said. "Given the circumstances, anyone would have done the same."

Dan shifted topics, his eyes narrowing ever so slightly. "As you can see, we Kanjou are a peaceful people. We farm, we build, and we live among these high walls. Our cliffs and the priesthood who watches over us have long protected us from the aggressions of the outside world. You are one of the outsiders who have come heavily armed into this land. We have watched as you cut down trees and use animals to drag them back into your canyon. Your arrival has caused many a concerned voice to be raised at council. The most prevalent of these fears was that your people would attack us, steal our crops, or even take our valley. But if you are representative of your people, perhaps we can put those concerns to rest."

He turned to look at Darl. "Do you have any questions to ask our guest?"

The fat man eyed her. "What are you running from?"

The directness of the question took Carol by surprise, but she answered in kind. "We have indeed fled another land. My father was a noble in a distant king's court. When the old king died, the monarchy fell to his despotic son, who set about eliminating all perceived threats. We left to avoid war."

"Will that king pursue you here?" Darl asked.

Carol paused before speaking, considering her response. "I don't believe he could, even if he wanted to. We have come a long way, crossed the Mogev Desert, a journey that has taken many months. I think we are well beyond his reach."

Darl leaned back. "Then I, too, place myself at your service and welcome you as a friend."

When the meeting with the men came to an end, Carol spent another two hours in pleasant conversation with Kira before the woman escorted her back down the ladder to where Storm was hobbled.

Carol said her farewell and swung effortlessly onto Storm's back. With a wave, she turned and trotted out of the valley. As she reentered the narrow fissure that formed the only entry or exit from the cliff dwellings, an uneasy feeling caused her to turn in her saddle to look back over her shoulder.

Despite not seeing anyone, the feeling she was being watched stayed with her as she moved out into the wide valley beyond. Only when she was back within the gorge that led to Areana's Vale did the sense of foreboding fade.

6

Coldain Estate—Southeastern Tal
YOR 414, Mid-Summer

Sixteen-year-old Garret Coldain strode across the keep's courtyard on the heels of the messenger who had come to him in a state of excitement. In tan pants tucked into tall riding boots, his white shirt open at the neck, the tawny-haired young lord considered himself quite the dashing figure. He knew that his father had seen more than good looks in him, though. That was the reason the earl had left Garret in charge during his absence.

At the open gates, an ancient figure in robes of midnight blue sat astride a bay horse before the guards who blocked his way, his long gray hair and beard merging into a mane that draped chest and back. The man clutched a staff in his right hand.

Recognition struck Garret with such force that his stride faltered. But he steadied himself against the shock and made his way past the guards. "Gregor," said Garret, "I am surprised to see you. I had heard that you were infirm."

"Your eyes should put the lie to that, Lord Coldain. I have journeyed far to bring you most pressing news. Can we go someplace where we can talk privately?"

Signaling his gate guards to let King Rodan's former wielder pass, Garret led the way to the keep. Outside, Gregor dismounted and handed his horse over to a waiting groom. Then he followed the young lord through the entryway and into Earl Coldain's meeting chamber. Behind closed doors, Garret motioned for Gregor to sit at the table and then assumed his father's seat at its head, his curiosity aroused.

"I was told that you were catatonic," Garret said.

Gregor stared at him through eyes that narrowed. "I tried to destroy Blalock, but he defeated me. But I had one last trick for him. I let him and the people in Hannington Castle see what I wanted them to see. A beaten and mindless old man. And all the while I waited and watched. Those around me paid me no heed. Why would they?"

Garret leaned forward, his pulse pounding. He had not known of the confrontation between Gregor and Blalock. That knowledge added an ominous tone to the wielder's words.

"And what you learned brought you here, to my father's estate?"

"It did." Again Gregor paused to study Garret. "It turns out that the king's wielder, whom we have always known by the name Blalock, is really Kragan. He has deceived us for years."

"What? Impossible. The one from the legends died four centuries ago."

"So we believed. But he has dropped all pretenses and become an even greater abomination. He now walks the land, clothed in the body of Kaleal, the Lord of the Third Deep."

Gregor frowned. "Through the last four centuries, everyone has believed that Kragan and his ambitions to enslave this continent were dead. With his return to public view, I think that he seeks a way to dispel the Endarian time-mists that isolate our territories from Kragan's homeland across the Great Sea. For there lies the true seat of his powers."

"Cannot the king stop this?"

"Hannington Castle has fallen to Kragan's foul army. Gilbert is dead. I barely managed to escape with my life. You are the acting head of the third noble estate I have warned."

Gregor interlocked his fingers. "Mine is a vain quest. There are not enough fighting men left in Tal to oppose Kragan. Even now his horde marches, overrunning one keep after another, enslaving the people and pressing fighting-age men into his army. That army is now on its way here."

A wave of fear froze Garret as the visualization of what Gregor had said filled his mind. Earl Coldain had left his only son as master of this keep in his absence when he had taken the gathered army of Tal in pursuit of High Lord Rafel and Rafel's legion. And aside from peasants and tradesmen, the earl had left behind a force of only three hundred soldiers and one wielder to defend the keep and protect his family. Barely able to utter the words, Garret asked the question to which he dreaded to hear the answer.

"How many?"

"Kragan commands a force of well over a hundred thousand vorgs and men. Besides himself, his army also has dozens of wielders."

Garret felt his eyes widen despite his attempt to give no visible reaction to this news. He had known that any force that could sack Hannington Castle would be vast, but this number had not been heard of since the Vorg War, three decades ago.

"I suggest," said Gregor, "that you gather what forces you have, take your mother and two sisters, and flee."

Ever so slowly, Garret felt his sense of the man his father expected him to be reemerge. "That I cannot do. I will not disgrace the house of Coldain by slinking away with my tail tucked firmly between my cheeks."

"Then you and your family will die alongside your people."

Garret rose to his feet. "We Coldains do not die so easily. My father charged me with protecting his lands. No matter the cost, I will do my duty."

The old wielder leaned back in his chair and sighed. "I expected no less. Since there are no more noble estates for me to carry warning to, I will lend what strength I have against the coming horde, for what little good it will do."

"Thank you," said Garret. "I will take you to a room that you may claim for your own."

As Garret turned and led Gregor out of the meeting room, he suppressed a shudder at the thought of bringing this news to his mother, Mina, and his two eight-year-old twin sisters, Elena and Erica. Before he performed that unwelcome task, he would meet with Commander Volker, the head of Coldain's Guard, so that he could begin making defensive preparations. Garret would also send out a dozen rangers in search of the army of Tal, in hopes of getting word of Blalock's treachery and the wielder's true identity to his father. At least his father could seek vengeance.

Climbing the torchlit stairway that led to the upper residences, the flames brought to Garret's mind images of the keep burning. Despite his brave words to Gregor, he wanted to take his mother, sisters, and three hundred soldiers and flee this place. But his father was a man who valued duty above life, or even love. So Garret would remain in this keep and do his very best to defend it, hoping that his father had learned of the recent events within Tal and was even now marching home.

It was a hope Garret would cling to in the weeks to come.

7

Areana's Vale
YOR 414, Mid-Summer

In the weeks that followed, Carol returned several times to visit with Kira and Katya. Since she had delegated most of her tasks within Areana's Vale to others, her workload had lightened. She soon had three people teaching within the settlement: Cora, a matronly woman of fifty; Dianne, a slight, blonde girl of twenty; and David, a bookish lad of eighteen. All three had different strengths, and the children liked them. Carol was thrilled that they did not require much instruction in their duties, enabling her to devote a good portion of her time to the Kanjou.

Because Carol's inspections ensured that work within the vale stayed on schedule, her father raised no objections to her twice-weekly trips to see the tribe. These visits built within her a growing love for those who made their homes in the high cliffs.

She also developed a close friendship with Darl. Carol found that he had a keen wit and a remarkable insight into people as well as a love for discussing philosophy. One day she brought one of her books with her, a tome that discussed irrigation and the advantages of certain methods over others.

Darl was fascinated not only by the book but the entire concept of being able to record ideas in writing and leave them for others to read and study. He immediately determined that he would learn to read and write and asked Carol if she would teach him.

The pace with which he absorbed the lessons amazed her, as Darl was soon able to transcribe an entire book in days. So hard did he work that over the course of two weeks, he used up Carol's paper and ink. This presented a problem, especially since Rafel's high priest, Jason, refused to give away any of his supplies.

"My writing materials are needed in the training of my acolytes and not for schooling the cliff dwellers," he told her, and no amount of cajoling could coax him into changing his mind.

But Darl was not to be stopped. He set about experimenting with a variety of plant dyes and soon devised an ink that Carol thought superior to any she had seen. Paper presented a bit more difficulty, but after extracting all the knowledge he could from Carol on the subject, Darl set about attempting to manufacture his own.

He talked Dan into letting him have the use of two workers to assist him. After several tries, he was rewarded with a form of usable parchment. Nevertheless, this was not satisfactory. As the weeks passed, his paper improved, slowly at first, and then, as if by some burst of pure inspiration, he arrived at a technique that produced a light tan material of extremely fine quality.

Darl was overjoyed. He soon had five subordinates working to produce paper and ink regularly. Carol began buying both products for use in the vale schools. When Jason discovered that she had a source, he also initiated his own purchases. The trade between the communities continued to grow, with Rafel's people providing metal instruments and other crafts while the cliff dwellers supplied vegetables and cloths of various types, along with paper and ink.

Carol became so busy that she began to fall behind in her other administrations. Not only was she working to establish the schools in

Areana's Vale, but Darl had talked Dan into letting her begin to teach the children of their tribe to read and write.

Despite the progress she was making within the vale and with the Kanjou, Carol felt an ever-increasing sense of frustration at her inability to overcome the fears that prevented her from casting spells. The meditations needed to wield her power continued to elude her. She had hoped that by visualizing a fortified sanctuary atop a mountain peak and continually adding details, she could retreat there within her mind, locking the terrifying memory of her branding outside. Every time she tried to meditate and did not succeed, she added to the sanctuary, but the technique failed to provide her the protection she required.

She badly wanted to be able to wield magic once again. Without access to her magic, she had no hope of gaining the power to bring about the meritocracy that Thorean had described within the pages of her most prized book, *Liberty*. Of all the works she had maintained in her collection back at Rafel's Keep, she considered this the masterpiece. Thorean had spent his life studying the philosophy of the erudite Endarian culture, specifically the structure of its meritocracy. The Endarians chose a ruler, male or female, from among a group that the high council deemed most intellectually accomplished. And they replaced that ruler whenever another's talents surpassed hers or his. Fear of the ideas expressed within this tome had driven King Rodan to order Thorean's execution.

And something else was troubling her. As time went by, Carol began to feel that Darl was keeping a secret. As the days passed, she grew closer to the adviser, almost as if he was filling the gap left by the loss of Hawthorne. Their growing relationship revealed that something was troubling him. She noticed that, once, when she talked of High Priest Jason and the way the people of the vale looked to the church for their spiritual and physical care, the jovial man grew serious and silent.

She pressed him to speak openly and plainly, but before changing the subject, Darl simply responded that his reaction was nothing of importance.

Then the shadows arrived. One morning as Carol made her way up along the cliff walls to the area she used for her classes, she saw a figure clad entirely in black, with a hood pulled over his head. The man was on another rope ladder, staring across the divide at her. When he noticed Carol looking back, the man hurried upward and disappeared into one of the dwellings above.

"I saw a man in black as I climbed up here," Carol said when Kira met her at the door to her house. "Do you know who he is?"

"That was just one of the protectors. Nothing to be alarmed about."

"The protectors? Who are they?"

Kira directed Carol to one of the cushions against the wall and sat down beside her. She leaned back, pulling her knees to her chest and wrapping her arms around them. "They are the priests of my people."

"He didn't look like any of the tribe members around here."

"They aren't from here. The priests have a temple far to the northwest. They come every summer."

"You said that they're priests. Does that mean that they're healers, or do they conduct religious ceremonies?"

"They protect us from evil," Kira said. She was rocking back and forth on the cushion. Carol could feel a tension building in the air.

"I'm sorry," Carol said, putting a hand on Kira's shoulder. "I didn't mean to inquire too deeply into your beliefs. Anyway, I must be going to my classroom now. It's almost time for instruction to begin."

Relief showed on Kira's face. "So soon?"

"I'm afraid so. My duties in Areana's Vale will require my presence this afternoon."

Carol hugged Kira at the door, then stepped out and made her way along the maze of ropes to the open amphitheater that served as a classroom. As usual, the children ran forward to gather around, touching her or just wanting a hug. They were kids, much like any others she had known, except warmer and more innocent.

The morning classes passed more slowly than usual. She kept thinking about the strange priest and had to force herself to concentrate on phonics. When noon arrived, she dismissed the students and hurried to meet Darl. Perhaps he would fill in some of the missing details.

The adviser, however, was nowhere to be found in any of his usual haunts. Neither Kira nor Dan had been able to say where he was, although they did not appear concerned.

"No doubt off studying something," said Dan.

Short on time, she abandoned her search and climbed back down the rope ladders to the valley floor. Mounting Storm, Carol made her way home.

When she reached the outer walls of the lower fort, she knew something was wrong. Too many soldiers were on the wall that blocked the way into the canyon; there was a stir of activity.

A squad rode out to meet her. She recognized the sergeant leading the group.

"Lorness Carol, your father sent us to escort you back to the fort," the sergeant said.

"What has happened?"

"Jaradin Scot has been attacked and badly injured. The bastards killed the ranger who was with him."

Without waiting for the escort, Carol urged Storm into a run. The mare swiftly outdistanced the horses of the surprised guards as she raced across the drawbridge, through the lower fort, and out its rear gate. She passed through the midfort in the same manner, crossed one final drawbridge, and pulled Storm to a sliding halt inside the upper fort.

Carol dismounted and tossed the reins to one of the grooms before running to her father's council chambers.

The courtyard was bustling. Several soldiers crowded around the doorway to the central hall. The soldiers split and moved aside as Carol approached. She moved quickly between them, pausing just long enough to let her eyes adjust to the dim light inside.

Her father stepped forward to meet her. "You've heard about what happened?"

"Only that Jaradin was badly hurt," she said as the two walked toward the large center table. The high lord sat at the head of the table, with Gaar, Alan, and Broderick seated around him. Carol joined them.

"When I find out who did this, they will wish they had never stepped close to the vale," Rafel said.

"Until Jaradin regains consciousness, we won't know the identity of the attacker," Broderick said.

"Can't Derek and his bear track them?" Carol said.

"Derek said that there was no sign of anyone else having been in the immediate area," said Broderick.

"Could Jaradin have hurt himself in a fall?" she asked.

"No," said Gaar. "Jaradin and another ranger, Fredrick Han, were on routine patrol near the Great Forest. When they didn't return on schedule, Derek went in search of them. He found Fredrick dead and Jaradin clinging to life. Someone cut him up with a knife to send us a message."

The high lord pounded his fists on the table. "I look forward to returning it."

"Where's Derek?" Carol asked.

"He's leading one of the five ranger patrols that I sent out to try to pick up the attacker's trail," Broderick said. "If anyone can find it, that ranger and his bear can."

"You should have let me go, too," Alan said.

"You're a good fighter, but you're not a ranger. It's time to let them do their work. But when it's time to battle, I won't hold you back."

"Where's Jaradin?" Carol asked.

"In the infirmary," said Gaar. "Jason and two acolytes are attending him."

Carol stood and walked outside. The soldiers had moved away from the doorway and returned to their duties. The shadows from the high valley walls had just begun to creep over the fort, and an unusually cool breeze brought goose bumps to her arms. The fiery pulsing of the elemental mark on her shoulder stood in sharp contrast to her cold skin.

The infirmary consisted of a large room on the western side of the fort. She paused outside the entryway, took a deep breath to compose herself, and stepped inside.

Jason stooped over Jaradin's body, which lay on a long, narrow table. Two acolytes clad in white robes, now heavily bloodstained, assisted him. The old priest looked up as Carol entered.

Her first sight of Jaradin pulled a gasp from her lips. His body was a mass of jagged wounds, knives having crisscrossed over him, not to kill but to torture. The ranger's face was worst of all. Flaps of cheek hung open, and an eye had been gouged from its socket. Carol wanted to scream.

"It's not pretty, is it?" Jason said.

"Will he live?" she asked.

The priest bowed his head for a moment, then went back to work sewing up the wounds. "I have seen men die from lesser injuries, and I have seen men live through worse."

"Why would anyone do this?"

"To scare us." The priest paused as an acolyte leaned over to wipe his brow. "I have been afraid something was going to happen for some time now."

"What do you mean?"

"Someone doesn't want us here. I've felt it on the edge of my thoughts as I go through my daily prayers."

"So you've felt it, too!" Carol said. "I was hoping my dreams were just the result of the hardships of the journey and would pass with time."

Jason continued to stitch, but his voice carried a troubled undercurrent. "Tell me about these dreams."

"I wish I could. For several weeks now, I've awakened in a sweat from some dream that fades into mist. I almost came to talk to you about the dreams, but I didn't. What was there to discuss? I can't even remember what they were about."

She reached out to lay her hand on Jaradin's head. The memory of how he had fought alongside her when a bear had attacked Derek filled her mind. Like his brother, he had always been so rugged and strong, the very definition of a ranger. Now, as Carol looked down at him as he clung to life, a sense of helplessness enfolded her. The sound of his ragged breathing pulled forth a vision of Hawthorne gasping out his last breaths in her arms. Carol shuddered.

"May the gods help you save him," she said, then turned and walked out of the room. Carol looked up to see her brother standing just outside the door.

"You look a little pale," he said. "Are you all right?"

"I needed air."

"I did, too, when I first saw Jaradin. Do you think it could have been someone from the nearby tribe?"

"No. Even if they weren't peaceful, I don't think they could have taken Jaradin unaware. I don't understand how that could happen."

Alan shook his head. He gripped the handle of his ax so tightly that muscles coiled all the way up his arm and into his shoulder. "If anyone can find who did this, Derek will. You should have seen his face as he left."

Alan placed a hand on her shoulder. Then he turned and strode off toward the blacksmith shop.

Carol walked directly to the stables. A boy directed her to the stall that held Storm, and she made her way into the vale. She realized that she was late for her meeting with the three teachers, but she did not care. The way she felt, they were lucky she opted to keep the appointment. Mundane tasks would help to calm her mind.

The remainder of the day, short though it was, passed slowly. Carol reviewed the progress of classes and later traveled up the valley, leaving Colindale, as the first village had been named, passing through Fernwood, and finally stopping at Longsford Watch. This last site had been named after a famous battle from the Vorg War. Carol thought the fight was an incredibly stupid thing after which to name a town, but Rafel, Gaar, and Alan loved the choice. Men needed to be reminded at every opportunity of past glories lest someone forget they were men.

Thunder rumbled in the distance as she unsaddled Storm and began grooming the mare. Carol saw huge thunderheads piled high above the southern walls of the valley. The bottoms of the clouds were shadowy and threatening, standing out in stark contrast to the brilliant scarlet cloud tops. Lightning splintered downward and laced the entire skyline, followed several moments later by two louder booms. Carol could see sheets of rain spewing from the clouds so that the end of the valley disappeared behind a veil. When the first fat drop spattered her face, she ended her reverie and moved to get out of the coming storm.

Carol left the stables and made her way toward her home, a simple two-room cabin on the southeastern edge of Longsford Watch. She had insisted on a cabin on the outskirts of town for reasons of privacy.

The house was on a small knoll and had a large front window looking out over the valley to the north, provided the shutters were open. The front room also had a hearth and a set of bookshelves, as well as a table and chairs. The front door opened out onto the one true luxury that Carol had allowed her father to have built for her: a covered porch with a board floor and its own set of chairs.

Her bedroom was small but comfortable, with a wood frame bed and shuttered window. The only inconvenience was the walk of about fifty paces down the hill to the nearest of the community outhouses. She considered this a small price to pay for the satisfaction she got from the cabin.

Rain suddenly poured down from the sky, sending the lorness racing the last few paces to her porch. There she paused to shake the water from her hair and clothes. The sound of the rain on her porch roof was wonderful, as was the light show being put on by the lightning. The storm brought with it a deep darkness and the good smell of air washed clean by rain.

She flopped down in one of the porch chairs and leaned back. With thunder rumbling all around, she lost herself in sleep.

—∾—

Carol awoke with a start. It was quiet. The storm had died. Despite the chill in the air, she was drenched in sweat and breathing heavily, as if she had just finished running. She looked around, trying to pierce the thick blanket of night with her eyes. She couldn't see anything, but from the sound of the steady drip of water from the roof and the feel of her chair, she knew that she was still on her porch.

She stood up and walked forward, going slowly, feeling her way along the boards with her feet. Her outstretched arm bumped into one of the porch supports, and she stopped to lean. An image flashed into her mind, and then it was gone. She had dreamed again, but this time it seemed different, more urgent, demanding to be let out of her subconscious mind, desperate, seeking. Carol struggled to recall the image, but she could not. Some force was blocking her, as if something did not want to let her subconscious do its work.

She found her way back over to her chair and sat down. She inhaled deeply, then let her breath out slowly.

In quiet desperation, she steadied her pulse and began the meditation. She was floating, pulled from her body by the wind. She willed herself upward, through the clouds. Something sped up after her, something she could not allow to catch her. Her will pulled her onward, faster, higher, until finally she arrived at a temple atop a snow-covered mountain. She rushed inside, slamming the huge doors behind her. As she closed the bolt, something smashed into the door from outside. Carol staggered backward. The door had to hold, at least long enough for her to accomplish her task.

The battering on the doors intensified. Carol ignored the sound, turning her attention back to her dream. Her mind was clear and sharp, a state she had not experienced since the incident with the fire elemental. Suddenly a massive blow hit the doors, sending splinters flying inward.

She reached out for the image left by the dream. It appeared, but at such a great distance that she could not make out details. Another terrible blow struck the door, shattering part of a panel. In desperation, she pulled the image to her.

It was dark, not the total darkness of night, but rather the darkness of evening twilight. She was in the valley of the cliff dwellers, in the center of the amphitheater. All of the Kanjou had gathered, filling the seats for row upon row, even sitting along the cliff walls where they could gain purchase. They stared down at Carol. No. Not just at her. Others were there, too. She looked around. Dan stood close by, as did Kira, and Darl. Kira looked as if an unuttered scream was trapped upon her lips. The men were tense, drained of color. Still.

She turned again. Katya lay on a stone slab, staring skyward. Her eyes were dazed. The black figures of several priests, like the one she had seen earlier, moved to surround the girl. One of them turned to face Carol.

"This is what you have wrought with your meddling," he said, pulling a curved dagger from his cloak.

The priest turned back toward the girl, and a chant arose from the others, climbing in pitch as he gripped the dagger with both hands and slowly raised it above his head. Carol struggled to move but could not, caught in some force that held her in place. A low chuckle escaped the priest's lips as the dagger descended.

Carol screamed as the doorway to the temple shattered and the familiar terror returned. The mental image dissolved, and her consciousness plummeted back to her body. She jerked up from the chair.

8

Areana's Vale
YOR 414, Mid-Summer

The sky in the east was just beginning to gray when Carol bounded off the porch and strode down the hill toward the stable, moving as rapidly as she could manage in the predawn light. Storm nickered an acknowledgment of her presence.

Saddling the mare, she led Storm out of the stable and leapt astride. Turning Storm's head, Carol urged her steed into a ground-covering lope. She reached the ravine just as the first rays of sun touched the mountain peaks. Passing through the series of upper fortifications, Carol pulled to a halt at the lower fortress's raised drawbridge.

Two soldiers scrambled to meet her.

"I'm sorry, Lorness. Our orders are not to let anyone in or out until the shift change at eight o'clock," said the larger of the two.

"Has any order like that ever applied to me?" she asked.

The soldier paused. "No, but—"

"Then open the damned gate now!" The soldiers stepped backward.

"But—"

"I said now!" Her voice echoed between the canyon walls.

"Yes, Lorness," the soldier said.

He turned to yell at his compatriots inside the guardhouse. "Lower the drawbridge."

When the far end of the bridge reached the ground, Carol raced down Areana's Gorge at full speed. As she exited the canyon, she slowed to a gentle canter. There was little chance that anyone would try to catch her. Her father would be furious about her leaving at such an hour, but there was little he could do about her decision.

The morning was still young when Carol brought Storm to a halt outside the slit in the wall that led into the valley of the Kanjou.

Dismounting, Carol hobbled Storm and set her saddle and bridle under a tree. Then she turned and walked into the fissure. She emerged on the far side and headed toward the rope ladder that led to Dan's house. The workers in the fields showed no signs of anything out of the ordinary having occurred. They were used to Carol's arrivals and did not pause from their work.

She climbed the ladder, taking in the area when she reached the rock ledge. Seeing no sign of the protectors, she made her way to Dan's house and knocked on the door. Kira opened it, and Carol stepped past her into the room. Dan, who was sitting on one of the cushions, looked up in surprise.

"Listen to me," Carol said. "I don't have time for you to ask me how I know this or for you to argue with me. I came to tell you that Katya is in great danger from the ones you call the protectors. I believe they were responsible for the serious injury of one of my father's top rangers and the death of his companion. You must come with me quickly. I will take you and your family to Areana's Vale, where you will be safe, and then my father will deal with these criminals."

"How perceptive of you," said a deep voice from her right.

Carol spun to see one of the priests step from the shadows. She raced toward the open door, but something struck her, sending her flying. As she bounced off the rock wall and tumbled to the floor, a faint red mist swirled. Then everything went black.

—∾—

Distant voices mumbled, gradually gaining clarity. Damn it. Why couldn't they let her sleep? Then her memory returned, jerking her back awake. Carol was in a small room. Where exactly, she couldn't tell. But she was standing. Now that was odd. She couldn't remember getting up.

From her right, she heard Darl's voice.

"Are you all right?"

"I think so. My head hurts."

She tried to turn to look at Darl but found that she could not. In fact, she could not move anything but her eyes. She looked downward to see how she was bound, and gasped. She was suspended in the air a pace off the ground. No ropes held her. Rolling her eyes to the right, she barely managed to glimpse Darl. He hung in suspension just as she did.

"What's happening?"

"I'm sorry," Darl said. "I feel responsible for getting you mixed up in this. If I had known our friendship would come to such an end, I would never have asked you to teach here."

"Why?"

"The protectors. I was hoping that by educating the children, their parents would begin to learn some of the teachings of your writers, and that, in time, they would be able to discard the superstitions that have led us to rely on the protectors. I hoped my people could throw off the yoke of servitude imposed on them."

"Servitude?"

"Or slavery," said Darl. "Whatever one chooses to call it. The protectors come here every summer, supposedly to provide guidance, but in reality to take one child of every ten to serve in their temples, to become like them."

"And you let them?" Carol asked, shocked at the revelation.

"We don't have a choice. The protectors do not tolerate opposition. In the past, those who confronted them were made to serve as examples to the others of what happens to heretics."

"And that is what they plan for us?"

"I'm afraid so," said Darl. "I had hoped that they would not learn of your activities, that they would come, take the grain and children, and go. I underestimated them."

"Can Dan stop them?"

"Dan is hanging right behind you. He has not regained consciousness."

Carol struggled to move, straining with every muscle in her body.

"No use fighting," said Darl. "Only a protector can free us from these bonds."

Carol ignored him, reaching inward with her mind, searching for a center. Tension drained from her body, so that once again she was floating, drifting toward the light, the peaceful light surrounding her, soothing her, etching a brand into her shoulder in living flame.

She screamed, her voice filled with terror and rage.

"What's happening?" Darl asked.

"Nothing," she said, sobbing. "Nothing at all."

Several minutes passed before she regained her composure. "I'm sorry," she said. "I didn't mean to lose control."

"It's nothing. I feel that way as well."

"What . . . what happens now?"

"We wait for sundown," said Darl. "The protectors like to gather the people at dark to watch these ceremonies. Afterward, their lesson given, they will take their portion of our harvest, along with the selected neophytes, and depart. But not before they have appointed a new chief. They have concluded that Dan is no longer fit to rule."

"When I don't return this evening, my father will come looking for me."

"Too late, I am afraid. Either way, I don't think he could do anything to stop them. As you can see, their dark gods grant the protectors great power."

Carol paused. She had intended to discuss the subject of magic with Darl earlier. However, doing so would inevitably lead to a discussion of her own use of magic, her subsequent branding, and the circumstances of Hawthorne's death, uncomfortable topics that she had put off.

"That is where you're wrong," said Carol. "They wield magic no different from that used by others I have known."

"Does your father have one of these wielders?" Darl's voice carried a hopeful note.

Carol paused. "Not anymore. The wielder in our group died several months ago."

"I am sorry to hear that."

The afternoon wore on, and the shadows lengthened. Dan awakened but refused to speak. As evening crept into the valley, a protector entered the room and gestured. The magically bound prisoners floated after him as he departed. The protector moved methodically upward in the cavern, heading toward the amphitheater. Carol had often traveled this path to conduct classes for the children. This lesson would not be so pleasant.

The three prisoners floated to a stop near the center of the stone amphitheater. The entire valley's population filled the semicircular rows of seats. On the raised central dais, six more protectors, the hoods of their robes pulled up, waited beside the rock slab that she had seen in her vision. Katya lay atop the slab, silently staring upward.

"Oh no," Carol said in a hushed breath.

The voice of the priest in the center echoed through the amphitheater. "My people! Hear me!"

The murmur of voices in the crowd died.

"I made the journey south from our temple at Mo'Lier with the same great anticipation as always, looking forward to the warmth and love that our visits with you bring. I looked forward to giving you the wise words of our high council and conducting the traditional ceremonies of renewal. Imagine my disappointment upon discovering that an outsider moved among you, teaching forbidden skills, spreading heresy. Thank the dark god that we arrived in time to end this treachery."

Just then, Kira rushed forward from the crowd to fall on her knees before the priest.

"Oh, Holy One," Kira wept. "I beg of you. Do what you will to my husband and me. It was truly our fault. But please spare my little girl. Surely, in your great wisdom, you can find the mercy necessary to—"

"Do not tell me what I can and cannot do!"

Kira stumbled backward before the priest's harsh words.

"The gods are angered by your actions. Only the sacrifice of an innocent may appease them."

"You filthy bastards!" Carol hissed. "When my father catches you, he'll cut your evil hearts out and then journey north to burn your temple to the ground!"

"Silence!"

The priest waved his hand, and Carol felt the sleeve of her shirt torn away to reveal her living brand. With another gesture, she began rotating slowly, bathed in a brilliant light so that all could see the elemental mark on her left shoulder.

"Behold the elemental-marked witch who seeks to corrupt you."

A low chant arose from all seven priests. As the chant mounted, the sky darkened, and the priests on the platform moved to form a circle around the stone. Carol struggled to break free, to center her mind, anything. Rage coursed through her body, making her left shoulder throb in rhythm with her pounding pulse.

The chant reached a crescendo as the high priest drew from his cloak an obsidian dagger, veined with thin red lines that seemed to pulse with anticipation. The protector turned and walked slowly toward the stone slab, where he bent to kiss Katya gently on the forehead. The fury that coursed through Carol's mind became a torrent, frothing with the bloody foam of hate.

The protector extended the dagger slowly, pricking a point just above Katya's heart, marking the spot for its entry. Then he raised the blade high above his head, turning his face to the heavens. "Mighty Krylzygool, I give you this girl that you may taste her blood and be appeased."

Carol reached out with her mind for the fire elemental, felt fear's clutch try to stop her, and let her rage burn that fear to dust.

"JAA'DRAAAAAAAAAA!"

Carol's yell thundered through the valley as her mind lashed out, snaring the fire elemental in a grip that it had never felt before. With a shriek that crackled through the air, the elemental descended on the dagger, turning it into a molten blob that fell upon the protector's face, burning through flesh.

The priest crumbled to the ground. The other protectors stood frozen at the sight. A hush fell over the crowd as their chanting stopped. Carol stepped forward in the air, suspended now by her own will. Storm clouds boiled over the canyon walls, and lightning arced downward, one bolt connecting to the next in an undying web as thunder shook stone.

Winds howled through the crowd, sweeping up the priests and depositing them together in the center of the dais. Three of the protectors raised their arms to summon spells of their own, but they perished before they completed the tasks, their bodies crumbling into brittle piles of ash swept aloft by the wind. The remaining priests dropped to their knees, whimpering, begging for mercy.

Carol settled to the ground and stepped forward, not pausing as she passed Darl and Dan, who had tumbled from their suspension when the first priest had fallen.

"I will give you fifteen minutes to be gone from this valley forever," Carol said, facing the cowering protectors. "Any of you I lay eyes on after that will long for the deaths I gave the others."

She paused, then said, "The sands are draining from your hourglass."

The protectors scrambled to their feet, knocking some of the others down in their haste to flee the amphitheater. In seconds, they had all disappeared over the wall leading down to the valley floor. Carol lifted her eyes to the lightning that crawled through the storm clouds above, savoring her control of Lwellen, the lightning master, increasing the strength of her casting so that the stone beneath her feet vibrated with the thunder's echo. Best to lend speed to the running feet of the fleeing protectors.

Slowly she let the lightning fade.

She turned and stepped toward the stone slab where Kira cradled Katya's head in her arms. An eerily familiar scene. Carol could hear Dan issuing orders to some of his men, telling them to watch the priests and ensure that they had departed. As she reached Kira's side, Carol placed a hand on her shoulder, gently moving her out of the way.

She looked down at Katya. The child's eyes had glazed over, and her breathing was extremely shallow, the rise of her chest barely perceptible.

Carol concentrated, and a gentle light bathed the platform, enabling her to see. What had the priests done to the child—drugged her? She placed her hand on Katya's forehead. The girl was on fire with fever, but her skin was dry. Heatstroke?

She reached out for Jaa'dra once more, grabbing it more gently, willing it to the child, directing it to absorb some of the heat from Katya's body. Then the presence of another fire elemental within the girl's mind stopped Carol cold. A name formed inside her head, one she was unfamiliar with: Oganj.

"Oh no!" she whispered.

"What is it?" asked Darl, who had come up beside her.

"The protectors have caused a minor fire elemental to possess her."

"Can't you do something?" Kira pleaded. "You're more powerful than the protectors."

"I'm afraid I might hurt your daughter in the attempt. But our high priest can advise me on this. I will take Katya to him."

A low wail escaped Kira's lips and was carried away on the dying wind. As Carol knelt there, gently stroking the child's face, a worm of regret crawled through her mind. How could she have let the protectors who did this return to their temple? She had not seen the last of them.

Carol gazed in the direction the priests had departed. Fresh lightning branched through the sky above the cliffs. Then, sheathing her anger for later use, she let the lightning die.

9

Eastern Coast of Tal
YOR 414, Late Summer

Far below where Kragan stood atop a coastal hill, campfires twinkled like a great swarm of fireflies on the plain, fifty leagues southeast of the ruins of Hannington. The night air was still and cool, with just a hint of moisture, and it carried the sound of distant laughter to his ears. Kragan's eyes drank in the sight. As his army had progressed eastward through Tal, conquering the noble estates one after another, the war camp had grown as thousands of new conscripts and slaves had been pressed into Kragan's service. The smell of smoke wafted upward from campfires that would be left to burn themselves out with the coming of dawn.

Kaleal's voice rumbled in Kragan's mind: *The silent one in the west has awakened.*

The feel of the night, the smell of smoke on the breeze, and the sound of Kaleal's voice in Kragan's head pulled forth the brutal memory of the moment when, at Kragan's urging, the primordial lord of the elemental planes had merged with the ancient wielder. The pain Kragan had endured as his body had changed, gaining in height and breadth, had burned itself into his mind. Tendons and tissue had rippled into place, stretching skin until it burst, only to reknit itself, then burst again. Gradually the cycle slowed, the skin thickening, taking on a bronze hue that eliminated all traces of the scars that had covered much of Kragan's body.

When his suffering had ended, the sight of himself in the mirror had made the agony Kragan had endured worthwhile. Golden eyes stared back at him from a feline face atop a body that was a thing of seductive splendor and authority. But far more important than his appearance was the combined power of their shared minds. In the coming months, Kragan and Kaleal would enslave this continent and open a path to the outer world that had spawned Kragan all those centuries ago. He would not allow Landrel's she-wielder to stand in his way.

Returning his focus to Kaleal's comment, Kragan clenched his clawed hands, sinews rippling. "I know," said Kragan aloud.

She is getting stronger, said Kaleal. *When so much time passed since last I felt her, I began to think that perhaps some accident had befallen the woman. The sooner we deal with that one, the better.*

"Her strength is irrelevant. No matter what, she cannot prevail against the power of our joint wills. When I have conquered the last of the noble estates and gathered enough conscripts to augment my army, I will begin preparations for the invasion of Endar. In the meantime, I will dispatch my allies in the west to deal with the prophecy's witch and her father."

Rafel's daughter easily dispatched a group of Jorthain's priests.

"A small group of underlings," said Kragan. "High Priest Jorthain has many more powerful protectors in Mo'Lier and will raise an army to deal with Rafel's legion."

Kaleal laughed, a low rumble that escaped Kragan's lips and rolled out over the encampment.

For several moments, all other sounds ceased as the immense army of men and vorgs glanced about uncertainly. Then, with nervous laughs of their own, the members of the horde returned to their preparations for the next day's march.

PART II

During my long life, I have faced many enemies. But never did I think that my own people would cast me out.

—From the *Scroll of Landrel*

10

Areana's Vale
YOR 414, Late Summer

Arn, Ty, John, and Kim sat atop their horses in a canyon leading toward the place where two towering rock walls pinched together. As he watched the group of twenty heavily armed riders trot out of the opening to meet them, Arn thought back on the months of searching the western lands after his group departed Endar. The long search for Rafel had finally yielded word of a large group of newcomers. And that news had brought Arn here.

"This is quite some country your old boss picked out," said John.

"And he's sent a reception party out to welcome us," Arn said, pointing toward the approaching riders. "Just be composed, keep your hands off your weapons, and let me do the talking."

Ty snorted in disgust but sat calmly atop the big stallion as they continued toward the approaching soldiers. The four riders brought their horses to a stop as the soldiers spread out. Several had crossbows leveled in their direction. Many stared in wonder at Kim.

"Are you folks lost?" the young captain in charge asked. "Because you're sure heading toward a dead end. There's nothing this way but a valley."

"If that's where High Lord Rafel has settled in, then we're on the right track," said Arn. "I'm surprised you haven't recognized me, Hanibal."

"Blade!" The captain's face showed a moment's shock, but he recovered quickly.

A murmur ran through the line of soldiers.

"It must have been him that cut Jaradin up," one of the soldiers said, pointing at Arn. "There's not many who could manage that."

Angry mutters rippled through the ranks.

"At ease!" Hanibal commanded.

The soldiers immediately snapped back into military form, although their eyes betrayed the depth of their anger.

"Jaradin Scot's been hurt? I'm sorry to hear that," Arn said. "I always thought highly of him and his brother. Fine rangers, those two."

"Drop your weapons and accompany us back to the fort," said Hanibal. "One of my men will pick them up. I'll return them to you if High Lord Rafel allows it."

Arn smiled. "I know you mean well and I'm sure you're following standard procedure, but I surrender my weapons to no one. The same goes for my companions. But we will ride back with you, and you can have your crossbow men ride behind us. When we get back to the fort, we'll wait outside the outer walls, under guard, until you have an opportunity to talk to Lord Rafel. Then we'll do what he commands. Fair enough?"

Hanibal considered the offer for a moment. Arn knew that Hanibal was aware that he had been a protégé of Rafel's.

"Agreed," Hanibal said.

The captain signaled, and a dozen riders with crossbows fell in behind the four companions, while others flanked them left and right.

The way John fingered his bow concerned Arn, but when Kim leaned from her mount to place a hand on her husband's arm, that worry eased. Beside them, Ty sat on his mount, remarkably calm.

Hanibal turned and led the four toward the narrow ravine.

Arn gazed in awe as they passed between cliff walls that stretched skyward on either side, feeling an urge to dismount and test his climbing skills against the rock faces. A league up the canyon, as the gap between the cliffs reached its narrowest point, the riders came to a halt where the rushing stream blocked their access to the fort that stood on the opposite side.

"Your friends have been busy," Ty said.

Arn nodded. High Lord Rafel, Conqueror of the Vorg Hordes, Commander of the Army of Tal, was a leader who accomplished what others thought impossible. Arn looked forward to seeing him once again, an anticipation that had been growing since Galad had escorted them out of Endar.

Hanibal wheeled his horse toward the four travelers. "You will wait here. My men have orders to shoot to kill if you make any move toward your weapons. That applies to the Endarian as well."

Arn noticed the dangerous light in John's eyes.

"That'll be fine. We'll sit here until you return with Lord Rafel."

"If that is his desire," said Hanibal, turning his horse and passing across the just-lowered drawbridge and into the fort.

A loud braying from Arn's right echoed off the gorge's sheer walls. He turned to see Ty sitting backward on the palomino stallion, arms folded, head tilted back, golden locks matching his horse's mane. A booming rendition of one of the raunchier tavern songs popular along the border spilled from his lips.

Oh, I had a girl, from the town of Traborg,
She was one half grun, and the other half vorg,
She was minus one eye, her face full of pits,

What she lacked for in brains, she made up for in tits,
She had three on the left, and four on the right,
To feel them real good took me nearly all night . . .

The soldiers relaxed as they recognized the ditty, and laughter spread through their ranks. Even the men atop the wall seemed to be enjoying the concert, the lyrics of which droned on interminably.

"Let's hope the high lord gets here soon," John said. "I don't know how much more of this I can endure."

Kim had long since learned to ignore Ty's crude attempts to nettle her. Arn noticed a bored expression on her face, although he also thought he caught the hint of a smirk. The Endarian princess had grown comfortable with her companions, and even John no longer felt it necessary to shelter her from Ty's wit.

Mercifully, they were not forced to endure Ty's lilting verse for long, as Rafel trotted across the drawbridge mounted atop a bay warhorse. Upon seeing Arn, he leapt off the mount and tossed the reins to one of the soldiers.

"Put those crossbows down!" his voice boomed as he strode toward Arn, who slid out of the saddle and extended his hand to the warlord. Rafel took the extended hand and shook it heartily, clapping his other palm down firmly on Arn's shoulder.

"It's good to see you, son. We had heard some rumors that you might be dead."

The depth of the elder man's feelings rang in his voice.

"It's good to see you, too, High Lord," Arn said, returning the grip and the feeling. "As you can see, I'm still around."

"I apologize for the greeting. Something happened yesterday that's got everyone spooked."

"No need to apologize. You can tell old Gaar that I'm impressed with that son of his. He's turned into quite a leader."

"You're right about that. Gaar will be glad you noticed."

"Speaking of good soldiers, how is Lord Alan doing? Last time I saw him, he was getting pretty damn good himself."

"Just don't let him hear you say it. He is strong as an ox and afraid of nothing. That's his problem. He understands tactics and strategy but loses himself to fury in the heat of battle. He might turn out fine if I can keep him from getting himself and everyone around him killed."

Arn could hear the contrasting currents of disappointment and hope in the high lord's voice.

"And how is Carol?"

The question sounded like small talk, but Arn broached it painfully. As a teen, he had adored her like a beloved little sister whom he had watched over. It was painful to think of how she had come to despise him when he rejected her advances—not that he'd wanted to. But at her seventeen to his twenty-two years, such a turn in their relationship would have felt wrong. And the call of Arn's darker side would not allow him to give up his longing for vengeance.

Rafel's face clouded. "She's fine, though I'm worried about her today. She snuck off to go riding when I didn't want her to leave the vale, what with all this trouble yesterday. She's just as strong-willed as she's always been, though. I can't hog-tie her."

The high lord shifted his attention to the others. "Introduce me to your companions, and then we'll go somewhere where we can have a more leisurely conversation."

Arn turned toward the trio, who had also dismounted. "This dark-eyed fellow is John, the big wild man is Ty, and the lovely one of the bunch is Princess Kimber of the Endarians."

Rafel shook the hands of John and Ty as they were introduced, but stopped, stunned before the princess. After several seconds, he managed to recover his composure enough to speak, bowing his head gracefully as he took Kim's hand in his.

"Excuse my stumbling greeting, Highness," Rafel said. "It's just that you remind me very much of someone I used to know."

Kim laughed, a melodic sound that lifted the spirits of all who listened. "You could not have greeted me in a more pleasing way. I have looked forward to meeting you for a long time."

Rafel stared for several more seconds and said, "Follow me back to the fort, where we can talk more comfortably. I am anxious to hear your story and to answer any questions you may have of me. I have a few for you, too, Arn."

The high lord mounted his horse once again. Arn and the others followed suit.

Rafel led the riders across the drawbridge. Inside the fort, ladders led up to a high walkway that allowed troops to shelter behind the forward battlements.

Arn and his companions followed Rafel out through the fort's rear gate. Farther to the east, at another bend in the river, he saw a second fort and understood. If the lower battlement fell to attackers, Rafel's men would use its rear wall to fire down on those within. And when they were forced to retreat, they would fall back into the fort that blocked the gorge farther upstream.

The road led to the place where another drawbridge had been lowered across the creek. As they passed into this fort, the nature of the high lord's defenses dawned upon Arn. The fortifications were a progression of small forts built where the rushing water approached the canyon's northern or southern walls. Then, as the watery maelstrom cut across the canyon to the other side, the next drawbridge led to another fort. This sequence of switchbacks blocked by forts repeated itself again, the sole access to each being the drawbridges.

This third and final fort was larger than either of the lower forts but was clearly a work in progress.

"Impressive," Arn said as they came to a halt and dismounted.

Rafel nodded. "It's coming along. We still have much to complete." He turned toward one of the soldiers. "Have the grooms take care of these horses."

"Yes, High Lord."

"I'm afraid I'll have to go with your grooms," Ty said, "at least until I get this stallion settled in. He won't let anyone else touch him. I'll join you in a few minutes."

"That'll be fine," Rafel said.

He turned and led the others into one of the buildings. Arn ran his hands over the rough-hewn logs that formed the wall as he entered. They were large, with a deep, rust coloring that he had not seen before.

"What kind of wood is this?" John asked.

"It's taken from trees that grow along the high slopes just outside the canyon. We have teams of men cutting and snaking the logs down. Dangerous work, but we've been lucky and haven't lost anyone so far."

The warlord led them into a large room lit by a handful of lamps. He motioned for Arn and the others to be seated as he sat at the center of one of several long tables.

"Well, my young friend," Rafel said, "tell me, what fortunate set of circumstances has guided your footsteps here to my valley?"

"Gladly," Arn said. "But first, I feel obligated to let Kim tell her part of the tale."

Rafel leaned back in his chair as Kim rose and walked toward him. Her next action startled everyone in the room. The princess placed her hand in Rafel's, dropped to her knees, and began to weep.

The high lord leaned forward and placed his other hand under her chin, lifting it so he could look in her eyes. "What is it, Highness?"

Several seconds passed before Kim recovered her composure to the extent that she could speak. When she did, her voice trembled with emotion. "I am sorry. This is not how I planned to say this. My mother, Queen Elan, sends her fondest greetings and her undying love."

Rafel looked stunned. "What? Elan? Your mother?"

"I . . ." Kim struggled to continue. "I love you, too, though all I have known of you came from my mother's shared memories of you. For you see, I am your daughter."

Rafel froze. Suddenly he leapt to his feet, sweeping the Endarian woman up in his arms, embracing her as though time had lost its meaning. Tears ran down his cheeks onto her upturned face. Several long minutes passed before he could speak.

Finally Rafel released his hug, holding the princess instead at arm's length, staring into her sparkling eyes. "Gods! You hit me with a vorg war hammer, daughter."

"I hit myself with it as well," Kim said, wiping her tear-streaked cheeks with her hands. "Arn introduced you to John earlier. What he did not tell you is that John is my husband."

When the high lord turned his gaze on John, it was as if he was seeing the man for the first time.

John reached out to shake Rafel's hand, but the high lord swept him into a powerful hug that the smaller man returned somewhat awkwardly. Rafel released him and stepped back.

"What a day. Not only do I learn that I have another daughter, but I also discover that I have a son-in-law. Welcome to the family, son."

"I'm honored," said John.

Rafel led them back to their seats.

"Well, well, I guess it's about time that I hear this tale of yours, since it brought you on this long and dangerous quest, in somewhat questionable company I might add," he said, arching an eyebrow at Arn.

"I can tell that your words do not truly state your opinion of Arn," Kim said. "For that, I am very glad, since these two, along with Ty, saved me from the vorgs and allowed me to find you."

Clearing her throat, Kim began the tale of her mission to find her father, of her long and dangerous journey from Endar Pass, eastward across the Northern Plains, and then southeast across the Borderland Range toward Tal. She spoke of the vorgs who had attacked her party, killing her guards and taking Kim to the town of Rork, where she was to be sold at auction. She had been fortunate indeed that John and Arn had been there to rescue her and then, along with Ty, helped her escape her pursuers.

Ty rejoined the group during the telling.

When Kim reached the part in her tale of their discovery of the existence of Lagoth, long thought destroyed, she let Arn tell of his and Ty's excursion into Kragan's ancient stronghold.

Arn spoke of the slave city beneath Lagoth and the spell Kragan had cast that caused anyone not loyal to the wielder to become slaves themselves. But it was his revelation that a twenty-paces-tall statue of Carol stood in a chamber beneath the city that widened Rafel's eyes.

Shortly thereafter, a hearty woman and two helpers carried several trays of food into the room. Conversation stalled as the four traveling companions heartily consumed the meal.

The telling wore on through the afternoon and into the evening, moving around the table as Arn, John, and Ty each added their portions to the story, followed by Rafel's account of his own group's journey. As he drew to a conclusion, Gaar entered.

"Sir," Gaar said, "I think you need to see something outside."

Rafel rose from his chair. "What's going on?"

"That you'll need to see for yourself."

Arn followed Rafel through the door, with the others trailing along at his heels. As he emerged from the building, he observed that the sky was darkening rapidly, not just with the gathering twilight. Huge thunderheads boiled overhead, moving at a pace that belied explanation. Lightning flashes chased each other across the sky, followed by the loud crackle of thunder. Some bolts struck so close to the fortress that a sound like the ripping of paper preceded the boom.

"I've never seen clouds move like this," said John.

"I hope it's your magic wielder doing that and not someone else," Arn said, turning toward Rafel.

The warlord shook his head. "I'm afraid not. Hawthorne died on the trail."

"Sad news, indeed," said Arn.

Rafel strode rapidly to the fort's western wall and climbed one of the tall ladders that led to the upper walkway. Arn and the others followed him as he moved to the point that overlooked the center of the canyon. From such a vantage, they saw that the clouds were rushing toward one central point, several leagues distant.

"Carol's out there," Rafel said. "She's in that damned canyon with the cliff dwellers."

The high lord turned and ran along the walkway toward the ladder, cutting off the question that rose to Arn's lips. He raced after Rafel, catching up as he neared the stables.

"Get me my horse now!" Rafel bellowed. "And tell Hanibal I want thirty men ready to ride in five minutes."

Two soldiers scrambled away to comply with their high lord's orders.

"I'd like to come along," Arn said.

"Us, too," said Ty.

"Fine. Except I want Kim to stay here," Rafel said. Then, seeing her flashing eyes, he added, "Don't worry, Kim. It's not that I doubt your ability to handle yourself. This is strictly a selfish decision. I have one daughter out there already. With two of you in danger, I would be too worried to function."

His kindly smile washed the anger from the Endarian's face.

John took Kim's hands and leaned in to kiss her. "I will return."

"I do not doubt it," she said.

Ty led Arn and John to the stalls where their horses were being kept. The three men were soon mounted and waiting for the soldiers, who began arriving shortly thereafter, falling into line just before the drawbridge.

Arn was pleased to catch sight of Alan among the soldiers. The young lord had grown from a strapping lad into a man since he had last seen him. Alan was the same height as Arn, but with his barrel chest and thick form, he weighed as much as Ty, who stood a head taller.

Hanibal arrived with Rafel, cutting short Arn's recollections. "Lower the drawbridge!"

The rumble of a heavy winch and the creaking of thick ropes followed the warlord's yell.

"Column of twos. Fall in!" Hanibal's command brought the soldiers into a double column. "At the trot . . . forward!"

Rafel was already through the raised gates as Hanibal led the column of soldiers out. Ty, Arn, and John trotted out after them. As the column passed through the two lower forts to exit over the final drawbridge, they picked up a ground-burning canter that Arn and the others matched.

As the lightning died out, darkness descended rapidly, forcing the riders to slow to a trot.

Suddenly Rafel's voice rang out. "Halt!"

The word echoed eerily among the surrounding canyons.

Hanibal's voice broke the silence. "Every third rider back on the left, light up a torch."

Arn heard the sound of steel striking flint, followed shortly by oily rags sputtering alight. Before long, lit torches illuminated the entire column of soldiers, casting a glow outward for several paces.

Arn rode up beside Rafel.

"Sir, John has the best night vision of any human I've ever seen. If you put him up front so he's not dazzled by the torchlight, I think we'll make better time."

"Tell him to move on up," said Rafel. "We want to make our way around that ridge on the left and then south into the valley beyond."

Arn nudged Ax back along the column of soldiers to where John and Ty sat.

After he relayed Rafel's instructions, the three companions rode several paces out in front of the column, with John in the lead. At

Hanibal's command, the column picked up a walk that was the best they could manage with the reduced visibility.

Arn found that he could not see much of anything, other than the occasional faint glimmer of torchlight reflected from a rock or tree up ahead. He could listen, however, and by doing so, kept himself close to John's horse. John pressed the pace, calling out when the soldiers behind began to drift off track as he led them to the west, around a ridge, and into a canyon that led off to the south.

"Rider coming!" John yelled back.

Arn saw a distant rider surrounded by a bright circle of light approaching them.

"Double echelon right!"

Hanibal's voice brought the column of soldiers around into double ranks, spread out and facing the front. The soldiers holding the torches formed up in the fore, while the others fell in several paces behind them, out of the torchlight.

"It's a woman on a gray horse," said John, "and she's carrying a child across the saddle in front of her. There are runners off to either side, staying out of the light. I can't tell what's causing the light. It just seems to move with her."

"What does she look like?" Rafel's voice held a note of urgency.

"Slender, long brown hair." John paused. "Holds herself erect like royalty."

"Carol!" Rafel said. "Let's go!"

With a command, Hanibal brought the soldiers back into a double file, advancing at the trot. As the gap between the woman and the soldiers closed, Arn felt tension rising within. Would Carol shrink away from him as she had the last several times they saw each other? The pain of those memories spiked his brain.

Carol came toward them now at a canter made possible by the bright circle of light that extended around her horse for ten paces in all directions. She pulled to a stop beside Rafel.

"Father, this little girl is badly hurt. I've got to get her back to the fort quickly to see if Jason can save her. I'm afraid she'll die. Her parents are following behind. Would you please provide them escort to our infirmary?"

"Certainly," said Rafel. "Hanibal, see to it. If the parents are willing, let them ride double with two of your soldiers."

As Arn watched Carol, his eyes locked to her stress-lined face. Everyone else faded into his peripheral vision. A tremor made its way into his hands, and he clenched them into fists before anyone noticed.

She looked up and saw Arn within the circle of light. "What?" Carol's voice sounded hollow, as if it came from the depths. "How?"

She suddenly sagged in the saddle and would have fallen had Rafel not reached out to catch her. The floating light suddenly went out.

"Hanibal," Rafel yelled as he supported Carol and the child. "Get one of your men to carry the little girl and another to take Carol's horse. Gently now; she's been injured. And bring a torch over here. Carol's head is bloody."

With a heavy heart, Arn wheeled his horse around and rode away from the group into the blackness of the night. A sudden constriction swelled his throat, making breathing difficult, as if he had taken an unexpected blow to the midsection. Carol had seen him and had passed out from shock and revulsion.

She was hurt, yes, but that had not been bad enough to topple her from her saddle. Only the sight of him had been sufficient to accomplish that. Arn had seen the look of bewilderment on her face before she collapsed.

The ride back to the fort seemed endless, as if time and space had been distorted. The darkness took on a dismal, oppressive quality that left Arn cold. He felt a sudden need to be alone. Perhaps that was his problem. He had let himself get too involved with other people, too open to feelings that he had long denied himself. He was left vulnerable to the kind of hurt he had not felt since he had turned his back on Carol to enter the king's service.

Arn shook his head as he rode along, trying in vain to clear it of muddied and repetitive thoughts. How could such a simple encounter affect him this way? Carol's revulsion should not have surprised him. She had avoided him for years, turning away on those rare occasions when they had chanced to meet during his travels to Rafel's Keep to discuss the king's business.

"What's up?" John's voice brought Arn out of his reverie. "You look like you've seen a ghost."

Arn turned toward him. "I keep forgetting about those eyes of yours. What if I said I had seen a ghost?"

"I'd say you were full of it."

"Yeah. And you'd be right about that, too."

John fell silent but continued to ride close to Arn, as if he somehow sensed his comrade's yearning to fly off into the darkness.

Arn's mood lifted somewhat as the group reached the westernmost fort and had almost returned to normal by the time they entered the upper fortress and dismounted. Carol had recovered during the ride, confirming that her head wound was relatively minor. However, what shocked Arn was the brief glimpse of the mark on her shoulder as Rafel lowered her to the ground.

He had gazed upon that same brand on the left shoulder of the huge marble statue of Carol beneath Lagoth. That statue was the mirror image of the illustration contained within the *Scroll of Landrel.*

Arn shifted his attention to the child, whose eyes stared outward without seeing. She was clearly unconscious. If he did not see her chest gently rising and falling, he would have thought she was dead.

Rafel led the way rapidly between angular structures, turning into a lighted doorway in a building that butted up against the fort's eastern wall. It was an infirmary, with several rows of wooden beds completed and a number of others under construction.

Arn was struck by the room's cleanliness. Despite the ongoing construction, there was no sign of sawdust or dirt. A young man in the white robes of an acolyte came toward them as Hanibal laid the little girl on a table.

"Go get Jason," Carol said, seeing the questioning look on the acolyte's face. "Tell him to come quickly."

"Yes, Lorness."

The young man turned, breaking into a run as he exited the building. Carol's hand stroked the child's forehead, tears welling in her eyes.

Just then, Kimber entered and stepped up beside the lorness. The Endarian princess paused for several seconds, her eyes passing over the child and then lingering on Carol, who met her gaze with an unmistakably awed expression.

Rafel joined them. "Carol, this is Princess Kimber. I'm sorry that I'm not able to introduce you under better circumstances, but she is your half sister."

Carol's eyes widened in shock. Several moments passed with an ever-deepening silence before she threw her arms around Kim. When the two parted, questions spilled from Carol's lips.

"My sister? How did you get here? Did Arn bring you?"

A sudden charge, as if he had just rubbed his head with a wool towel, raised the hair on the back of Arn's neck. Carol had said Arn and not Blade. She had not called him by his given name in ages. What could it mean?

Arn told himself she was just caught up in the emotions of the moment and forgot who he was. His hard mood returned as quickly as it had lifted.

"I will tell you all about our arrival when I have a chance," Kim said. "But right now, I need to examine the child. I have some skill with healing."

Just then, Jason hurried into the room, his priestly robes swirling about his legs as he strode rapidly to the table where the little girl lay.

He bent over her, placing his hand on her forehead, gently lifting each eyelid. After several seconds he stiffened and turned to Carol.

"This child is elemental possessed."

"I am aware of that," said Carol. "Can you help her?"

Kimber leaned over the table, murmuring softly beneath her breath. The lights in the room dimmed visibly.

"By the gods," Rafel said.

Arn placed a hand on the high lord's arm. "It's Endarian magic."

Almost instantly the tension seeped out of Rafel's body. At that moment, Hanibal escorted a man and woman into the room; they were the little girl's parents. The man's face was frozen into a mask of dread, while the woman wept openly. She clearly wanted to move to her daughter's side, but seeing Kim and Jason examining the child, the man held his wife back.

Kim spread her fingertips above the girl, starting at the feet and moving slowly upward. When Kim's hands reached the girl's head, she stopped. Along the right side of her skull, an angry red glow laced with orange and green crawled beneath her fingertips. Several seconds passed as Kim studied the spot before she turned toward Carol. With the dropping of her hands, the lights in the room returned to their earlier brightness.

Kim shook her head, sadness shining in her eyes. "The elemental has injured a major blood vessel in this child's brain. Right now, that elemental is the only thing keeping the vessel from bursting. If it is expelled, the vessel will rupture, and the girl will die."

Arn saw Carol's desperate gaze switch to the priest, but Jason merely shook his head.

"I am truly sorry, Lorness. There is nothing I can do for this child."

The moan that escaped the mother's mouth as Carol wrapped her arms around the woman shrouded the room in sorrow.

11

Areana's Vale
YOR 414, Late Summer

It was well past midnight when Arn stood outside gazing up at the moonlit cliffs that enclosed the hidden valley. The rustle of footsteps caused him to turn toward the newcomers. With John in tow, Ty halted and gazed skyward.

"Would you look at that sky?" he asked.

Arn snorted in disgust. "Is that why you searched me out? So you could ask about the stars?"

"A little testy tonight, are we? I didn't realize that High Lord Rafel affected you that way . . . or is it his daughter?"

The mild irritation Arn had been feeling flared up into unadorned anger. "Go away."

"Don't get worked up over nothing," said Ty. "I didn't realize I was prodding a raw nerve."

Arn doubted the truth of the statement but he didn't feel it worthwhile to argue the point.

"What I was trying to get you to notice is how bright the stars are tonight," said Ty. "There's not a trace of cloud in the sky. Doesn't that strike you as being strange after the thunderstorm we had earlier this evening?"

"Not really. Storms build and dissipate quickly in the mountains."

"Not as quickly as that one came and went. Apparently you didn't notice how the clouds just faded away into nothingness a short time before we found High Lord Rafel's daughter."

"What are you getting at?"

"Did you see the way that circle of light moved with her, then went out when she fainted? It strikes me that we may have found the wielder doing all that conjuring."

"I had the same thought," John said.

The revelation stunned Arn. "Deep spawn! I was so surprised to see Carol again that I was blind. I knew that she was a pupil of old Hawthorne's, but I never dreamed that Rafel would let him train her in magic."

"What we just saw," said John, "matches Landrel's prophecy."

Arn paused, rubbing his chin. "Whenever high-powered magic is at work, strong opponents are usually involved. If Carol was calling the storm, whom was she fighting and why?"

"We're not going to find out until after she gets done caring for the little girl," said John. "And from the look of her, Rafel's daughter is going to need some sleep. We won't get the whole story until morning."

"I must be groggy myself," said Arn. "I wasn't thinking too clearly this evening."

"I doubt that lack of sleep is causing your fogginess," said Ty.

"Is that supposed to mean something?" asked Arn, feeling his irritation flare once again.

"Ty," said John, "can't you tell that this female wielder has affected Arn's mind? She seems to have placed him under a powerful enchantment."

"I'm getting the urge to do a little cutting," Arn said, his anger fanned by the enjoyment these two were taking in seeing him uncharacteristically flustered.

"You're right, John," said Ty. "She has enthralled our dear friend here, turning him against his friends."

"Shocking," John said.

"That does it," said Arn, turning to stalk off down the alley, letting their jeers fade into the distance.

He moved quickly, eliminating any chance that the others would follow him. Rounding a corner, Arn found himself facing the fort's log wall that butted up against the south face of the cliff. He thrust his fingers into a crack between logs and began climbing. The wood was rough, knotty, partially covered with peeling strips of bark. The evergreen smell was still strong in the logs, and the sticky sap clung to his hands.

At the top of the wall, Arn paused. He moved sideways, running his hands along the cliff face. It was vertical, nearly smooth, with hairline cracks and small edges jutting here and there. Once again he began climbing, his pace much slower now, wedging a finger into a crack here, jamming a toe against a small outcrop of stone there, all the while feeling his way upward along the stone face.

Sweat beaded on his forehead, then dripped downward to sting his eyes or dangle at the end of his nose, defying the chill of the night air. A ledge above his head made itself known to his exploring fingers, then yielded to a swinging heel as he hefted himself up. The ledge was only as wide as his hand, but it was enough for Arn to sit upon to peer out over the fort below.

The light of the full moon lit the opposite cliff. Arn guessed that he was at least a hundred paces above the top of the log walls, barely a start at climbing the towering wall that rose above him. He sucked in a deep breath and released it slowly. His irritation had departed and been replaced by the exhilaration of the climb. He tilted his head sideways against the stone and gazed upward.

Something about free climbing had always fascinated him. To stand on the edge of a high wall, feeling the magnetic pull of the depths, made his pulse pound. The danger magnified life, stretching the eternal now, altering time in a way that nothing else did. The exertion required to climb a sheer wall added to the feeling, so that all the nerves in his body seemed to vibrate.

Arn's mind drifted. The young woman he had so adored had become a wielder of considerable ability. She had been marked with an elemental brand and somehow survived. A fresh storm of emotion rocked him at the thought of Carol's body being scarred. Once again, he thought of the giant statue in the caverns beneath Lagoth. What exactly was happening?

He slid off the ledge, turning in the air to catch hold of it. The descent took longer than the climb, mainly due to a dead end at an overhang that he could not see in the darkness. This forced him to climb back up ten paces and move to his right before resuming his descent.

Arn made his way down the log wall and through the empty streets, working his way back to the infirmary. A light still glowed through a crack in the door, dimly illuminating the guard who stood just outside. This fellow was shorter and stockier than the one who had been on duty several hours earlier.

"Hello," Arn said, stepping forward.

The surprised guard jumped backward, struggling to pull his sword at the same time.

"Hold on," Arn said. "I'm no enemy, just one of the travelers who came in yesterday."

"What do you think you're doing, jumping out of the dark at me at this hour of the night? You could get yourself killed doing stuff like that!"

"I'll try to be more careful in the future," Arn said.

"See that you do."

"Mind if I go inside?" Arn asked.

"My instructions are to let you and your friends come and go as you wish. You just caught me by surprise."

The guard was still muttering as Arn moved through the door and closed it behind him. A hooded lamp burned dimly on a table across the room. The little girl lay unconscious on a padded bed against the far wall, covered with a thick quilt. Carol lay on a mat close to the child's bed, with John and Kim sharing an adjacent mat while Katya's parents slept on another, all bundled into warm-looking quilts. One of the priest's apprentices moved about the room, seemingly lost in prayer. There was no sign of Ty, who had apparently gone off to sleep elsewhere.

Arn moved to a corner opposite the child's bed and lay down against the wall. As his head sank to the floor, a wave of fatigue took him, whisking away the last of his busy thoughts, leaving his mind an empty place where sleep could gently settle.

—~~—

"My, that looks comfortable." The sound of Kim's voice brought Arn awake.

He raised himself up onto an elbow, momentarily disoriented. "Ow," he said, rubbing his stiff neck.

"We do have beds around here, you know," Carol said.

"By the time I came in, I didn't see the point of disturbing anyone."

"This is intelligence," Carol said, making Kim chuckle.

Arn got to his feet, yawned, and rubbed his hand through his hair. His tresses had gotten long and shaggy on the journey from Endar. And his two-day growth of beard didn't enhance his appearance, either.

"How is the child doing?" Arn asked.

"There is a possibility that we may be able to help her," said Kim.

"It will be risky," said Carol, "but with Kim using her Endarian magic to heal while I expel the elemental, we might be able to save Katya."

"Couldn't Kim act alone?" Arn asked.

"No," said Kim. "For this to work, the two of us must join minds. I can only do that with someone of my blood."

Arn looked from one to the other. "But Carol isn't Endarian."

"She's my half sister. Tonight, in a grassy clearing, we will perform the ritual. Today I must prepare."

"Then I will leave you to it," he said, rising to his feet.

Carol surprised Arn by following him outside. "Let's go find my father. It's time that I told him what has happened."

"Lead and I will follow," Arn said.

Carol seemed somewhat ill at ease in his presence. That, at least, was familiar, if unpleasant. Although he had intended to broach the subject of Landrel's prophecy, he remained silent, discomfited by the moment.

She led the way to the building where Arn had met with Rafel. This morning, however, the space was empty. She stopped at a long, low structure that served as a dining hall. Along with Ty, the high lord sat eating with several officers and soldiers. All of Rafel's men rose as Carol entered, while the Kanjari remained seated.

"Come sit with me," Rafel said. "Gaar will move over to make room."

True to his statement, the grizzled battle master scooted down the wood bench, forcing everyone else to move down. Two lieutenants on the end of the bench grabbed their plates and shifted to the next table.

"What happened to you yesterday?" Rafel asked his daughter.

"First I need to eat. Then I'll share all the details."

"Fine."

Carol rose from the table and looked down at Arn. "Come on. Let me introduce you to our cook."

Arn rose to his feet and fell in line behind Carol. "I'm looking forward to making his acquaintance."

The line had decreased in size to the point where only a dozen soldiers waited in front of Carol and Arn. The two grabbed tin plates and utensils and made their way to the counter, receiving eggs, sausage, and bread. Arn grabbed a mug of hot tea, noting the odd smell that wafted up from the steaming brew.

Seeing his questioning look, Carol explained, "We've had to use some of the local plants as substitutes in our brew. An acquired taste."

"So long as it has a little kick to get the day started," said Arn.

Carol smiled. "Don't worry about that. I think you'll find that the stimulant property is not one of this tea's weaknesses."

A quick sip confirmed Carol's comments. The tea had an aroma that cleared the sinuses, but Arn found the flavor to his liking. The cook was out of the kitchen, and so Carol could not make an introduction, but that hardly mattered to Arn's stomach. They resumed their seats, and conversation died out.

He had forgotten how much he had missed real food prepared by cooks who knew their trade. Carol also seemed to be enjoying the repast, as the time between bites allowed for little chewing and no speaking.

Carol's face was as stunning as he remembered but held a maturity that had not been present when he last saw her at Rafel's Keep. The stress of the caravan's long journey had hardened her, but determination and strength of spirit still shone in her brown eyes.

Finally Arn mopped the last of the eggs from his plate with the remainder of his bread, wiped his mouth on his sleeve, and pushed himself back from the table.

Then, remembering his manners, he said, "Sorry. It's been a while since I ate at court."

"This is hardly court," said Rafel, "and we seem to have a shortage of napkins or people to wash them. I suspect it will be some time before we have regained that level of civilization."

He turned to look at Carol. "And now, if this headstrong daughter of mine is done eating, maybe we can head over to the meeting hall for a full council."

As Carol rose to her feet, she placed her right hand on Arn's shoulder as she stepped over the bench, steadying herself. The gesture brought heat to his cheeks. Ty's mischievous grin did nothing to settle his rampaging heart.

—~—

The morning passed swiftly as Carol told the story of her encounter with the protectors. Arn sat silently as Rafel, Gaar, Jason, and Alan peppered her with questions. Ty and John, who had quietly entered the hall after the larger group, looked on as well.

The high lord alternately cursed and frowned as he listened to his daughter's account. He turned to Arn. "What do you think?"

Arn looked at Carol, trying to override his reluctance to be critical. But they all deserved his honest assessment. "It would have been better if you'd killed them all."

"Exactly!" said Gaar.

"I cannot bring myself to kill those who have surrendered."

"When Derek hears of this," Gaar said, "there'll be no holding him back. It's a sure bet that they are the ones who cut Jaradin up and left him for dead."

"We can send him and a squad of rangers after them," Rafel said.

"Sending Derek out won't accomplish the mission," said Arn. "These beings are wielders. But my knife protects me from magic. That makes me the only one who can do this work."

"Maybe so," Rafel said, "but this isn't your fight."

"My lord," Arn said, "I like this place of yours, and if it pleases you, I'd like to remain. That makes it my fight."

Rafel placed his hand on Arn's shoulder. "I want you to remain. You don't need to prove yourself to me."

"I know. But this task calls to me."

"We're going as well," John said.

"You'd better believe it," added Ty.

"Not this time," Arn said. "The wielders will have placed wards around their camps that will alert them if anyone comes near. Only I will be able to pass through them undetected."

Ty grasped his battle ax. "So, we wait outside the line of these wards while you do your thing. At least you'll have us there to pull your butt out of the fire if something goes wrong."

"No," Arn said.

"You can say no all you want to, but I go where I please."

"That goes for me, too," said John.

"Your friends are right," said Carol. "It's stupid to operate without a reserve."

"That may be true in military endeavors but doesn't apply to me," said Arn.

John picked up his bow and rose to his feet. "We're going."

Arn shook his head in exasperation and rose from the table.

"Gaar will outfit you with supplies for the journey," Rafel said. "Good hunting."

With that, his two comrades followed Arn out into the afternoon sun.

They were soon mounted and passing westward through the lower fortress and into the canyon beyond. Carol, Kim, and Alan escorted the trio to the spot where the priests had left the canyon of the cliff dwellers. John and Kim dismounted to embrace, a sight that filled Arn with envy. He caught Carol gazing at her Endarian sister sharing a tender kiss with her husband and, for a fleeting instant, thought he saw a yearning cross Carol's face.

But she nudged her gray mare to the right, bringing her horse alongside Arn's. Once again, Carol placed her hand on his arm. "Take care" was all she said before moving away as Kim and John mounted up.

As he turned Ax toward the trail, Arn glanced back to see Carol wave, a gesture that he returned, battling the emotions that filled his heart.

—ʬ—

The trio of riders made their way rapidly down the valley and into the forest, where the tall trees deepened the gloom of evening. As the light faded, Arn realized how glad he was to have his two friends along. The sense of companionship lifted his spirits, and John's ability to see in the dark enabled them to stay on the protectors' trail.

At dawn, the trail turned northward, skirting along the foot of the mountain range, where scrub oak and grass became the dominant vegetation in rolling hills cut by streams. Ty was the first to spot the campsite. A small pile of ash marked the location of the dead campfire. John reached down to feel the ashes, stirring them with his fingers.

"They're cold," John said. "The protectors are still a day ahead of us."

"That's okay," said Arn, stepping down from Ax's back. "By the look of things, I'd say they were fairly confident that they weren't being followed. You don't build a campfire when you think you're being pursued."

"Nope." Ty stooped to examine the tracks. "They rode hard for about twelve hours and then settled in for the night."

"Why not?" asked John. "Carol had let them go with a warning. Wouldn't they assume that nobody would pursue them?"

"I wouldn't make such an assumption," said Arn. "Still, it looks like they did. Let's rest the horses and grab a bit of sleep. Then we'll pick up the trail again. I'll take first watch."

"Sounds good to me," said Ty, who released the palomino and flopped down on the ground. He was asleep almost immediately. John grabbed a bite of dried meat, unsaddled, and followed Ty's example.

In three hours, they were moving again. The sun shone brilliantly, although the temperature had dropped since dawn. A cool breeze cascaded down the mountain slopes from the northeast, whipping up bits of dust and leaves and sending them whirling through the air. Arn picked up the pace, sending Ax trotting along the trail that plainly showed the passage of the priests' horses.

The day faded quickly. As evening encroached, the men came upon signs of a second camp. This time the ash-covered coals were warm.

"They can't be more than about six hours ahead of us," said John. "I'll bet they're setting up camp for the night right now."

Suddenly the hair on the back of Arn's neck stood on end. He dived sideways, catching John full in the stomach with his shoulder, driving him down into the dirt. A river of fire flowed out of the woods, striking the tree where the archer had been standing. Ty dived behind a boulder just as another ball of flame erupted above him.

Arn was already up and moving through the woods. He angled to the right, then turned abruptly back to the left and off to the right once again. He moved by instinct, his mind no longer functioning on a conscious level. Brush tore at his buckskin shirt, scratching his face. He ignored the pain, plunging ahead with the speed and silence of a great cat, seeing not with his eyes but with his mind.

A priest appeared with his back to Arn and died barely realizing that his throat had been cut. Arn caught the body, cushioning its landing so that no sound issued forth. He continued moving, turning to the left. He felt the presence in front of him in the darkness before he saw the wielder. Darkness within darkness. Stillness within stillness.

The protector was aware of danger, crouched, a faint magical chant slurring from his frightened lips.

Arn smiled. The priest's magical wards would not serve him this night. The chanting stopped as Slaken entered the protector's skull just behind his left ear. Warm blood spurted across Arn's hand, accompanied by the cloying, copper smell of death.

A loud yell accompanied the sound of another fireball crackling through the cool night air. Arn heard the twang of a bow, clear and pure as the plucking of a guitar string, followed by a swish and a soft sucking sound as an arrow wrapped itself in flesh. A heavy thud was followed by the sounds of a man running across the glade. The sound suddenly stopped.

"By the deep!" Ty said. "I didn't even get to swing my ax."

"Will you shut up so we can tell if anyone is still out there?" John said from somewhere off to the right.

Arn listened carefully, not just with his ears, but with the sixth sense that was never quite separate from him. Indeed, it felt as if they were now alone. He made his way over to where a priest lay on the ground, his leg twisted beneath him unnaturally. A black-feathered arrow pierced the protector's right eye.

"If this isn't the craps," said Ty. "Here I almost get my hair burned off, and I don't even get a crack at the bastards who tried it."

Arn moved in a slow, ever-expanding circle around the campsite before returning to John and Ty. "Nobody's here."

"Yeah," said John. "Between the one I shot and the two that you cut up, that accounts for the three priests that Carol said she let go."

Arn bent to examine the ground closely. In the gathering gloom, he was unable to see clearly, so he motioned to John. "Take a look at these tracks."

John leaned down, then slowly paced back along the trail several paces. "They made camp just long enough to get a fire going and toss scraps around to make it look like they stayed for a while. Then they made the trail out of camp, as if they'd kept going. And just over there, they doubled back and split up for the ambush."

"These guys wanted to be followed," said Arn.

"You're saying that these bastards are good," Ty said.

"And that's bad news," said Arn.

Arn moved to each of the bodies. Satisfying himself that the dead protectors had nothing of import, he turned to face the mountains. "Back it is then."

Ty whistled, and the palomino stallion raced into the clearing.

As Arn swung and mounted Ax, he felt his eyes drawn to the northwest, the direction in which the dead protectors had been traveling. Somewhere out there a storm was building, one that threatened the woman he loved. But for now, he would return to Areana's Vale to brief Rafel and resist the urge to ride toward the danger that called to him, ignoring Slaken's call. Taking a calming breath, Arn turned to follow John and Ty.

12

Areana's Vale
YOR 414, Late Summer

Standing three paces from where Katya lay faceup in the lush grass, Carol watched Kim, as did Dan and Kira from the edge of the clearing. The full moon bathed the meadow in a ghostly glow. The Endarian princess moved as if in a trance, her feet barely touching the ground, or so it seemed in the moonlight. Stopping beside the child, Kim began to sing softly, the verse raising gooseflesh on her skin. Dew gathered rapidly on the grass, a soft glow hanging in the air of the clearing.

A thought popped into Carol's head unbidden, calling forth stories she had not heard since childhood, the memory of which made her long to be a girl once more. The air had taken on a thick feeling, not of dampness but like the charge in the atmosphere before a thunderstorm breaks, the feel of too much energy confined in a small space and seeking release.

A sudden breeze sprang up, cool and soothing against Carol's damp skin, blowing her hair across her face. The glow in the clearing coalesced, condensing like the dew until it had formed tiny orbs of light that clung to blades of grass. The breeze whirled slowly around the clearing, bending the grass as it spiraled inward. Along that path, the drops of dew and light began to flow, slowly at first and then building until they formed a gentle stream moving around and around, ever closer to the Endarian and little girl at the center.

Carol's heart ached, tears running down her cheeks to fall in the grass and be swept along with the dew. The enchantment of the song built upon itself, too haunting to bear, too full of love and longing to endure, too mystical to resist.

Kim turned, and Carol saw that the stream of dancing lights had reached her so that it splashed up onto her bare feet, clinging to her skin to climb upward with the breeze. The stream flowed along Kim to form beads of light that floated around, up, and away. A gentle wind caught Kim's hair, bathed in a soft halo of light and mist. Her hand gestured toward Carol, who felt herself pulled toward the Endarian, almost as if she were floating.

Kim reached out with both hands, feathering them lightly along Carol's cheeks, her index fingers coming to rest on her sibling's temples. The ground shifted so that Carol lost her balance. She was falling, trying to cry out, but she could not.

"Relax, my sister. I have you." Kim's voice wafted soothingly into her mind. Carol relaxed.

"Where am I?" she asked.

"You are where you have always been, but have never seen. You are in our world."

"The Endarian world?"

"You are in our world, yours, mine, everyone's. Look around you, not with your eyes but with your being."

Carol released her awareness. She was in the glade. She was in the ground. She was in the plants. An incredible living energy flowed through the surrounding plant life, drawing from the soil, drinking in the nurturing strength like a babe suckling at its mother's breast. She was aware of insects buzzing, birds chirping in the forest, animals moving deep in the woods. Their energies flowed from the same great source.

Once again she felt reality shift, this time almost imperceptibly. She was dimly aware of a deep throbbing. As she tried to locate the source, she felt her awareness expanding outward. Something moved within the ground, growing steadily more distinct. A great energy throbbed within. On her world's surface, mighty oceans moved, tides rising and falling in a steady rhythm, water flowing through a million streams. She felt small.

Then the globe itself diminished, and she was falling through an eternity of stars in a bottomless sky, falling even though her body was still rooted to the tiny world that tumbled with her through the incredibly vast expanse. Carol's breathing became ragged as vertigo assailed her. Then once again she felt the pulse of other orbs hurtling through the vastness of space, a deeper, more distant sound on the edge of consciousness. The universe itself thrummed with life. She found herself struggling to comprehend all that she saw.

The enormity of the revelation overwhelmed her. Once again, she focused on her world and its land, growing to encompass her awareness. So filled with life. She let the awareness wash through her, its enormous presence imparting a sense of security, of the rightness of nature, of her small but wonderful part in nature. And then she felt something else: a faint sense of wrongness, small but terrible. The world was ill. A cancer was spreading, although she could not determine its origin.

"The elemental realm." Kim's voice spoke in Carol's mind. "They aren't of this universe. A great many years ago, a man of arcane knowledge discovered a way to tear the fabric that separates the dimensions. In so doing, he enabled the elementals to gain access to this world. Their magic is not our magic. Endarian lore draws upon the powers of this universe, relying on balance, the transfer and shaping of natural energies.

"Humans and Endarians are not so different, yet we are an older race. We are much more attuned to the Mother, the world that lets us draw upon her powers as she in turn draws upon the energies of the cosmic. Your mind has been allowed to link with mine because I am your half sister. Some of the same blood flows through our bodies. Some part of each of us is the same. That, and only that, will enable us to do what we must. Where I have only touched your consciousness up until now, we must now join our minds. While this is common among Endarians, it is almost never done with humans. While I do not know what each of us will experience, the process will be a shock. You will gain all my awareness, memories, knowledge, and feelings while I gain yours. A lifetime will pass between us in less than a second, something wonderful, terrible, both.

"The reason we must do this is apparent. It is the only way we will be able to coordinate our efforts to save Katya. I will work to heal her wounds as you control the elemental and keep the entity from doing more damage. Once my work is complete, you will be able to cast the elemental out. Are you ready?"

Carol centered her consciousness. "Yes."

The merging was instantaneous and devastating. Carol/Kim reeled, enduring the mutual shock as she/they worked to establish a frame of reference. What had seemed firm and well understood crumbled beneath the weight of a new understanding and confusion. Time lost meaning. A lifetime lasted hundreds/tens of years. Endarian/human emotions calmed and raged.

Carol heard her Endarian voice cry out with terrible sadness and longing as Kim's human voice rang with excitement. She remembered racial memories from eons past, and in her mind the moon whirled around this orb as it circled the sun. Humans lived half-lives, walking the land for such a brief time before they were swept away in the mighty surf of time. Such strange creatures, so intense and brief.

And for Kim, time moved ever more slowly. Emotions, so hot and out of control, so barbaric that they could not be tamed, coursed through her brain. No wonder the humans were seduced by elementals. Surely these feelings were akin to those of their tempters. Kim/Carol reached to snare one with her/their mind, hungry to control it, to make the elemental pay for the evils done to her people since the rift. Such power.

"No." Carol/Kim's thoughts echoed, reflected between personalities. "Stay focused on the task at hand." They clung to the thought.

Slowly their dual consciousness stabilized, merged but separate in purpose. Communication flowed between them at the speed of thought. They were learning, feeling out how they would work in tandem, each performing different tasks with complementary purposes.

They reached into Katya's mind and seized the infecting elemental, binding Oganj so that their will became its own, limiting its functions to maintaining Katya's life. They pulled the earthen energy inward, letting it flow through them and into Katya's body, moving in tiny ribbons to heal damaged vessels and cells, stimulating natural responses.

Oganj had been busy; the entity's inflicted damage was extensive and subtle. As the moon moved across the sky, the two women worked patiently, and as their joint effort drained their energy, the Endarian side drew more heavily on the Mother.

And then it was done. They drove the elemental out of Katya, hurling Oganj into the netherworld from which it had come.

With another wave of vertigo, Carol felt their minds separate. Her feet slipped from beneath her body, and she sat down hard in the suddenly dead, brittle grass. Kim sagged slightly, then straightened, once again her regal, Endarian self. Carol gazed up into her sister's eyes, seeing them soften with loving knowledge and acceptance. They now shared a bond greater than any blood tie. They had each lived the other's life.

A sigh escaped from Katya's lips, and the girl's eyes fluttered open. Carol climbed to her knees and took Katya's hand in her own as relief washed over her.

"Is the bad dream over?" the child asked weakly.

Carol smiled at her as Dan and Kira raced to kneel at their daughter's side.

"Yes, Katya," Carol said. "You are going to be just fine."

—~—

Tired as she was after the effort she had expended helping Carol, Kim could not afford to sleep just yet. John had come to her with news that the ranger, Jaradin, had developed an infection that was not responding well to Jason's treatment. Thus, she made her way to the room beside the infirmary, where Jaradin was being cared for.

She arrived to find Jason and Derek in attendance at the ranger's bedside, Derek's face full of dread. Jason stepped aside to let her in. Her first sight of Jaradin made her wince. Although she had treated a wide variety of badly injured people, the depravity of those who would stoop to such torture infuriated her.

His left eye had been gouged out, along with the eyelid. Dark striations traced veins surrounding the empty socket. The other cuts in Jaradin's face and upper body had been expertly stitched closed and smeared with a medicinal salve with which she was not familiar. But the area in and around the eye socket radiated the highest fever.

Kim's healing magic was strongest at night, when she could best observe the subtle flow of life energy within her patient and the living things that surrounded him. The next best thing was to find a deeply shaded spot in the forest.

She turned to Derek. "I need Jaradin moved to a place within the forest where the shade is the darkest. We should hurry."

"I know just such a place not far from the fort."

The ranger did not hesitate. His long strides carried him out the door, and he whistled to get a soldier's attention. Moments later he led two men carrying a stretcher into Jaradin's room. After placing the stretcher on the floor, Derek and the other two men gently set Jaradin on it, then lifted and carried him out.

When they reached the forest, Derek quickly guided them to a place shaded by interleaved branches of three spruce trees. As they prepared to place Jaradin on the bed of pine needles, Kim stopped them.

"No," she said. "As much of his body as possible must be touching a tree. Especially his head."

She guided them through the process. Jaradin lay on his right side, curled around the youngest of the trees in a fetal position, his head resting on an exposed root.

"Leave us alone," Kim said. "I cannot have distractions for what I must now do."

Jason and the two soldiers nodded and moved off through the woods. But Derek remained. When Kim gave him a questioning look, he responded in a husky voice. "Whether or not you're able to save him, I will remain with my brother until the end. I will make no sound or movement."

Kim understood.

She seated herself cross-legged behind Jaradin's head and softly began to sing. The song had nothing to do with the magic; it was an ancient Endarian melody that helped her attune with the life energy that flowed through the forest. At first, she saw nothing, but as she moved deeper into the trance, dim beads of light crawled beneath the bark of the young tree, barely visible in the light of this day.

Kim turned her attention to Jaradin's face, now seeing the sickness spreading through the ranger's veins in a greenish light as opposed to the healthy bluish white of the tree's life energy. Continuing to sing her gentle melody, she reached out to place her left hand on the tree trunk and her right hand upon Jaradin's face, circling the eye socket with her thumb and index finger. She formed a channel.

When the exchange began, a tremor passed through Kim's body as the sickness funneled through her in exchange for the health she drew from the spruce. The two competing energies flowed through her in opposite directions, and she suffered, both from the corruption she pulled from Jaradin and from the knowledge that she was killing one of nature's treasures, one that had as much right to live out its life as the man she was working to save. As she wielded the life-shifting magic for good and for bad, she silently mourned.

13

Areana's Vale
YOR 414, Late Summer

With Arn's warning that Kragan was alive and seeking to kill Carol in the forefront of her thoughts, Carol spent the next three days reinforcing Hawthorne's magical wards that she had placed around the vale when the caravan had first arrived, adding to their complexity and range. The process was tricky in that it required her to release control of the elemental she had bound to each ward, but to respond rapidly with a harsh punishment should the entity attempt to break its bonds. The danger was that another wielder might identify the elemental being used and take control of it before she could regain full command.

Thus Carol set up two layers of protection. The outer layer was monitored by a weaker elemental, whose only purpose was to alert her of any disturbance to the inner layer, the ward itself. Carol found that she could immediately detect variations in the wards and counteract an attempted breach.

The lorness was alive once again. To have her magic back felt beyond wonderful, giving her hope for the future she had always envisioned.

Perhaps she would yet accomplish enough to make Hawthorne proud, to be the wielder her people needed.

One day, as she practiced manipulating and augmenting her magical defenses, Arn surprised her when he stepped into her open doorway. She knew that he and his comrades had returned from hunting down the protectors, but she had been avoiding him, arguing with herself until she reached the decision that now seemed inevitable: She might scare him off, but she would go no longer without Arn understanding how she felt.

"Mind if I come in?" he asked.

"Sit with me on the porch," she said, extending her hand as she rose.

She led him to a bench that looked out over the valley beyond. As they sat down, Arn set the small package he had been holding on the bench beside him.

"I'm so glad you came," she said. "I've needed to talk to you."

Arn's look of surprise was quickly replaced with his customary stoic smile, but he did not pull his hand away. "What about?" he asked.

Carol swallowed, holding his hand between both of hers. Her heart beat wildly as she pondered what she was about to say. It was lunacy for her to blurt out what she felt, but here he was, and the time for such revelations might never be right. The memory resurfaced of how she had admitted her love for him during the Ritual of Terrors despite her wish to distance herself. Because of that love, she could now wield magic. Because of her love, Kaleal had failed to possess her.

"I'm not sorry that you've come to Areana's Vale," she said. "I've wanted that quite badly, wanted to tell you that I don't hate you. I thought that you were dead and that I'd never have the chance to let you know how I really feel."

She frowned. "And now that I finally have the chance, I'm babbling incomprehensibly."

Arn's stoic look disappeared, and Carol detected a slight tremor in the hand she held. She tilted her chin upward ever so slightly, looking deep into brown eyes, eyes that held nothing of the icy chill that had made them famous. She took a breath and said the words she had held inside for so long. "I love you."

Arn stiffened as his eyes seemed to lose their focus. His next breath sounded like someone breaking the surface of a lake after a long dive to the bottom. He struggled to his feet, but she did not release his hand, rising alongside him.

"As a brother, you mean," Arn said. "I'm sorry for my reaction, but you must understand that I have longed for your acceptance for as many years as I can remember."

He glanced down at her hands holding his. "I am, of course, thrilled," he said, "but I came only to bring you a package. Now I have lost my train of thought entirely."

Carol smiled at the stammering man before her. "Did I say brother? Funny, but I don't recall using that word."

"What?" His knees seemed to almost buckle.

Carol stepped in close to him once more. "I love you, Arn Tomas Ericson. Not as brother or uncle or cousin, but as I love life. I don't know how my girlish crush on you transformed into this, but I do know when I realized it, and that was during our journey to this wonderful new home. I will no longer play the timid girl."

At that moment, something seemed to break within Arn. He moved so swiftly that Carol almost thought she imagined his reaction, his arms sweeping out as if he were wielding his blades. But he held no weapons. They encircled her waist, lifting her into his embrace. As her lips parted to meet his, her body heat was all-consuming. She felt herself carried back inside the cabin. And as he laid her down on her bed, the desire she saw in his eyes was a perfect match to her own.

The sheath holding the ensorcelled knife he called Slaken hit the floor beside her bed. Carol gasped. Suddenly she could feel his presence and spirit as she had never before managed. The depth of his longing swept her away, a ship tossed by a storm. The tide of emotion tore through her mind, fanning desire's flames.

When at long last their naked bodies were spent, their passions abated, Carol put her head on his damp chest. Her right arm wrapped around him, as if she could not pull his body close enough to her own, and she slept.

Carol awoke with her arm still wrapped around Arn's shoulder, shuddering as the last traces of an unremembered dream drifted just beyond her grasp.

She lifted her head to look at Arn's form and stroked him gently in the fading afternoon sunlight. His body looked as though someone had stretched rice paper over twisted wire. So many scars, so many horrible wounds.

He sighed and shifted slightly so that his long hair moved away from his left ear. Part of it had been cut away, leaving the ear pointed. Carol kissed it gently and cuddled him again.

"I guess we both carry our scars, don't we, my love?"

Then, ever so gradually, despite the dull ache in her shoulder, sleep claimed her once more.

The small package that Arn had brought was left, forgotten, on the back porch.

—~—

Arn awoke from his best sleep in ages, stretching in the simple but luxurious bed, feeling Carol snuggled against him. Her soft breathing told him that she was still asleep, and that sound, mingled with the early-morning twitter of birds, formed the most entrancing melody he had ever heard. He did not want to move lest the motion disturb Carol's slumber. He just wanted to lie there and feel normal.

He did not know what had brought him to this new and wondrous situation, but he thanked whatever god or gods must have intervened. That small voice always guiding him in the back of his mind doled out reassurance. But Arn also knew that he would have ignored his instinct's traditional call to leave. He had no inclination to analyze, question, or fight this reality in any way.

When Carol awoke, they arose together. She dressed unselfconsciously, smiling at Arn as he watched her from the other side of the bed.

"You have given me what I dared not dream of," Arn said, pulling on his boots.

"And what is that?"

"Hope," he said. "Hope for my future, which until yesterday seemed a fairly bleak prospect." He had never uttered such words to anyone.

Suddenly Arn remembered what he had left outside. "I brought something that you will want to see."

He walked to the back porch and retrieved the wrapped package. Turning, he handed the bundle to Carol, who had followed him.

A small gasp escaped her lips as she unwrapped it, revealing an ancient leather-bound tome with odd symbols on the cover and the clasp.

"I found this book on the body of a wielder with a company of vorgs led by a commander, Charna."

The memory of the vorg who had killed his mother tried to claw its way to the forefront of Arn's consciousness, but since that would rob him of this moment's pleasure, he reburied it.

"I'm thinking that perhaps his death wasn't accidental," Carol said as she continued to study the book and its clasp.

"He made the mistake of trying to kill me and my friends."

She walked across the room and sat down in a chair, placing the book in her lap. After several moments, Carol closed her eyes. Then with a word and a gesture of her hand, the strap and clasp vanished from the cover of the tome. Ever so carefully, she opened the book to reveal the pages within, brittle with age despite having been treated with a preservative.

Carol's excitement was plainly visible as she scanned through the pages, then flipped back to the front to begin studying the discovery more closely. After several minutes, Arn cleared his throat. She glanced up in surprise.

She set the book down, stood up, wrapped her arms around Arn's neck, and kissed him. "Thank you. You couldn't have brought a gift that would mean more to me."

Arn gazed into her upturned face. The memory of the giant statue of her in the throne room beneath Lagoth flashed into his mind. The thought sent an icicle of dread through his chest. He would have to tell her about that and everything he had learned about Landrel's prophecy, but he could not bring himself to do it on this most wonderful of days.

"We have a bit of a problem that we should discuss before I get my day started," Arn said, "and that is the awkward situation our relationship may put you in publicly. I know that Lord Rafel is fond of me, but I don't think that he'll be thrilled with the idea of an assassin being romantically involved with his daughter."

"My father knows I'm my own person," she said. "I would welcome his approval, but in the end, I'll be happy whether he approves or not."

"The idea of me as a potential son-in-law may cause him a great deal of difficulty."

"Are you asking me to marry you?"

Arn struggled to maintain his composure. "Gods. I certainly didn't mean to ask in such a clumsy manner."

Carol took his hand in hers, stepping in close. "Then say what you mean."

Arn opened his mouth, then closed it as he fumbled for the words, mortified by the time it was taking him to form a coherent thought. With his left hand, he wiped away beads of cold sweat from his brow.

He said, “I came here to protect you. You know what I am. Now I fear that my selfish longings will place you in even greater danger.”

Seeing the old hurt creep back into her brown eyes, he forced himself to continue. “But my love for you is so strong that I cannot deny it. So, yes, I am asking. Will you be my wife?”

Relief flooded her face. Then she threw her arms around his neck and kissed him as he pulled her close.

When the kiss ended, she let out a shuddering breath. “I’ve wanted you to ask me that since I was seventeen.”

Dizzy with wild joy, Arn swept Carol up in his arms and carried her back into the cabin.

14

Areana's Vale
YOR 414, Late Summer

"Ah, there you are." Rafel stepped forward to clap a big hand on Arn's shoulder as he walked into the high lord's meeting chamber. "I expected you first thing this morning."

Despite the tightness Arn felt in his chest, he reached for a bit of levity. "I guess I must be getting old, oversleeping."

"Ha. I shall not live to see that day. I have some news that you will find of interest."

Rafel led Arn to the rough-hewn wooden chairs that surrounded the sand table used for briefing his commanders. "We are going to be invited guests tomorrow night."

"One of the local tribes?"

"Actually, Ty ran across a patrol from a clan of horse warriors while he was out riding, and they escorted him back to their fortress city about a day's ride north of here. While there, he arranged to introduce me to their leader, whom these warriors refer to as the khan. Your Kanjari friend is a rather presumptive fellow."

"No doubt about that, but knowing how he hates socializing, he must have had a damned good reason for doing it."

"He thinks the clan may be distant kin to the Kanjari. I suspect that their chief wants to learn if we pose a threat. I'd like to find out the same thing about them."

Arn strolled slowly around the sand table, one hand resting on the carved wood siding, rubbing its rough surface.

"If Ty's right about these people being kin to the Kanjari, or at least similar enough for him to regard them as such, then they're warlike," Arn said. "They'll be highly protective of their domain. Any perceived encroachments or challenges to their prowess will invite an attack."

"So you think turning down their invitation would be regarded either as fear or an insult?" asked Rafel.

"Most likely," said Arn.

"It wouldn't hurt to cultivate an alliance with our neighbors to the north, if possible. I want you to accompany me, along with Broderick, Ty, John, and a small group of rangers."

"Are you sure you don't want to bring at least a company of soldiers? A show of some strength never hurts."

"Our people have their hands full with what I want done here," said Rafel. "Besides, that amount of force wouldn't be of much use if something goes significantly awry."

"Carol, Gaar, and Alan are not going to like being left behind."

"Carol is second-in-command and would need Gaar to help her if something happens to us. As for Alan," the high lord said, his face darkening, "I am reluctant to take him. He tends to be reckless, ready to fight at the slightest provocation."

"If you ask me," said Arn, "the trip represents a good training opportunity."

"You see straight to the heart of the matter. Carol has a natural feel for the right thing to do, but Alan needs to learn. I'll bring him along."

Arn locked eyes with those of the high lord, taking a deep breath before he changed the subject. "I need to talk with you about something else."

"I've never known you to be shy. Spit it out."

"I'm in love with your daughter."

The high lord stared at Arn, arching his left eyebrow ever so slightly.

"Are you planning on telling me something I haven't known for eons, or is this what you thought I needed to be braced for?"

"I asked her to marry me, and she said yes."

For a moment, the warlord froze, and Arn braced himself for the worst.

Then the steel-gray eyes sparkled with a strange light as Rafel stepped forward and crushed Arn in his famed embrace. "Arn, you witless fool. I've long wondered when you two would see what was clearly in your hearts. You've finally given me the hope that I'll get to hold some grandchildren of my own."

Rafel stepped back. "Did you doubt that I've loved you like my own son?"

"No. But there are prodigal sons as well. With me, she inherits many enemies. And I'm confident you're aware that tongues will wag unfavorably at our union."

"Prodigal perhaps, but the best protector that has ever served any lord or king. As for wagging tongues, the day I start running my court like some waifish wisp of a courtier, then you are welcome to put an end to my misery. I suppose you think that she inherited only friends from me. Though I will not hesitate to come to their aid, the world we live in is a treacherous place, and I will not shelter my children from the glorious dangers that the adventurous confront."

Arn started to respond but found that a strange lump in his throat had appeared. He swallowed hard and finally managed to speak. "Thank you."

He gripped Rafel's forearm, maintaining his hold as a wave of emotion rocked him. Then, turning swiftly on his heel, Arn strode from the room.

—~—

Rafel moved up onto the fort's east wall and watched as his future son-in-law melted into the woods beyond, a broad grin lighting his features. Gaar's arrival interrupted his reverie.

"What's so funny, High Lord?"

Rafel turned, leaning back against the rough logs. "Old friend, there are moments in this life that make a man wish he was young again, that he might experience the glories of this world for ages yet to come."

"I'll have the priests check the purity of the water supply," Gaar replied. "You seem to have consumed something that does not agree with you."

The sound of Rafel's happiness drifted out on the breeze and echoed through the reeds and hollows. The young soldiers lifted their eyes to the walls in wonder, having never heard that booming laugh. Those who were older and more experienced merely continued their work on the fortifications. That joyous sound almost always preceded battle.

15

Coldain Estate—Southeastern Tal
YOR 414, Late Summer

Coldain's Keep was perched atop the white cliffs against which the ocean pounded far below, its stone ramparts having stood in place for three centuries. Never had it fallen to an enemy. On the western wall, Garret Coldain stood atop the ramparts, backlit by the red glow of the approaching sunrise. Clad in leather armor beneath a chain-mail shirt and wearing his iron helmet, he studied the three hundred soldiers who would soon fight to hold the wall against the horde gathering to the west of this fortress.

Garret lifted his eyes to the siege engines that moved at the forefront of Kragan's army. Should the gates withstand the magical assault that Kragan and his wielders were certain to unleash, this keep would still fall. But there would be those who would whisper the name Coldain in reverent memory of the fight Garret would deliver on this day.

Atop the tower behind him, Gregor stood, his dark blue robe billowing out in the stiff morning breeze, staff in hand. On the wall to Garret's left stood his father's skeletally thin wielder, Panko, in a coral-colored robe, bearing a staff as white as ocean foam. Alongside these masters of air and water, Garret would soon give battle to his enemies.

As he surveyed the long lines of marching vorgs and brigands that merged into the gathering horde, Garret clenched his teeth, trying to still the tremor that had crept into his sword hand.

—~—

Kragan stared up at Coldain's Keep, using the air elemental, Ohk, to lens his view so that it seemed that he looked through a far-glass. It was not the image of Coldain's son standing atop the wall that shocked him. It was the sight of Gregor standing on the tallest tower, his robe the blue of the ocean that extended beyond the keep to the distant horizon. Somehow, Rodan's wielder had deceived him, making Kragan believe that he had broken Gregor's mind when they had contested in the chambers beneath Hannington Castle.

Clearly Gregor posed a much greater threat than Kragan had believed. And Gregor was not the only enemy wielder visible to Kragan. Coral-robed Panko stood atop the western wall beside Garret Coldain. Although these two were masters of controlling the powerful elementals of air and water, they were adept at wielding elementals from the other planes as well. This battle would not go as easily as Kragan had hoped.

Kaleal's thought rumbled in Kragan's mind. The primordial's comment did little to improve Kragan's mood. But he did not allow his anger to force him into hasty action. Instead, he chose caution. He would unleash his army and allow the dozens of wielders within the horde to deal with this unexpected turn of events. By his so doing, Gregor and Panko would be forced to reveal what strength they could bring to bear. Only if needed would Kragan directly involve himself in the fight. He trusted that would be unnecessary.

—~—

Garret Coldain watched from the courtyard as the tree-size battering ram, propelled forward by dozens of vorgs, crashed into the gates with such force that its metal tip split the thick wood. It was nothing short of a miracle that the keep's defenses had held until midday. That had been thanks to the combined efforts of Gregor and Panko as they battled the magic of dozens of enemy wielders. But as they tired, Kragan had floated up above his troops, his inhuman form visible for all to see.

Through his far-glass, Garret had stared into those malevolent eyes, having to work to keep his knees from buckling. He had beheld a being from the deep and was afraid.

Then Kragan had reached out a hand, and the shielding Gregor had erected over the keep shimmered, glowing red. A terrific blow struck it once, twice, three times, creating a thunderous boom that threatened to deafen the soldiers and townspeople within the keep's walls. The last of these invisible attacks created a spiderweb of black cracks in the shielding above the tower where Gregor battled. These cracks spiraled inward, widening until the entire shield gave way. The gray-bearded wielder staggered, then tumbled from where he stood.

In horror, Garret had watched Gregor's body smash into a bloody mess on the paving stones of the courtyard below. But the young lord had not remained frozen in place.

"To the gates!" Garret had yelled as the vorgs carrying the battering ram charged forward, protected from arrows by walls of shield bearers. He had rushed down a ladder into the courtyard as Commander Volker sent dozens of soldiers carrying support beams to the gates as a hundred soldiers formed into battle ranks behind them.

Now Garret assumed a battle stance beside Volker, at the front of those soldiers. As Garret stood, shield raised, sword at the ready, a new sound pulled his eyes up to the ramparts above the gates. Panko turned eastward to face the sea. He lifted his arms, palms up, and the mist rolled in, curling over the cliffs and rising above the keep. The mist boiled, turning from white to gray as it thickened into clouds, growing darker with each passing moment. Beyond the gates, a downpour began, quickly increasing in intensity as Panko's face tightened in concentration.

Garret had never seen a rainstorm such as this. A massive waterfall from the sky splashed to the ground, flooding the invading horde and sending spray onto the guards manning the battlements above. A fireball exploded around Panko, its flames engulfing the wielder and setting his robe on fire. Panko screamed, then stumbled forward, plunging out into the maelstrom beyond the wall, taking the last of Garret's hopes down with him.

Suddenly the weakened gate exploded inward, propelled by the floodwaters that Panko had unleashed. Garret found himself knocked off his feet and swept along with other soldiers across the courtyard. Dropping his sword and freeing his left arm from his shield, he struggled to right himself, but the weight of the chain mail prevented him from doing so.

Then Garret's head struck stone, and darkness took him.

—∾—

The overwhelming odor of raw sewage tugged Garret back to wakefulness. He opened his eyes but could see nothing in the darkness. He tried to thrash about in his panic, but his body was pinned to wet muck beneath a pile of debris. Steeling himself, he lifted with all his might and felt the pile move. Again he tried, ignoring the pain that hammered his head, and felt something give way above him. Some of the rubble slid aside, allowing him to push more of it off his body.

He managed to roll to his knees and then crawl forward through stinking sludge, ankle deep, until his outstretched hand felt a stone wall that curved upward. Tracing the wall with his fingers, he felt it arch to form a ceiling just above his head. If he tried to stand, he would knock himself senseless again.

Then he understood. This was the sewage channel beneath Coldain's Keep. How far down he'd been washed, he didn't know. But Garret knew he was fortunate to not have drowned. If he had not been jammed into the pile of debris that partially blocked the tunnel, his body would have washed out through the exit spillway to tumble down the cliff and into the roiling sea.

Kneeling in sewage, he reached up and winced when his fingers found the knot where his head had connected with stone. How long had he been unconscious? If his parched throat was any indication, he had lain here for at least a day.

He reached down into the foul stream that trickled past him, finding he was currently facing the direction from which it flowed. Good. This would take him back to the storm drain into which the water had swept him.

As he began the painful crawl, his thoughts turned to his mother and sisters. Garret had promised his father that he would take care of them, along with the people who resided on the Coldain estate. Instead, Garret had never even raised his sword against the enemy. He knew that he could not have stopped Kragan's horde, but at least he could have given his life with honor.

He dared not think about what had happened to his loved ones while he had lain unconscious. His desperation to get to his mother and sisters lent strength to the arms and legs that propelled him back up the channel.

The smell of smoke becoming stronger than the stinking slime through which he crawled alerted Garret to his proximity to a storm drain. That and the distant shaft of sunlight that speared down through the hole. When he reached the drain, he squinted as his eyes adjusted to the bright light. Then, ever so slowly, he straightened and climbed the metal rungs embedded in the wall, dreading the moment when he could peer out at the keep beyond.

That moment took his breath away. Garret peered out from beneath an overhanging stone shelf at the burned-out ruins that had been Coldain Keep. Nothing moved among the rubble. The dead lay scattered everywhere. Although the fires were out, smoke still wormed its way upward, as gray as the overcast sky above.

Garret crawled out of the drain and wandered aimlessly through the courtyard, struggling to keep from vomiting at the sight of dismembered corpses and the line of impaled bodies that led from the destroyed outer gates into the ruins of the village at the base of the hill. The horde that had done this was gone, apparently having taken survivors with them.

He turned away from the sight and walked to the burned-out inner keep, stepping across fallen beams as he made his way into the interior. Although he had intended to go first to his family's living quarters, higher in the tower, the horror that he saw as he passed the earl's audience chamber brought him to a halt. There, in Earl Coldain's high-backed chair, bound hand and foot to its arms and legs, sat his mother, her final screams frozen on her seared face. If it had not been for her seashell necklace and bracelet, he would have failed to recognize her.

For a moment that stretched into eternity, Garret stood there, frozen in place. Then, as his knees gave way, he sank to the floor and wept.

16

Val'Dep
YOR 414, Late Summer

Rafel's party assembled at the stables at sunrise. Arn watched as a handful of rangers led by Derek Scot sat silently astride their horses, waiting for the signal to fan out on the flanks. Alan sat atop his warhorse near John, Ty, Arn, Broderick, and his father.

Carol had accepted the logic that kept her back in command of the valley. Gaar was not happy about being left behind, either, but he understood the risks of sending the entire leadership on the trip.

Arn watched as John and Kim each reached out with their right hand to caress the other's cheek, an Endarian custom between husband and wife when parting. John straightened in his saddle, the light of the morning sun filling his dark eyes.

"Gods," Ty said, "can we move along?"

When John and Kim ignored him, Ty continued. "We will be traveling north along the foothills once we leave the vale. The khan's escort riders will meet us about four hours north of here and will guide us the last several leagues to the fortress city of Val'Dep. Once our escorts join us, you can pull the rangers back in. From that point, there will be no further need of our own watch."

"I don't like that idea," said Broderick.

"Since we are already committed to going in small numbers," Rafel said, "it makes no sense to act skittish once we're in the midst of our hosts. We'll do as Ty suggests."

The high lord turned to the guards. "Lower the drawbridge."

Broderick pulled his rangers in for a quick conference, and then the group of riders trotted out onto the trail that led out of the vale. The rangers moved out quickly, disappearing around the nearest bend in the trail, while Ty rode beside Rafel. With a nudge of his heels, Arn put Ax into motion beside John and Alan.

As they rode northward, the coolness of morning gave way to a warm afternoon. Arn saw the first of the khan's riders at the same time as Ty. Two dozen warriors raced toward them at a gallop. A much larger group of horsemen sat their mounts on the ridge that formed the west side of the valley. Arn looked up the eastern slope but did not spot any additional riders.

As the warriors drew closer, Arn had to admit that they reminded him of Ty, although these men wore considerably more armor than his Kanjari friend did. Rough chain-mail shirts covered upper torsos. Legs sported tough leather breeches tucked into knee-high boots. Leather gauntlets studded with small metal spikes adorned forearms. Battle-axes hung from saddles. All had bows and quivers slung across their backs.

Rafel held up a hand, bringing his contingent to a halt. The rangers rejoined the main group so that all formed a double column. As one, Rafel and Ty trotted forward to meet the coming riders of the khan. The horsemen pulled their mounts to a sliding halt in a tight semicircle around Rafel and Ty, raising a cloud of dust that briefly obscured all. Alan's hand drifted to his ax, but Arn laid a restraining hand on his arm, and the young lord relaxed.

Almost before the dust had settled, Rafel and Ty concluded a brief conversation with the leader of the riders, swung their mounts around, and returned to the group. The riders of the khan swept into a loose formation surrounding Rafel's party. With a yell from the leader of their new escort, both groups of riders headed up the hills to the north.

Cresting a ridge, they entered a broad and fertile valley that narrowed and steepened perceptibly as it turned to the northeast. After several leagues, the valley narrowed. Arn watched as several hundred warriors spilled from the surrounding hills to fall in behind them.

In front of Arn, a twenty-pace-wide chasm crossed the valley from east wall to west. The valley floor had apparently collapsed at some point in ages past. From high up on the chasm's eastern wall, a plume of water thundered down, becoming an underground river. Along the far side of this chasm, a fortress wall formed a barrier to the stretch of land that led to the city visible in the distance.

Two ten-pace-wide cantilevered ramps swung forward from the top of the outer wall to touch down where Rafel's party and the khan warriors approached. The ramps could be lifted and swung back onto the far wall, leaving no path for an enemy force to cross the fissure.

Watchful guards manned the top of the outer wall, which had crenels for firing arrows along with troughs and buckets for pouring hot oil. The riders picked up a gallop, hitting the wooden ramps and racing up over the chasm and onto the top of the wall beyond. As the horses hit the twin ramps, the chasm amplified the thrum of their hoofbeats until the sound echoed from the canyon walls.

As his horse galloped up the ramp, Arn's heart raced. Never had he felt something as exhilarating as the ride up one of the fifty-pace-long wooden ramps to spill out on top of the broad granite wall. But the group didn't stop to admire the view. Instead, the horsemen raced down a sod ramp on the wall's back side onto the parade and training grounds beyond.

The riders leading Rafel's party pulled to a sliding halt before an elevated dais in the center of the parade field. Rafel's group matched them at the halt. The hundreds of riders who then poured over the wall raced around the field counterclockwise, forming a circling vanguard around the group in the center.

Arn gazed up at the top of the dais, where a throne carved from white stone sat. A man with graying blond hair and beard, glittering armor, and an ornate ax looked down at Rafel.

The man stood and raised the great ax high in the air. Circling riders slid to a stop as one, wheeling their horses around to face their leader.

"Khan!"

The word thundered from every throat and echoed off the valley walls.

"Unhorse!"

At the khan's command, every one of the horsemen dismounted, their feet striking the ground in unison. Only Rafel's group remained astride their mounts.

The khan took a step forward on the dais. "I gave a command! You are new here, so I do not expect you to know our ways, but you will react to my commands as do all others in my domain."

Rafel's deep voice carried through the natural amphitheater. "I am Rafel, commander of the legions that defeated the vorg hordes, high lord of the free people of Areana's Vale, here by invitation of the one known as Khan. I bend knee to no man or god. If you are not the one who invited me, then take me to him and stop wasting my time with petty attempts at intimidation."

Arn felt a barely perceptible ripple pass through the scores of warriors surrounding those who came from the vale, a mixture of shock and outrage threatening to overwhelm iron discipline. The moment dragged on as a stifling silence descended on the field. Rafel's group sat on their horses at ease, including Alan, who watched his father, mirroring his expressions.

The khan suddenly leapt to the stairs, descending them at a run. At the bottom of the dais, he jumped astride a black warhorse held by a squire and closed the gap, pulling the animal to a stop beside Rafel's.

Arn saw the khan's sparkling blue eyes locked with Rafel's steel-gray ones.

"Let's step down together, then. What say you?" said the khan.

"Agreed."

The two leaders swung off their warhorses, a movement matched by the rest of Rafel's party. As their feet hit the ground, the khan extended a hand, grasping the outstretched forearm of Rafel.

"Well met," the khan said. "I see that my Kanjari friend did not exaggerate in his description of you."

Arn felt his body relax. Today would not be their day to die after all.

17

Val'Dep
YOR 414, Late Summer

The fortress city of Val'Dep stretched out above and before them, climbing the canyon walls on the right and left in a series of steps carved into steep hillsides that ended at the cliff walls. It looked like a multitiered cake that had been cut in two, with both halves having been rotated back to back, a narrow gap separating them. Alan believed that the buildings had been constructed of white limestone, offering peaked tile roofs.

A twenty-pace-wide lane between high walls was blocked by a series of iron gates. This defense was augmented by the fortified city walls on either side, from which arrows could be fired from the hundreds of crenels lining their tops. More of the cantilevered ramps connected the opposing city walls, allowing troops to traverse Val'Dep above those jammed into the killing zone below.

High on the steep slopes of the right-hand portion of the city, a white palace perched, its turrets and rooftops covered with brightly colored tiles. A prominent flag with crossed ivory axes on a bloodred background fluttered above the tallest tower. Rafel's small group, having followed their guide along the road that separated the two halves of the city, found themselves in a broad box canyon that extended several leagues to the northeast. Like Areana's Vale and the home of the cliff-dwelling Kanjou tribe, the sheer cliffs had been carved eons ago by the glaciers from which the mountain range had gotten its name. Half of this pastoral canyon bottom was farmland, while the other side was used as grazing land for several thousand horses.

Here the roadway split, with one portion leading around the city wall on the left and another branching around the city wall on the right. Alan marveled at the detail and thought that had gone into Val'Dep's design and construction. He also noted that the food and water supply could not be cut off without an army having made the trek to this point. And a large cavalry could be assembled in the broad box canyon to greet attackers as they emerged from the narrow gap between the city walls.

Taking the rightmost branch of the dirt road into the broad valley, they were led around the wall on the right half of the city and up yet another ramp through a gateway beneath a raised portcullis and into the city streets beyond. The streets were paved in cobblestones, ancient and worn from centuries of passing feet, but everywhere they looked, the buildings and streets were meticulously clean and well maintained. The doorways into the houses were either open archways or constructed of dark wood with iron latch handles. All of the houses and shops connected, periodically separated by narrow alleys. Small windows were decorated with colorful cloth curtains, most pulled to the sides and tied with cords. On the larger homes, stone balconies provided a standing or sitting area from which one could look upon the vista below.

Several things attracted Alan's interest. Where were the dirty smells and other evidence of the sewage and garbage problems associated with a town of any significant size? He could see none of this, and no foul odors drifted to his nostrils. Men and women moved about their business, pausing to stare at the strangers as they passed. A group of young children began to gather, clad in bright colors, the boys in short pants with colored suspenders and the girls in a wide variety of skirts, dresses, or short pants. Several of the children followed along behind the procession until a guardsman rode back and sent them scurrying to their mothers.

Alan studied the women who moved through the streets, noting with surprise that their hands showed the calluses of physical labor. Then he saw women hard at work in the shops that lined the main street. All of the tradespeople appeared to be women. They were the butchers, bakers, bricklayers, and blacksmiths. And these women were not slaves. They appeared to be firmly in charge of all the professions that made the khan society function, freeing the men for the profession of arms.

Rounding a bend in the street, Rafel's group turned onto a broad avenue that meandered upward toward the gleaming white walls of the palace. The palace gate consisted of a raised portcullis under a thick stone archway between towering walls. Guards strode methodically back and forth along the tops of those walls, their armor gleaming in the sunlight as they paused to peer over the side at the riders below.

As the riders entered the palace courtyard, several squires came forward, the eldest taking the reins of the khan's stallion and the others securing the horses of the remainder of the group. Dual rows of guardsmen lined the entrance to the great hall into which the khan ushered his visitors. With a wave of his hand, the khan indicated that those from the vale were to follow the guardsman who awaited them just inside.

Alan and the rest of Rafel's group followed the attendant through a pair of thick doors and up a spiral stairway to an ornate apartment, in which a fully provisioned table awaited.

"My name is Fallon, and I am here to ensure you are properly accommodated. I trust you will find the food to your taste," the guardsman said. "Should you need anything, pull on the bell rope, and a server will fetch whatever else you desire. The khan has directed me to inform you that this is merely a small meal to take the edge off your appetites.

The feast will begin promptly at sunset. I will return to guide you to the banquet hall at that time. Please make yourselves comfortable and enjoy the view from your balcony."

Walking over to the draperies on the far wall, Fallon pulled a cord, and they parted, revealing a broad balcony overlooking the courtyard and the valley below. The scene brought exclamations from the entire company.

"That is truly a sight worth many a day's travel," said Rafel.

"I have never seen the like," said John. "And that is saying a lot after spending the winter in Endar."

With a slight bow, Fallon strode from the room, closing the door in his wake.

Alan walked out onto the balcony and leaned out over the ledge, gazing down on the grounds below, taking in the courtyards and lower walls to the compound, and then letting his gaze move down over the twin halves of the city and the chasm that separated them in the center of the ravine. The way the city hugged the two steep sides of the canyon, molded into the shape of the rising hillsides onto which the twin halves clung, was a sight from a children's tale.

The sounds from below could have been those of any busy locale that he had experienced except for the lack of harsh, guttural tones one picked up in the cruder sections. The closer calls of officers, directing soldiers in their duties, floated up on the breeze. An occasional gust of air flapped the many red and white pennants that fluttered from the walls, both above and below. As Alan listened, he could dimly make out a deep thrumming rush of water through the rock.

"Magnificent," Rafel said, coming to stand beside his son on the balcony.

Alan saw that their entire party had assembled to look out over the scene.

Ty stepped up to the balcony's edge as a sudden gust whipped his mane. "For horse warriors to lock themselves in place by building a city," Ty said, "is more than passing strange."

The group followed Rafel back inside the large apartment and seated themselves on the cushioned chairs and sofas that formed a semicircle around the empty hearth. The high lord stood at the focal point.

"We're among the wolves now. I do not think that we have seen the last of their aggressive testing of our character," Rafel said. "What do you think, Ty?"

"We've merely passed the first of a sequence of tests, although they don't think of them in that way. These people, like the Kanjari, are slow to warm to outsiders. At this point we've only been deemed worthy of admittance."

"They haven't cut our throats," said Broderick, "but I wouldn't give two pieces of eight for our chances should we stumble."

"Keep that in mind," said Rafel. "I want everyone to follow my lead in both manner and action. Our comportment will be a delicate balance between confidence and brashness, but we must not allow ourselves to lose our tempers."

The high lord glanced at his son.

As the sun set in the west, Fallon appeared to escort the vale travelers down to the site of the banquet. This turned out not to be the great hall they had observed upon entry to the palace but a smaller room entered through a set of double doors. The banquet hall was perhaps thirty paces wide and about the same length.

A set of thick oaken tables formed a U shape that occupied most of the room, with the khan seated at the center. Warriors were seated along the tables, servers scurrying back and forth among them, bringing platters of food and pitchers of ale. Candelabras festooned the walls and the tables. Nearer at hand, servants turned two roasting pigs on spits above a bed of glowing coals.

The khan, clad in a white tunic over gold trousers, his hair braided and hanging down his back, stood and raised his glass, an action immediately followed by the fifty or so warriors who occupied places at the tables. "Hail to our guests."

"Hail," the assemblage echoed.

"High Lord Rafel, I have reserved for you a seat next to my own."

Rafel led the others around the tables on the right, directing them to be seated in a section of empty chairs. He continued on and assumed a seat beside the khan. Alan deduced that the warriors who had been invited to the feast represented the leadership of the khan's kingdom. Yet Alan found it odd that no women were present aside from some of the female servants. Even though women's roles within Tal's society were limited, lornesses were certainly welcome at the tables of the nobles. The khan's feast suffered by comparison.

The attire of the warriors was uniform and matched that of the khan exactly: white tunic over chain mail, with gold-colored cloth breeches. Hair was blond or red throughout, twin braids down the back, with beard and mustache braided to form twin forks. Metal-studded leather gauntlets covered the wrists and forearms of the khan's men, although his gauntlets were of gold. Three of the warriors sported black eye patches and scars down their faces.

The khan rose to his feet once again. With a scraping of chairs, everyone followed his lead. "First, we drink, then the entertainment, then we eat and drink again. To comrades in arms!"

"Comrades in arms!"

The khan and all present drained their mugs and sat down. He clapped his hands twice, and a pair of warriors bearing two axes each entered the center area between the tables. "High Lord Rafel, you will now enjoy a demonstration of martial skill the likes of which you have not seen before."

He clapped once more, and the two warriors, one redheaded, one blond, immediately whirled around, axes rising and falling in a frenzy of motion as each attempted to dismember the other. Each blow rang out as it was blocked and countered. The pair danced about each other in a continuous blur of motion that would have seemed choreographed had the clash of steel been any less deafening.

The redhead slipped beneath the other's blow and brought his great ax down on his opponent's head, somehow stopping the descending blade as it cut into the blond warrior's skin from forehead to chin. Despite the blood that leaked from the wound, the warrior remained standing. Alan knew that the injury would leave a scar but was not life-threatening. The two combatants lowered their axes and clasped wrists in mutual respect.

"Bravo!" Rafel roared his approval, standing and clapping long and hard, a move emulated by his men.

As they resumed their seats, Rafel addressed the khan. "Ty has told me of the skill of your warriors, but that demonstration was truly amazing. My compliments to you and your men."

"Thank you for your words," the khan replied with a nod of his head. "It is unfortunate that we did not have a chance to inform you of our customs before you arrived. Our tradition demands that all parties at a feast of acquaintance offer a demonstration of martial skill. I can hardly judge your lack of preparation."

"Khan, I would not expect you to suffer such an insult. We, too, are a warrior people, and as high lord, I am never unprepared. Perhaps you will find our own demonstration to be of some passing entertainment."

Rafel signaled to Arn to rise. "Khan, I present to you one whom most people refer to merely as Blade, the finest knife fighter I have ever seen. The king of Tal would often ask Blade to demonstrate his skills before the court."

"As you wish, High Lord," Arn said, moving around the tables to reach a position in the center of the U and in front of the khan and Rafel.

Alan watched as Arn stooped slightly. His hands barely seemed to move, and a pair of daggers appeared, having left their sheaths in the tops of his boots to tumble lazily above his fingers. Two more knives materialized as well. These were in turn joined by Slaken from its spot at his waist. The pattern carved by the black blade was a whirling motion occupying the center of the circle formed by the other four. Arn's hands blurred as the speed of the knives increased until only a sequence of shadows could be seen by the light of the candles. And in the very center of the shadowy ring, the spinning Slaken carved a hole.

"Is that all?" the khan asked. "I show you fighting skill, and you give me carnival juggling? Gods, I have servants that can juggle better than that. Gunthar, grab some knives and show him."

A young servant scurried forward holding a small armload of carving knives, which he soon had whirling above him. He moved in toward Arn until they faced each other, barely a pace apart, the younger man with several more knives in the air than the five that spun before Arn.

"Pitiful." The khan roared with laughter, and his warriors roared with him, sloshing their ale in fits of mirth.

Alan felt his hand creep toward his ax as the blood thrummed in his temples. But a sharp look from his father kept him in his seat despite how he wanted to beat the insolent bastard of a khan into a bloody pulp.

Suddenly Arn moved, or at least it appeared that he moved. A rapid sequence of slapping sounds brought stunned silence as the assembled group suddenly realized that the servant boy no longer held any knives. These now resided in a tight pattern embedded in the nearest of the slowly turning pigs.

The brief hush was broken as one of the khan's warriors sitting across from Alan rose to his feet. "A trick with a woman's kitchen utensil. Can you not handle a real weapon?" he yelled, hefting an ax.

"Knives are my weapon of choice, not axes," Arn said, continuing the blur of steel before him.

"As I thought." The warrior hurled his ax at Arn. Somehow the weapon did not reach the assassin, turning as it came within the whirling circle of knives and coming to a halt with a *thunk*, embedding deeply in the oaken edge of the table directly in front of the khan.

"As I said," said Arn, "I don't like axes. Since it appears you don't want to keep yours, I return it to your leader."

Roaring, three more warriors rose and hurled their axes at Arn, who, shifting position slightly, sent them spinning to hack into the khan's table adjacent to the first. In seconds, more axes were thrown from different sides of the room so that Arn spun in a tight circle, redirecting them to find their place in the line embedded in the table in front of the khan. And all the while, the whirling halo of knives spun in the air.

Three warriors now leapt from their places at the nearest table, hefting their battle-axes in a rush toward Arn. The first reached him, swinging his ax in an arc that swept down through the space where Arn had been only a second before, the weapon clanking loudly on the floor and sending stone chips spinning into the air. Somehow Arn had shifted out of the ax's path effortlessly, while still juggling the knives. As seen through the bloodred vision of his escalating rage, Alan almost believed Arn wielded magic instead of his blades. The second and third warriors swung simultaneously, their results no better than that of the first. Again and again the three struck at Arn as he shifted subtly between strokes, moving with the grace of a jungle cat, the whirling cutlery never changing its rhythm.

As several more warriors rose to join the fray, a booming yell shook the hall. Alan stood, lifting the long table at which he sat high above his head before sending it crashing to the floor. Ripping his ax from its place at his side, he smashed it into the table's legs, removing them cleanly and hacking the oak structure with such force that it split asunder.

"If it's ax play you want," Alan said, keeping his voice steady despite the way his heart hammered within his chest, "then I'm dealing. I'll have your limbs, and then I'll chop this castle down to form a gravestone fitting for such a pack of fools."

Holding the ax out in front of him, Alan spun in a circle, feeling for all the world like he was part of an ancient tribal dance.

Amidst the commotion, John, Ty, Broderick, and the rangers raced to place themselves around Arn, moving into positions between him and the warriors of Val'Dep.

"So, my lords," Arn said, still juggling the knives, "what say you? Has this been enough of a demonstration, or shall we move on to violence?"

The khan tilted his head back and bellowed rapturously, slowly rising to his feet and clapping his hands in a steady rhythm. "Young man, I salute you. A marvelously fine show of martial arts and plain foolhardiness by all concerned."

A wave of his hand sent his warriors back to their seats, except for the ones whose table Alan had destroyed. These latter stood at attention.

Turning to Rafel, the khan extended his hand. "Truly a worthy band you lead, especially that lion of a son of yours. Shall we then feast together?"

Rafel raised his mug. "Indeed."

"Clear a table for our guests. It seems theirs has come undone. Those of my men without seats shall eat cross-legged on the floor after the manner of our people when outdoors."

"Khan, since my son destroyed your table, he will eat on the ground with your men," said Rafel.

"So be it. Since the entertainment is at an end, let the feast commence."

As if they had never been in motion, Arn's knives were suddenly once again in their sheaths.

Lowering his ax, Alan forced his tensed muscles to relax. As he seated himself low beside the warrior who had been introduced as the khan's son, he caught the harsh gaze his father directed his way, a look of disapproval that only stoked his anger. Alan had once again failed to exercise the self-discipline the high lord expected.

18

Kragan's War Camp—Western Tal
YOR 414, Late Summer

At the center of his war camp, dozens of leagues northwest of the ruins of the Coldain estate, Kragan sat cross-legged on the black-on-red, spiral-patterned rug within his tent. He stared down at the fist-size scrying vase before him, the surface of the water within as smooth as glass. Jorthain, high priest of the protectors, possessed another of these crystalline orbs, each of which contained water that Kragan had drawn from a natural basin in the caverns beneath Lagoth. He had distributed these scrying vases among his key followers across the Endarian continent.

Kragan's mind reached out for Boaa, the water elemental that he had used to fill the small globes. As he concentrated, the water within began to move, crawling up the sides of its container, forming a lens that matched what was happening inside the vase within Jorthain's chambers. Inside the orb, a familiar room appeared. Jorthain stood near the balcony, his black robe hanging loosely from his frame as he conversed with another protector.

The sounds of their voices in that far-off room within the temple above the city of Mo'Lier vibrated the water within the scrying vase.

Like a tuning fork, Kragan's orb picked up the sounds, letting him hear the conversation between the two priests. Uninterested in the discussion, he interrupted.

"High Priest Jorthain," Kragan said, his voice transmitted through the distant vase, "I would have a word with you."

Jorthain turned to face his scrying vase, situated atop a black marble pedestal near the fireplace mantel, and dismissed the other protector with a wave of his gnarled hand. He stepped closer to peer into the orb. The high priest's eyes widened at the sight that confronted him. That did not surprise Kragan. Jorthain had only seen him once since he had assumed Kaleal's form. "My lord Kragan?"

Kragan paused to allow the other protector to exit the room, something the younger priest accomplished with alacrity after a glance at Jorthain's scrying vase. When Jorthain was alone, Kragan continued. "Focus on my words, not my appearance."

To Jorthain's credit, he adapted quickly to Kragan's intrusion. "What do you wish of me?"

"Do you know precisely where Rafel's stronghold lies?"

Jorthain glanced at the eye suspended in a clear preservative fluid within the glass jar atop his mantel. The eye that had once resided in the face of one of Rafel's rangers.

"I have placed a spy within Rafel's inner circle. That spy continues to provide me with detailed information about the high lord's location, fortifications, and army. In the Glacier Mountains, dozens of leagues to the southeast of Mo'Lier, Rafel has built a series of three forts that block the only entrance into the valley he has claimed for his own."

"Tell me of your preparations to destroy Rafel's legion and kill his witch of a daughter," said Kragan.

"Already, tens of thousands of vorgs and men have answered my summons," said Jorthain. "Every day, the war camp south of Mo'Lier grows. The army will be ready to march by midautumn."

Kragan's temples throbbed. "That is too late. An early snowstorm could seal off the army's path into the mountains."

The wrinkles in Jorthain's forehead grew even more pronounced. "It cannot be helped. The commanders must have time to instill enough fear into these new recruits that they can be counted on to follow orders. It will also take time to construct the siege engines that will allow the soldiers to breach or scale the fortress walls."

"What are your protectors for? Are you afraid that Rafel's daughter can fend off all of your priests?"

The high priest's lips pressed into a tight line. "Many of my protectors must remain behind. I will not leave Mo'Lier undefended."

"No. You will commit every bit of your available might to put an end to the threat that sits on your doorstep. And I expect you to direct this attack personally."

"Long ago I pledged to support you. But I will not endanger my city nor the temple that sits atop it."

Kragan did not speak or shout at the priest who now defied him. Instead, he focused his fury into the elemental plane of earth, seizing control of Dalg. Beneath him, the ground began to tremble and shake, a tremor that made its way into the scrying vase to be echoed in the crystal orb's twin inside Mo'Lier. Above the mantel on Jorthain's left, a large mirror jerked free of its mounting and crashed to the floor, spewing glass across the room. The old priest jumped away in fear.

As quickly as he had called it forth, Kragan released Dalg and let the tremors die.

The expression that had crept onto Jorthain's face told Kragan all that he needed to know. The high priest would challenge him no more.

19

Mo'Lier
YOR 414, Late Summer

Eleven days after Rafel's stay in Val'Dep, Arn sat astride Ax on a wooded ridge, looking through his far-glass, studying the expansive valley below. The meeting between the high lord and the khan on the day after the banquet had been productive. Although no formal treaty had been agreed upon, the khan had accepted Rafel's offer for him to visit Areana's Vale so that he could see its people and fortifications—a simple expression of trust and the second step in developing friendly relations between the two leaders.

Arn's attention was drawn to a glint of sunlight from the mirror shard in the hand of a ranger atop a distant hill. He sent a quick flash of reply. Two days ago, the rangers had spotted a scouting party with a protector and nine vorgs almost a day's ride from the vale. It was the opportunity Rafel had been waiting for.

With Arn watching from this hidden vantage point, the six rangers waited in ambush for the scouting party, while Carol provided a shield against magical attack. Rafel had ordered the rangers to allow at least two of the scouts to escape. And when they did, Arn would follow them back to their temple.

The two rangers in the valley below moved back into the wood line and began working their way toward the next hook in the valley. Beyond this, Arn could clearly see the scouting party making its way through the brush in the general direction of the vale, which lay almost a full day's ride to the east.

Down in these low foothills, the temperature was considerably warmer than in the mountains to which Arn had grown accustomed. From this vantage, looking off to the north, Arn's view commanded the valley for leagues, back toward the spot from which the protectors' scouting party approached.

Closer at hand, the rangers moved into a shallow draw that provided excellent concealment and dismounted to set up their intended ambush. One ranger led the horses around to the opposite side of the hill. Two others blocked the path leading to the west, establishing positions behind a group of boulders. The remaining three knelt in protected outposts among rocky clefts higher on the hill, but within easy bowshot of the path along which the scouting party rode.

A lone vorg scout rode point dozens of paces in front of the main group. The rangers allowed this one to pass safely through the ambush. But as the main body moved into the kill zone, the rangers rose up and launched their arrows, sending four vorgs tumbling from their horses. The robed protector spread his arms, and a shimmering shield appeared around him and his horse, deflecting the arrows that rained upon him. Rafel's men hidden higher on the hill rose and fired as the vorgs charged the two rangers who blocked the trail to their front.

Two more saddles emptied, leaving the protector and two of his vorg scouts alive. The protector gestured, and a bolt of flame flew from his fist, bursting harmlessly in the air a dozen paces in front of him. A new hail of arrows caused the priest to shift his focus to his own defense. Deciding that survival was at stake, the protector spun his horse and bolted back down the trail along which he had traveled, followed closely by the two vorgs. Rafel's rangers let them go.

For a week Arn followed the small group as they made their way northwest through wide valleys and rolling hill country, the weather steadily becoming warmer with the drop in elevation. When the priest arose at dawn on the eighth day, he appeared to have acquired an increased sense of urgency. He and the vorg scouts soon had their horses saddled and turned north.

Their pace increased, and by the time the sun set, they had covered another ten leagues. Up ahead, Arn could see a lone hill rising in the center of the valley, a hill from which a spire rose silhouetted against the horizon. Although he couldn't make out much detail in the fading light, he could see that hundreds of buildings draped the hill's sides.

In the rapidly gathering gloom, campfires sputtered to life on the valley floor to the south of the hill. Judging that he had identified the objective of his unwitting guides, Arn found that he no longer needed them. He urged Ax to greater speed, moving around the three until he arrived at a position well forward of the group.

He staked Ax close to a stream and then moved stealthily back through the woods, seating himself at the base of an aging oak. The clatter of horses' hooves on stone reached his ears, a sound accompanied by low voices speaking in guttural tones, perhaps twenty paces to his west.

Arn got to his feet and moved back through the trees, setting a course that intersected the protector's path, letting the sounds guide him to his targets. Soon he saw them, riding in a file with the protector positioned between the two vorgs.

Arn's hands flicked out, sending one dagger into the protector's throat. His second dagger buried itself in the lead vorg's left eye. Unable to see the other vorg, Arn darted forward among the rearing horses that raced past him as their dead riders tumbled from their backs to thud to the earth. The last vorg wheeled his horse away from the ambush, sinking cruel spurs deep into his mount's sides.

The animal screamed and reared, then gathered itself on its haunches in an attempt to bring the pain of its master's panic to an end with a burst of speed. Arn leapt across the horse's back, Slaken sinking deep into the stomach of the vorg as he struggled to draw his sword.

A rush of foul-smelling bile and blood gushed into Arn's face as he dragged the struggling vorg from his mount, the two striking the ground together, rolling into a thornbush. The dull black blade rose and fell several more times, and the vorg ceased his struggles.

Staggering under the weight, Arn dragged the vorg back out of the briars, then moved to search the other bodies. He worked swiftly, examining the corpses by feel in the darkness. The priest had a small pouch, a dagger, and little else of interest. The vorgs had nothing save their armor and weapons.

Arn stripped all three, discarding the clothing except for the priest's robe. Having completed the rifling of their belongings, Arn made his way to the stream and lay down in the water face-first.

With clothes dripping and boots sloshing, Arn scrambled up the bank, grabbed the bundle taken from the priest, and followed the stream bank back to the west until he reached Ax.

He swung up into the saddle and entered the stream, heading west at a walk, the *slosh splash* of Ax's hooves in the water forming the only sound in the night. He kept to the stream for several hours before turning back to the north. When Arn finally stopped to make camp, he allowed sleep to claim him.

When he awoke, the early-morning darkness was just beginning to fade to gray. He stretched himself and swore softly. Stiff with cold from sleeping in damp garments, his left calf cramped. For a moment he lay still again, letting the sharp pain in his leg bring him to full consciousness. Then he sat up and rubbed the knotted muscle until it gradually relaxed.

The last two days of scant food had left his stomach growling, a condition that he set about remedying with dried, salted strips of venison. Tearing off a tough piece of jerky reminded him of Rafel's terrier gnawing a strip of rawhide.

As the sun crested the mountains to the east, Arn sat atop Ax and raised his far-glass, looking due north toward Temple Hill, as he'd now come to think of the locale. In the early-morning light, the monastery was impressive in its austerity. The hill upon which it sat was conical, the temple dominating its crest.

The walls of the temple draped the upper third of the hillside and rose several stories, with windows spaced irregularly up its sides and a towering central spire. Thick walls at the base of the large hill surrounded the city. Within those walls, buildings were separated by broad streets and narrow alleys, but a green space separated the temple from the cluster that ringed it below.

The outer walls were formidable, with dark stripes down the sides, showing where hot tar or oil had been poured in times past. Circular turrets buttressed the walls at the corners, and the city gates opened beneath a raised portcullis. Despite impressive defenses, the stronghold had more of a monastic than military feel.

From this angle Arn could see that the hill sat perched on the edge of a large lake, the waters of which lapped fortress walls on the north side. Swampland stretched along the lake's edge, leaving only the south side of the city approachable by land.

Stretching out from the front gates, a vast tent city stretched across the valley floor, as if the hill was a rotting sack of potatoes that had split, spewing forth its vile contents in moldy lumps. Throngs of vorgs and men milled about within the military encampment, working to build siege engines and ladders.

Arn's thoughts drifted back to the dinner Rafel had given in honor of his and Carol's engagement the night before he departed. In the banquet hall, as they had dubbed the longhouse structure, they had eaten and been toasted by the high lord, his key personnel, John, Ty, Kim, and Alan.

He remembered Carol's attempt to hide her fears when Rafel turned the after-dinner talk to Arn's mission. How had the high lord phrased his command?

"Just delay the protectors until the first heavy snow closes these mountain passes," he had said. "If you can do that, the winter will prevent any attack until spring and allow us to complete our fortifications."

Arn gazed out at his objective, thinking about his return to the type of work that had been his life, feeling the familiar heat leach from Slaken into his blood. There were times when he wanted to be free of his connection to the blade that was a symbol of the vengeance he had vowed as he knelt beside his mother's corpse. This wasn't one of those times. The protectors had tried to kill Carol and were preparing an army to finish the job.

He reached down and patted Ax on the neck. "Well, old boy, it looks like I'm going to have to let you go. I can't take you where I now travel."

With that he turned the horse away from the fortress, heading back toward the meadows and stream he had spotted in the woods to his east. At the edge of the meadow, he unsaddled and unbridled the warhorse. Then, with a slap on Ax's rump, he sent the ugly beast trotting off.

Turning away, he stowed the saddle and his bedroll, keeping only the items he wore and the bundle with the priest's robe and dagger.

Then he turned toward Temple Hill and surrendered to Slaken's call.

20

Mo'Lier
YOR 414, Early Autumn

For two days Arn had patiently observed the fortress from a distance. Things were approaching a head in the encampment south of Temple Hill. The military organization outside the fortress walls appeared almost ready to move as the last of the siege engines and equipment approached completion. Arn had identified the tents of several of the vorg and human generals, not a difficult task considering the traffic of lackeys going to and fro.

Of particular interest to Arn were the comings and goings of the robed priests, who issued forth from the fortress walls periodically. They usually moved in groups of thirteen, passing through the crowds of soldiers in twin columns, hooded heads bowed. Vorgs and human soldiers scampered out of their way whenever they approached, although the top vorg leaders did not show this sort of deference, coming out of their tents to meet with the priests.

Arn easily observed that the priests were unhappy with the pace of activities and spent considerable time berating the army leadership in front of their own troops. The priests would then return to their fortress. After they departed each time, the vorg generals stormed up and down in a fury, throwing weaponry to the ground, slapping nearby soldiers, and hurling crude gestures in the direction of Temple Hill.

Arn moved back into the wood line, lay down on the ground, propping his head on the folded priest robe, and closed his eyes to await nightfall.

Darkness came. Arn killed a human soldier who strayed outside camp boundaries to relieve himself. He put on the ill-fitting and shabby armor, finding the helmet exceptionally uncomfortable but adequate for his purposes. He bashed in the corpse's face with a large stone and removed the few coins found in the soldier's pouch, spilling a couple on the ground beside the body.

The robbery completed, he shuffled off, entering the encampment but staying well away from the fires. He staggered drunkenly, slumping down adjacent to a trio of drinking vorgs.

"Gad," Arn muttered, staggering to his feet. "Oh, thought I'd soiled myself, but I see it's just some stinking vorgs. Why we has to have such trash in the army boggles the mind."

"Looks like a stupid human is about to get himself killed," said one of the vorgs, who rose to his feet and wheeled around to face the drunken soldier.

"Yeah? And who's gonna do it? Not you, unless you can ugly me to death."

"Kill the bastard and cook him," said another vorg as all three rose to their feet and rushed forward.

Arn sidestepped the first attacker, disemboweling him and whirling the dying warrior into the path of the two immediately behind while extracting his knife from its sheath. The trailing vorgs went down in a heap. Before they could arise, Arn turned and disappeared into the night in the general direction of the nearest human camp.

He ducked between tents and turned at a right angle to the direction he had been traveling, now heading toward the fortress itself. He assumed a walk, ignoring the growing clamor as a minor riot erupted a hundred paces behind him and off to the left. The sound of the large fight grew in volume, augmented by the yells of commanders who swore and barked orders as they stumbled from their tents, trying to figure out what was happening.

As he neared the wall, Arn turned toward the spot where the lake met its western side, stripping off the filthy armor. Satisfied that the attention of any guards was directed toward the army encampment where all the commotion was ongoing, Arn climbed the wall, swinging his weight effortlessly from the fingerholds he found in cracks between the stones. He paused just below the top to peer over. Two soldiers stood together atop the wall, about five paces east of where he clung, both gazing out at the camp that spread out below.

He vaulted silently up, landing on the top of the wall in a sprint. The guard on the left turned as he struck, Arn's vorgish blade rising and falling again and again, trailing a bloody spray. The second soldier staggered backward, struggling to pull his sword as Arn's fury struck him, cutting his throat and putting a stop to his building scream.

Arn tossed the bodies off the wall to break on the rocks below, dropping the vorgish sword onto the ground beside them.

Climbing down the nearest ladder to the fortress's interior, Arn disappeared into the gloom of the city streets.

—ʌʌ—

In Areana's Vale, a lone black wolf moved quietly through Carol's dreams, slaver dripping from its fangs as it moved among the spring lambs.

21

Endless Valley
YOR 414, Early Autumn

Four days into the eight-day ranger patrol led by Jalon Owens, Lord Alan had endured just about enough of the awe with which the rangers regarded Ty. He found the Kanjari seriously annoying.

Ty had needed less than a day to discover he could get under Alan's skin with needle-sharp comments. Once he had discovered the weakness, the Kanjari would not desist, particularly after noting that the rangers found his jibes entertaining.

What pushed Alan's good humor to the breaking point was the way the rangers assumed that Ty could handle himself in battle. As far as Alan was concerned, just looking good without your shirt on and carrying a fancy ax didn't mean a damned thing. Someday the blond barbarian would have to back up his reputation, and Alan wanted to be there.

As if on cue, Ty pulled Regoran into step beside Alan, his blue eyes sparkling with anticipation. "Ah, young lordling, I enjoy our talks."

Alan kept his eyes straight ahead, determined to ignore the Kanjari.

"I was just thinking about how you've missed your true calling," Ty continued.

Alan promised himself that he would not yield to anger, not within view of the rangers. He would not grant the barbarian that satisfaction.

"Based on the vigor with which you attacked the khan's table back in Val'Dep," Ty said, "I would imagine your skills more suited to a woodcutter than a warrior."

Gritting his teeth, Alan said nothing. He didn't need to. This time, Ty's comments failed to pull any merriment from the rangers, who apparently sensed the remark was cutting a little too close to home. Evidently Ty sensed their disapproval as well, because he sighed and urged Regoran into a trot that carried him away from the lord.

The rays of the sun cut golden swaths through the branches of a blue spruce when the sound of a loud splat and a chorus of cursing brought Alan's head around. Not ten paces away, Ty sat astride his stallion, covered in the biggest slop of bird droppings that Alan had ever seen, the center of impact having been directly on top of the Kanjari's head.

"By the deep!" Ty said. "A buzzard just dumped all over me!"

A wave of raucous braying broke out among the rangers, and Alan found himself swept away in the contagion. The harder he laughed, the weaker he became until he could barely maintain his seat astride his horse. Tears rolled freely down his cheeks, and the muscles in his face began to ache from exertion. The longer the rangers chortled, the redder Ty's face became.

"Okay, you bunch of jackasses. I'm going to go find a stream and wash up."

With that, Ty wheeled his stallion around and galloped out of sight through the woods.

The object of their good humor having departed, the patrol resumed its course, riding out of the wood line and up along a steep ridge toward a point where they could observe the country for leagues around. The group reached the promontory after fifteen minutes of rough riding due to the steep nature of the shale-covered slope.

Once off the slope and on the ridgeline, the view was breathtaking. Alan could see the hills drop away to the west in a washboard of canyons.

"Look there!" Jalon Owens pointed in the direction from which they had rode.

A league away, Alan could see a meadow through which a sparkling stream meandered. He could just make out the naked form of the Kanjari, his nemesis, splashing about in the water.

The chuckling that bubbled forth from the assemblage was cut short by the sight of two riders coming hard, heading directly toward the meadow through low brush, a group of vorgs rushing to overtake them as yet more vorgs poured down the hill to their front. And the whole mess was heading directly toward where Ty bathed, unaware.

"By the deep. How many are there?" Alan asked.

"Looks like twenty, maybe more," said Jalon. "I don't know if we can make it in time to be any help, but let's try."

Alan had already spurred his mount forward, plunging down the steep hillside in reckless abandon, followed by four rangers.

As his horse struggled to maintain its footing on the loose shale, his eyes remained locked on the scene unfolding in the distant meadow. The two horsemen had broken out of the trees into the meadow at almost the same time as the vorgs. One of the horses fell as an arrow cut short its flight, sending the rider rolling through the grass. His companion leapt off to stand beside him, battle-ax extended, as he stood across the body of his friend.

A wild cry split the air as Ty grabbed his weapon from its resting place alongside the stream and ran naked across the grassy opening toward the two men, the great ax glinting in the sunlight as he reached the leading vorgs.

Alan's path continued down the slope as he found himself unable to maintain a clear view of what was happening. He passed between trees that blinded him, brief glimpses of the distant battle revealing that Ty was still standing, cutting a swath through the charging vorgs that caused those nearest to him to hesitate. The moment of indecision swept them from the land of the living.

Alan's view of the scene ended as he reentered the tree line. He cursed in frustration as he ducked low across the big animal's neck to avoid the low-hanging branches. Although the horse was fast, Alan could not imagine how his mount could cover the distance that separated him from the battle before it came to a bad end. Still, he pressed on, the sound of the rangers close behind him.

Pressing the pace, Alan began to distance himself from his companions, the bloodlines of his warhorse coming to the fore, the animal's mighty lungs working like bellows as it propelled him toward his destination. Still, time slipped by, as did Alan's hopes of seeing Ty alive.

Bursting from the wood line to take the stream in one mighty leap, Alan needed several seconds to absorb the scene before him. Halfway across the meadow, the muscles in the Kanjari's arms and back flexed beneath a red sheen as the great crescent ax fell, splitting a vorg's upraised shield on its way through the head and body behind it, then continuing in an arc that severed the sword arm of the soldier's companion.

A handful of vorgs had dropped their swords and fallen back, desperately trying to fit arrows to their bows before the Kanjari could close with them. Upon seeing Alan burst from the wood line followed by the four rangers, they abandoned their efforts and fled, just as the last of the vorgs engaged with Ty after his companion fell to another stroke of the ax.

As Alan pulled his horse to a halt beside Ty and dismounted, the rangers raced past him, bows at the ready, hot in their pursuit of the fleeing vorgs.

The scene that confronted Alan lacked any semblance of reality. The Kanjari stood naked, his hair and body slick and dripping with the blood of his enemies. The crescent ax bled down from the blade along the handle so that no metal or ivory was visible. Only Ty's eyes shone through the crimson.

The horseman who had fought beside Ty was a familiar-looking khan warrior, his hair streaming down onto his armor and his beard gathered into bloody twin braids. The warrior's companion lay dead at his feet.

Suddenly the horseman dropped to one knee and bowed his head toward Ty. "Dar Khan."

Alan was not familiar with the word, but the mannerisms of the warrior indicated that he considered himself to be in the presence of royalty. No, that wasn't right. A god. The man seemed to think that Ty was some blood-drenched god of war. And as Alan shifted his gaze to Ty, he could not really blame the fellow for believing such a fantasy.

"I pledge myself to your service."

Behind a red mask, Ty merely stared down at the kneeling man. His response surprised Alan.

"You are the khan's son, Larok, are you not?"

"I am."

Suddenly Alan understood why this horse warrior looked so familiar. Behind that blood-coated beard was the face of the man the khan had introduced in Val'Dep.

"Then return the body of your companion to your people and tell your father of this," said Ty. "There may come a day when I will call for his aid."

"As you command, Dar Khan."

Ty turned to walk back toward the stream. From the look on his face, the prospect of yet another cold bath in the same day was less than appealing.

By the time Ty had finished cleaning up and getting dressed, the rangers had returned, having killed the vorgs they had chased. Larok told them that he and his companion had been scouting when they were ambushed by the vorgs. Beyond that, the khan scion would say little about his mission.

His reticence did not extend to the subject of Ty. Larok insisted that Ty was Dar Khan, the Dread Lord, a mighty warrior from the land of the dead. Legend said that he would eventually enter this world, taking mortal form for a time.

Larok told of how the Dread Lord would arise, clothed only in blood, and from his companions he would select a lone warrior to serve him. And that one, the Chosen, would draw to himself a group of mighty warriors who would fall gloriously in battle. These recruits would rise again in the land of the dead to fight alongside the Dar Khan.

Alan shook his head. How someone as battle-hardened as this bearded warrior could believe such a child's fable was mystifying. Even more surprisingly, a couple of the rangers seemed to be swept up in the myth.

Unbelievable.

The storytelling was finally interrupted by Ty's return to the group. Unwilling to talk about the subject in Ty's presence, the warrior draped his fallen companion across his horse, bowed slightly toward the Kanjari, swung up behind the dead warrior's body, and departed.

Alan watched the man depart with mixed feelings. As the rider disappeared into the tree line, he had the strong impression that he had not seen the last of the khan's horsemen.

22

Areana's Vale
YOR 414, Early Autumn

Carol stepped out of her cabin onto the back porch, the cold morning air in the Glacier Mountains turning her breath to thin puffs of steam. She stretched her arms wide, rolling her head to either side to loosen her stiff neck. She gazed out across the valley to the mighty cliff walls rising on all sides.

The day was so clear that it did not seem real. Birds twittered in the trees around her cabin. A pair of squirrels rooted around in the pine straw by a clearing, raising their heads to listen in unison. Then deciding that there were no threats in the area, they returned to their food gathering.

Running her fingers through her hair, Carol was shocked to discover its matted condition.

What had it been, two weeks since Arn had left? During that entire time, she had closeted herself in the cabin, examining in detail the wielder's book he had given her, only recently starting to read the tome from the beginning. She had requested of her father that absolutely no one was to disturb her while she studied her magic in preparation for the coming war.

First, she had wanted to satisfy herself as to the general nature of the book's contents and condition. She had also been very wary that perhaps it contained some self-destructive trap that would destroy it upon examination by an unwitting reader. But she had found no wards or traps. What she had found left her confused, baffled.

It did not appear to be a spell book. There was no organizing table or index of its contents like Hawthorne's book. Strange symbols adorned the four corners of every page, but the text itself was in the common tongue, although the handwriting, which began in a very clear and ordered hand, deteriorated to wild, barely legible scribblings toward the end of the manuscript.

The tome was written in a conversational tone, not unlike a diary or notes one would write to oneself. The language did not appear to be directed at anyone other than the author. Furthermore, the book was filled with what appeared to be meditative exercises, and judging from the length and complexity of the first one, the task of progressing through all appeared daunting.

But why would a wielder spend so much time writing to himself? After all, the notes appeared to be written from memory, not a chronicle of the results of experimentation.

Then there was the increasingly desperate nature of the handwriting, as if the author was trying to work out something important to him, something that seemed to slip farther from his grasp as his notes progressed. The handwriting toward the book's end had become almost indecipherable scribblings of short little blurbs, much briefer than the detailed ritual descriptions contained in the early pages. Perhaps the introductory exercises were the most thoroughly documented because they formed the basis of the work that followed, or perhaps the author had merely been driven toward madness. She decided that she would master the first exercise before delving deeper. There was nothing to be gained by taking unnecessary risks.

Carol rubbed her throbbing temples, turned, and walked back into her home. After being out in the dazzling sunlight, the cabin seemed too dark. She reached out with her mind, setting small flames atop candles and lamps around her bedroom. She felt . . . strong? More than that. She felt powerful in a heady way that begged her to exercise that power. She could feel the otherworldly planes, hidden from view but all around her, so full of elementals to contest with, so ready for someone strong enough to bend them to her will.

The book lay on the small table near the fireplace, binding strap firmly in place, the back leaning just against the base of the heavy candle stand. The manuscript had hardly been out of her mind since she had walked outside to clear her head. Carol was mildly amazed at how enthralled she had become, at how anxious she was to study the work. The brief scraps that she had read had inspired a curiosity she could barely contain.

The tightly packed, neatly appointed handwriting detailing the book's first exercise took up two full pages with the description of what the author referred to as katas, which Carol took to mean exercises or rehearsals. She read through the pages rapidly to get the general context, but that approach failed miserably. She could not decipher what constituted success.

No attempt had been made to describe what the exercise was supposed to accomplish. Only a sequence of very detailed steps appeared, the first of which was to bring oneself into a deep meditation referred to as a state of neutrality. Carol hoped that this was the same as what she thought of as finding her center, but she could not be sure.

She began again, working her way very slowly from the beginning, trying to understand the author's intention in each of the steps that followed.

When she looked up, the outside light was fading into early evening. Only the glow from her candles and lamp lit the room.

She leaned back in the chair, rubbing her face with both hands. Her temples pounded, a headache brought on by the frustration of trying to interpret instructions that relied upon knowledge she did not have. Several references had been made to establishing "the block" or to shifting "the filter." These were intermingled among instructions for visualization and concentration that she understood, but they would be wondrously difficult to perform.

She stood up, stretching her arms high above her head, and rolled her neck in several complete circles, a routine that produced an abundance of pops and crackles. If the first exercise was this difficult, how could she ever hope to understand the latter ones, exercises that must have been too much even for the ancient master, who tried frantically to assign their descriptions to paper.

Since the first step demanded the adoption of a deep meditative state, Carol would need to have all other steps committed to memory. More than that, she would need the other steps burned into her brain so that they automatically sprang to mind whenever she needed them.

Deep meditation was tricky. The very act of trying to remember something or even thinking about the way you felt would suck you out of the meditation and back to normal consciousness.

Luckily, deep meditation was something she had always possessed a great talent for. What was it Hawthorne had said? *My dear child, you can lose yourself more easily than anyone I have ever known.*

At the time she had not been certain that his words were a compliment. She missed the kindly old man with the long, flowing whiskers. But he was not here to advise her, so she would just have to get on with the task.

Memorizing all the steps was a task that just took concentration and effort. That would not be a problem. But Carol was worried because she did not know what the author meant by blocking and filtering. He had evidently thought it obvious enough not to warrant description, so maybe the terms would become self-evident as the exercise progressed.

Dangerous or not, she could see no way to discover the procedures contained within the book without attempting the katas, mastering them one at a time. If fragments were missing, she would just have to figure those pieces out as she gained context.

She focused on memorizing the steps in the first kata. Readying her quill, ink, and paper, she sent a mental thank you to Darl for providing them. Then she set to work transcribing kata number one.

She left plenty of room between lines and in the margins so that she could make notes on the impressions gained during her experimentation with this first ritual. She had always found that transcribing a text focused her thoughts in a way that made the content her own.

As she wrote, the ritual formed in her mind. The kata began with the achievement of a meditative state of neutrality and then progressed through a complex visualization. She would envision herself alone within a sea of darkness, expanding outward to infinity in all directions until she was merely a tiny speck at its center.

And into that black sea she would cast tiny pebbles, producing ripples, tiny colored spheres that expanded ever outward. All of these glowing orbs would pass through each other and over her form.

She would conclude the kata by transmitting her own mental images to the closest of the glowing orbs.

Carol shook her head in frustration at the cryptic wording of these aspects of the text. She made a few notes in the transcribed sections that she did not understand. She mentally played back the description of the kata, verifying it against her notes and the original text.

She repeated the process again and again until she knew it by heart.

The distant crowing of a rooster caused Carol to lift her head and look out the window. What time was it? She stood, sending a sharp twinge through her back, and twisted her torso slowly to and fro until the cramp subsided. Then she walked out onto the porch. The canyon was still dark, but a pale orange glow had spread across the eastern sky.

Her eyes felt as if she could not keep them propped open unless she resorted to using small sticks. A gust of cold, predawn air brought gooseflesh to her arms, and she shuddered, a brief but hard shaking that coursed through her body.

Her feet felt like two icicles attached to the bottom of her legs, contrasting sharply with the spot where the elemental brand burned on her shoulder. Since arriving at the vale, she had never felt this tired. Carol collapsed into bed, pulled the heavy quilts around her, and succumbed to a dreamless sleep.

—~—

She awoke with a ravenous hunger gnawing at her stomach. The late-afternoon sun slanted through the western window of the cabin, but upon throwing off the covers, she discovered that it held little warmth. She hurriedly donned her clothes and a thick jacket that she retrieved from her trunk.

She poured a small amount of water from a pitcher into the washbowl, scrubbed her face, and ran a brush through her tangled hair until she felt like a person again instead of some wild beast that had slunk from its lair.

She stepped out onto the porch, the cold wind pulling a gasp from her lips.

Carol walked to the woodpile, grabbed two small logs and several sticks, and carried them back to the hearth. She reached out with her mind and sent fire dancing among the wood, shooting sparks marking where the dried twigs roared to life. She hung her teakettle to boil over the blaze.

When she was finally convinced that she was ready to focus, Carol arose, moved to her desk, lit her study candles, and settled into her chair.

With a series of deep breaths, she centered, taking her mental self to a place she knew well, a place of peace and repose. All thought stilled, she allowed her mind to detach from her physical body and float free. Normally she was suspended in a gray cloud, but now she let that cloud fade to velvet nothingness.

She could see herself standing amidst the blackness, arms extended to the sides and slightly uplifted, palms upward. Her view was perfect in detail, down to the glowing elemental marking on her bare shoulder and her hair that fell in smooth brown swirls down her back.

She was slightly surprised to see that she had chosen a silk garment with pinpoints of light sprinkled liberally across it, the darkness of the gown against the emptiness of space giving the near illusion that Carol's hands and head floated free of her body.

Her viewpoint drifted around her body, zooming in and out, feeling the vast emptiness of the expanse within which she floated as if it were some thick ebony fog. Carol opened her mind ever wider, visualizing tiny disturbances that spread through the void toward her from a number of points, some close and some far away.

When the first of the expanding spheres rippled across her floating form, she experienced a sudden flash of images, sounds, and feelings that knocked her out of the meditation. She again found herself sitting at the small desk in the near darkness of her cabin.

Carol clenched her fists, angry with herself. When had she last lost focus during a meditation? Was she a novice?

If she had allowed something like that to happen in the midst of casting a spell, even a minor elemental may have been able to possess her. She stood up and walked over to the crackling hearth. She suddenly had the distinct impression that someone was watching her through the window. Carol stepped out through the door. Lights twinkled in the small village of Longsford Watch. The sky had acquired the dark blue of a bruise.

She moved out to the edge of the porch and looked around the corner of the cabin. "Hello?" She received no reply.

Though mindful of her previous premonitions of evil in the vale, she discarded the feeling that someone was watching her and walked back inside.

This time she had difficulty finding her center. She had allowed herself to get flustered to the point where nothing came easily.

She gradually sank back into meditation, taking herself deeper than before, preparing as if she were going to be contesting with a major elemental force. The first attempt at the kata had disturbed her deeply, and she would take no chances.

When the first of the orblike disturbances in the blackness passed over her, she felt something unidentifiable but let it pass by, maintaining the state of a passive external observer to what was happening to the wielder in the center of the maelstrom.

Wave upon wave of glowing spheres rippled across Carol's form in the blackness, painting it in refracted color amidst mutterings of sound, washes of sensation, and strong emotion. Carol eventually moved her viewpoint much farther from her visualized body until it became a tiny pinpoint of light among the ripples in the void.

While this helped to lessen the torrent of sensations that threatened to end the meditation, the range of feelings became an almost unbearable din.

She visualized a tablet, hoping to use it to filter the sensation storm, only to have it bulge as if it would burst. She looked outward, unable to locate her body in the blackness amidst the multitude of expanding spheres.

Then she saw it, the tiny speck of light that was her body, glowing oh so faintly now. What was it she had meant to do? That hardly mattered. She needed to get farther away from the pinprick being swamped with so many sensations it was bound to explode.

Explode? She looked at the image of the mental tablet, bulging so badly now that it was almost unrecognizable. She marveled vaguely. How could a construct be warped almost beyond recognition?

A sharp pain ripped through the darkness. Carol opened her eyes. She lay on the floor, the small table overturned on top of her. She rubbed at her forehead and felt a warm wetness run down her face to sting her eyes. She must have cut her head in the fall. Carol swam back to alertness. The candle lay overturned on the rug, the fringe of which had caught the flame so that it spread quickly.

She grabbed the near edge of the throw rug and rolled it into a bundle, smothering the growing flames within. Coughing, she staggered to her feet, opened the door, and tossed the rug off the porch. Blood dripped down her nose to fall on her shirt.

She stumbled off her porch. Her head felt like someone had been beating on it with a hammer. Bile rose in her throat, and she fell to her knees in the dirt, retching violently with dry heaves that seemed endless.

At last she was able to rise to her feet and stagger back inside. She poured water from her pitcher into the basin and gently bathed her face. She felt along the cut on her forehead. It was high up in the hairline, shallow and short in length.

She bandaged the head wound with a scarf, stripped off her clothes, and crawled into bed, overcome with a sudden fit of shaking that left her weak. Pulling her blankets up around her, Carol curled into a fetal ball and drifted into a troubled sleep, filled with faint whispers she could not quite make out.

23

Areana's Vale
YOR 414, Early Autumn

When Carol awoke, she discovered that she was still alive if pain was any indication. She sat up and almost sank back down again as the pounding in her head brought a small gasp to her lips. The grayness of dawn crept through the window above her bed.

Outside the wind howled in a cold fury, rattling the door on its hinges. She trembled and walked into the main room, carefully avoiding glancing in the mirror. The last thing she needed was the sight that her bedraggled form was sure to present.

The small study table and chair lay overturned where she had left them, the candles having rolled some distance across the floor. A small flame still nipped at the remains of the log on the hearth, its charred form diminished to a warped stub of its former self.

She walked outside, ducking into the wind to retrieve several sticks and another small log. She carried the fuel back inside, kicking the door closed behind her. Tossing the wood onto the hearth, she stood with her hands outstretched to the warmth as flames leapt.

"Well, that was a wonderful experience," she muttered to herself. "I can't wait to try that again."

A powerful odor caught her attention, accompanied by a savage hunger and a taste that filled her mouth with saliva. Blood. Then the sensation storm faded into nothingness. She stood alone before the flaming hearth, mystified by what had just happened.

She gazed into the fire, thankful that it had still been going. She was fairly confident that she could not even have managed the casting of the fire spell. Weary to the bone, she felt like she had just awakened from a long illness. Not really hungry, despite what she had felt only moments before, but knowing she needed something to restore her strength, Carol fixed a helping of bread and honey.

Having finished her repast, she felt a little better. By the time she had made her hot-spring bathing trip and dressed for the day, her headache had subsided completely, and she felt human. Examining her face in the mirror, she was pleased to see that the cut was almost invisible in her hairline, although she could feel the knot easily with her hands.

By the time she finished clearing the mess made the previous night, including repairing the burned edge of the throw rug, the sun had crested the rim of the vale, sending thin pale rays through a layer of high clouds.

As she moved past the window facing the porch, her eyes were drawn outside. Was someone watching her? She looked through the window, but apart from a pair of squirrels that stood on their hind legs, peering about nervously, she saw nothing. The duo scampered off as she grabbed her heavy jacket and stepped out.

Her uneasiness was almost certainly an aftereffect of last night's unsuccessful session. Deciding that the best cure for uneasy, lonely feelings was to visit some of her neighbors, she strolled down the path toward the nearby cabins in Longsford Watch.

Through the trees at the bottom of the hill, she could see the lights in the cabin of her nearest neighbors. Henry and Mary Beth

Abercrombie had built a three-room log cabin for themselves and their five girls. Attached to the back, Henry had erected a pen for his pigs and another for the guinea hens that provided fresh eggs for many in the small village. Accompanied by the distant squeals of the pigs, he was busy slopping out their breakfast.

Henry endured hard work providing for such a large family with no sons to help with the heavy chores. Carol shook her head at the man's lack of understanding of women's capabilities; she had no doubt that his family would continue to grow until that shortfall was remedied or until the valley overflowed with Abercrombie children.

As she neared the family's cabin, the pigs seemed to have picked up some of her own nervousness, running around their pen in an odd fashion, high-pitched squeals erupting in chorus.

Henry came around from the front of the house and then, seeing Carol, raised a hand in a cheery wave. He carried his bow in his left hand and wore a quiver of arrows.

"Lorness Carol," he said, stepping toward her with an outstretched hand. "It's been some time since you came down to see us."

"Too long. I've been somewhat preoccupied." She followed his gaze into the pen. "What's scaring your pigs?"

"I don't know. They only started behaving like this a few minutes ago. I thought I would take my bow and walk around a little. There must be a big cat or wolf nearby."

"Maybe that's it," she said, although her voice didn't carry conviction. "This wind has me feeling a little jumpy myself."

"There's nothing worse than a cold wind that's not packing any moisture."

"Does Mary Beth have some extra eggs that I can buy? I know it's not market day, but I could sure use a dozen."

"She does, although the guinea hens weren't laying well this morning. Walk on around front and knock. She'll be glad to see you."

Letting Henry return to his hunt, she walked around the cabin and rapped on the door. It opened to reveal a buxom, blonde woman with two redheaded twin girls, their hands holding tightly to her apron. Mary Beth smiled when she saw who had come calling.

"Oh, Lorness. Come inside and warm yourself by the fire," she said, waving Carol in through the door and shutting it firmly behind her.

As Carol made her way to the hearth, she sniffed. "Do you smell that?"

Mary Beth paused, a puzzled look on her face. "Is something burning?"

Carol cocked her head to one side, almost overcome with a fleeting sense of exhilaration that accompanied the coppery odor of blood. A burst of fear spread through her limbs, and she stumbled, catching her balance against a chair.

Mary Beth rushed to her side, the large woman's arms encircling the wielder's shoulders to steady her. Concern showed in the mother's eyes.

"Lorness, are you ill?"

Carol shook her head. "I'm all right. It was just a passing dizziness."

"You're so pale. Have you been eating well?"

"Actually, I've been so busy these last two days that I've been snacking on bread and honey."

"No wonder you look sick." Mary Beth directed Carol toward the kitchen table. "Sit down. I'm going to make some real food for you right here and now."

"Please don't bother yourself," Carol said, trying to rise.

Mary Beth's stout hand pressed her back down into the chair.

By the time she thanked her hostess and left the house carrying the eggs, Carol felt stuffed to the gills. She had eaten more chicken, potatoes, vegetables, and gravy than she thought she could cram into her body. As she departed, she saw Henry emerge from the woods with the body of a wolf slung over his shoulder. The pigs were still scared, but this was likely because their sharp porcine noses held little liking for the wolven smell.

As Carol entered her cabin, her sense of unease returned, and she glanced about nervously. What had gotten into her? She reached out with her mind, setting small flames to the wicks of a pair of candles. She tried something more difficult, bending an air elemental to her will, stilling the wind immediately around her home. Satisfied, she released it. No problems there.

She restoked the hearth, adding its cheery warmth to the interior of the cabin, and sat down to think through last night's failure. Her substitution of a mental tablet for the filters and blocks had failed miserably and led to the disastrous conclusion. But why had the mental construct become distorted?

Carol pictured the tablet as she had last seen it, bulging and warped as if crammed to the bursting point. The quantity of mental imagery and sensations in the void had overwhelmed her. Apparently she had chosen the wrong path by retreating from the waves of sensation. She would have been better off allowing those waves to disturb her from her meditative state rather than trying to contain them all.

A sudden inspiration brought Carol to her feet in excitement. In the midst of the meditation, she had shifted her mental viewpoint outward so that the visualization of her body had become a tiny pinprick of light in a sea of blackness sprinkled with millions of disturbances. She had retreated so far that she had almost lost sight of herself. If she had not fallen from her chair, she doubted that she would have ever managed to find her way back.

If she had done the wrong thing by retreating from her body, perhaps the answer involved doing the opposite. If she moved her viewpoint closer to her body, the act might limit the number of sensations she would experience. Perhaps this theory wasn't the correct filter, but it was worth a try.

The wind whistled sharply through the eaves, and she moved closer to the warm hearth. Sitting cross-legged on the floor, she began her preparations. For the rest of the afternoon, she meditated, shutting out the outside world with its cold wind and urgent whisperings, relaxing herself, allowing the restorative power of her mind to work its magic. By nightfall, she was ready.

With the waning light of day, she began again to implement the steps of the kata. This time, the sensations were as confusing as before, but her filtering trick worked. Carol found that by mentally zooming in and out from her body, she was able to have some degree of control over the sheer quantity of the disturbances that swept across her.

The problem now was trying to stay inside the meditation. Time and again, some wild emotion sprang up inside as ripples spread across her form in the void.

She felt alternately angry, scared, erotic, hungry, cold, hot, thirsty, sated . . . And then there were the images and sounds. Strange murmurings, fragments of words, flashes of imagery, all crashed into her mind and, time and again, knocked her out of her centered state.

Carol cursed and kicked the chair, pulling at her hair in frustration. She paced the cabin like a caged beast. How many times had she tried this tonight? Ten? Twenty? Always with the same result. All that time spent to achieve a deep center of meditation and begin performing the kata, only to lose it in a matter of seconds.

If elementals could overcome her mind this easily, she would have long since been possessed. Yet here she was, repeatedly frustrated in her attempts to perform the very first exercise in this deep-spawned book.

She considered giving the kata another try, but the mere thought of the effort made her head ache. Besides, angrily kicking chairs while pulling one's hair was hardly the indication of a mental state conducive to deep meditation.

Carol sighed and made her way back to her bedroom. She changed out of her clothes into a nightgown, washed her face, brushed her hair, and slipped under the covers, consumed by self-doubt.

24

Mo'Lier
YOR 414, Early Autumn

It was market day, and Freemarket Street was crowded with squalid carts selling produce, pots and pans, and assorted odds and ends. This was the day when the city gates were opened wide to all comers, whether you had a city pass or not. The street was the widest and seediest in the city that clung to the hill below the temple. A steady trickle of raw sewage sludge flowed through the open gutters on either side of the avenue, the aromas of which did little to enhance the marketability of the chickens, goats, and vegetables that adorned the carts or the outstretched arms of the merchants hawking their wares. Vorgs elbowed their way through crowds of people, shoving to the front of what could be mistaken for lines outside the taverns. Some paused to curse and kick at the beggars slumped near the doorways.

Clutching his filthy brown cowl tight about him, one of these unfortunates was unable to move his crippled form fast enough to escape a glancing blow from a studded boot. The beggar rolled over with a moan, then slowly shuffled farther from the door, looking something like a snail in the effort. The vorg turned away and barged inside with the others, eager to deplete some of the stout ale brewed at the monastery on the hilltop above.

Beneath the fecal-stained robe, Arn's legs cramped, rebelling at the strange contortions he was requesting of his limbs. Now was the time to sit and wait for the coming.

For the last week, he had roamed the streets and alleys of Mo'Lier, a task that was far easier than he had hoped. The city, which at one time must have been awe-inspiring in its grandeur, was filled with decay and hopelessness. The people who resided here lived only at the pleasure of the priesthood atop the hill. The society had become a perversion of normal life, a place where orgy, not piety, was the dictate of their priestly fathers. The protectors had needs driven by the desires of their deity, Krylzygool, fueling the baser instincts of man and vorg.

One of the purveyors of pleasure and pain currently occupied the beggar's attention. The priest was a brash and abusive young acolyte, high on the magical powers of the protectorate and bent on demonstrating his superiority to anyone in his path. The beggar's eyes followed the priest like those of a lion deep in the grass, patient, searching, ravenous. The hunger that burned like a hole in his belly was fed by an anger stoked by his revulsion at all he had beheld in the city.

The air in the narrow confines of the alley hung heavy with the smell of sewage and rotten food, piles of which periodically choked the gutters, routing sludge into the center of the path. The priest sidestepped these unthinkingly, elbowing past two old women who trudged down the hill toward the market below, laden with bundles balanced on their heads. Reaching the upper end of the alley, he continued at a leisurely pace up the steep trail that wound through the tree- and brush-filled park separating the dwellings and shops below from the base of the temple walls.

The trail twisted and turned, climbing steeply with the aid of stairs carved into the hillside. The trees, unlike any Arn had ever seen, encroached on the trail. The larger of these had trunks a wagon's width thick, branching widely about five paces above the ground. The roots of the tree sprang from everywhere, starting well above the ground and reaching out for new soil. The branches above dropped thin roots that buried themselves in the ground directly below, as if they were not happy to wait for nourishment that would be passed up through the central trunk. Vines draped these monsters, spreading from one to another, nasty-looking creepers infected with a sickly yellow blight. Thick fern fronds filled the gaps between the root-branched trees, and thus little could be seen beyond a few paces from the trail.

The beggar moved silently through this thick vegetation, his path cutting its way up the hillside to intercept the trail well ahead of the lone priest. He disappeared into an adjacent fern bed and waited. As the acolyte rounded the nearest bend in the trail, the beggar staggered out of the brush, sat down in the trail drunkenly, and struggled back to his feet.

The priest stepped back momentarily in surprise. Then, his face red with agitation, he dove upon the drunken tramp, his staff raised to deliver a lesson in piety. The staff somehow failed to land as the beggar ducked inside the blow, driving the blunt end of his dagger against the priest's left temple. The man's body went limp, collapsing into a loose pile of black robes. All semblance of drunkenness gone, the beggar tossed the limp form over his shoulder and glided back into the bushes. He made his way swiftly now, moving silently down through the thick brush despite his burden. He soon found himself before a decaying stone wall, the back of a building that had fallen into disrepair.

The beggar ascended the wall quickly, stepping easily from broken stone to crack, shouldering the priest's body up onto the roof before swinging himself up. Here the roof was slightly pitched and overhung by one of the large trees that filled the green space behind the building. Rooftops pitched and yawed at odd angles, almost touching each other except where the widest streets cut paths between them.

The rise and fall of the priest's chest was shallow and rapid. The beggar bent down and wrenched the priest's neck forward, a movement that produced an audible crack. The protector's breathing stopped.

Arn shrugged his way out of the foul-smelling rags, extracting the bundle that contained the robe of the priest he had killed days before. He donned the robe and the belt with the silver dagger.

Satisfied with his preparations, he lifted the dead acolyte's body onto his shoulder and moved along the rooftops. Arn jumped across several narrow gaps until he came to a sloping section where a portion of a building wall had collapsed into the alley below, forming a steep mound from which one could leap to grab a handhold on the roof. Climbing up the rubble pile, he stashed the dead priest's body on the roof. Drawing his hood up and over his head, Arn vaulted down, adopting a priestly stroll through the narrow alleyway that led down to Freemarket Street.

Arn bowed his head slightly as he turned onto the bustling avenue. His objective was an open doorway five paces to his right. A group of vorg warriors stood jammed in the entrance of the Red Tavern, a mud-floor dive with no redeeming qualities other than an endless supply of the monastic brew called blood ale. Repugnant to most humans, the drink drove the vorgs mad with desire for more, and thus, the warriors returned the majority of their pay back to its source on the hill above.

Arn bumped roughly into one of the vorgs, who turned and shoved him before recognizing that he was a priest. A look of surprise spread across the vorg's face upon recognition of his mistake. The warrior backed into a compatriot, who also turned to face Arn.

Arn hissed, drew the priestly dagger, and plunged it into the vorg's arm.

The vorg roared and charged, followed by several others. Arn turned and ran, dodging into the alley from which he had come. Ducking around the corner, he gained ground as the vorgs jammed into one another trying to make the turn. In a few steps, he reached the rubble pile, raced up it, and swung himself up and onto the roof.

As he disappeared over the top, he tossed the body of the dead priest down into the alley he'd just left. It landed with a thud atop the rubble. The enraged vorgs, thinking that the priest had slipped in his flight, converged with ferocity, kicking and pummeling the corpse. In their bloodlust, they hacked until the former protector was a torn and bloody mess.

Arn continued over the rooftops, stripping off the priestly robes. Reaching his point of origin, he retrieved the bundle he had left there.

Moments later, the drunken beggar stumbled out into the street, his interest momentarily captured by the stream of vorgs making for the gate as cries rang out for the city guard. Losing interest, the besotted tramp sank down in a corner with his bottle.

25

Mo'Lier
YOR 414, Early Autumn

Storm clouds roiled overhead, lightning arcing out and down, striking repeatedly around the gathered army. Temple Hill was wreathed in a churning fog. The shops and taverns, now deserted, had been left in such haste that the doors swung open in the howling wind. The priests descended from the mount in groups of thirteen, heads bowed, hands clasped beneath their robes.

The guards cowered on the walls as the first group carried the body of the dead acolyte out through the gates, followed by the others, thirteen groups of thirteen each. Atop the walls, even the commanders slunk within the parapets, cringing at each verse of the dull chant that rose from the hooded figures moving slowly out in their curling procession. A lone guard stood attentive to the proceedings, staring down at the scene below.

Arn's eyes peered through a far-glass from beneath the helmet. The change that had come over the encampment beyond the city walls was nothing short of incredible. Vorgs and men alike stood in perfect formations, scared out of their very minds by what they beheld.

Vorgs and humans hung from thirteen pairs of poles to which their hands and feet were staked, forming a great circle into which the priests carried the corpse of the young acolyte. The men and vorgs, all still very much alive, screamed in agony or begged for death. Lightning continued to arc downward, dancing atop each pole, followed by the tearing crack of thunder.

The priests entered the circle and moved to assigned spots in a carefully choreographed spectacle. The thirteen groups were soon arrayed in what looked like thirteen tentacles extending from a central core. In unison they knelt, bowing their heads to the ground. The deafening silence that accompanied the movement spread out like the clanging of a great gong.

"Krylzygool."

The chant, barely audible at first, picked up in volume as the kneeling forms of the priests began to writhe slowly in twitching, jerking movements that cascaded outward from the center. Arn blinked to clear the illusion that some monstrous creature was wriggling its way out of a deep hole.

A faint sound emerged above the chant, like the sound of thick mud as one is freed from its maw. Revulsion and dread swept outward as a new smell wallowed its way over Arn. He recoiled, his gut tightening into a hard knot.

On the grounds below, battle-hardened men and vorgs retched violently as, all the while, the chanting and the writhing of the priests increased in its frenzied need. Arn peered out over the wall through watery eyes, tears trickling down his cheeks.

The central core of the churning clouds overhead descended on the priests in a black sludge, transforming into thirteen thick tentacles that slithered outward and up the poles.

The agitation of the victims reached such a pitch that several tore a limb or two free of the spikes, leaving great shreds of their own flesh dangling behind. With their newly freed hands, they pried and tore at the fastenings that held them firm. Then with a lurch, the murky tendrils bulged and surged upward, engulfing the scrabbling forms.

Arn clenched his teeth as a wave of fear surged outward from the spectacle below. The tentacles bulged and bunched, some moving away from their victims, revealing people horrendously injured but still living.

The tentacles caressed the dying lovingly, and where they touched the bodies, great weeping sores spewed forth grubs that spilled onto adjacent skin, only to begin burrowing inside once more.

A huge vorg, which Arn recognized as one of those who had chased him, arched his body so violently that he tore himself completely free of the pole, falling to the ground with an audible thud.

The tentacle descended on the vorg, encompassing its form so that only a squirming bulge in the rubbery mass remained. And still the scene continued to grow in madness. The screaming bodies could not die, try as they might. Clearly, the dark god that held them would not grant them final release.

The central core of the monstrous mass was now throbbing with a rhythm that exuded a strange attraction, bringing forth a cry from all those it touched. The ranks of soldiers surged forward in a fervor, stopping short of the circle as terror returned, freezing them in indecision.

The great mass of the thing faded until only the swaying priests remained, uttering their dying chant. The bodies of the now mercifully dead hung limply from the spikes.

Arn staggered back from the wall, ill, but refusing to empty himself like the masses of the army below. He had seen and dealt death coldly, and that was not what sickened him. He knew that the summoned presence brought forth by the priesthood was the antithesis of all that was natural in this world. Something ancient and revolting. Something that hungered.

Arn closed his eyes in concentration, then turned on his heel and disappeared down the ladder into the alley beyond.

—ʍ—

Arn moved briskly through the gathering darkness of early evening, his purpose stretching out before him like a glimmering trail. In the woods just below Temple Hill, he slid through the brush toward his target, two priests engaged in deep conversation, heads bowed beneath their hoods, a mere forty paces from the great temple doors.

"Such overconfidence," Arn said, stepping from behind a tree.

Both priests raised their heads as Arn's hand flashed in an arc, which traced Slaken's path through their throats. Catching their dying bodies, Arn heaved one over each shoulder before either hit the ground and staggered back into the brush, moving down the slope toward the abandoned coal cellar he had found hidden in the vines. By the time he dumped his twin burdens down the steps, Arn was panting with exertion.

He wiped his blood-covered face on his sleeve, an act that failed to improve his appearance. Not taking any more time to rest, Arn turned once again into the night.

The evening communal gatherings in the city below Temple Hill would all be breaking up shortly, the populace having served up the periodic offerings and having received for their devotions the joy of continuing their miserable lives for yet another month under the "protection" of their priestly lords and masters. The scattered brethren would make their way in ones and twos up toward the high hold of the monastery above. His opportunity existed in the shadowed streets and wooded trails leading to the high gate, but that opportunity would not last long.

Changing tactics, he began killing priests and leaving their bodies temporarily hidden near where they fell, one here, two more there. The darkness, his old friend, hid the blood evidence that would alert passersby to his deeds come dawn. Just before midnight, he reached the desired quota and began the arduous task of retrieving the corpses and carrying them stealthily back to the hidden cellar.

Barely an hour before dawn, exhausted, Arn dragged himself through the shallow marsh that rimmed the lake beyond the easternmost of the city walls. This early in autumn, the shallow waters were only mildly cold. Arn moved out into the reeds, cut several, and selected one through which he could blow air. He placed one end in his mouth and allowed his blood-covered body to slip below the murky surface.

Arn let the cold and relaxation slow his hammering heart. Amidst that stillness, his mind drifted into a dream-filled sleep.

26

Mo'Lier
YOR 414, Early Autumn

Just after dawn, Jorthain was awakened by his aide, a cowering old monk with long gray hair falling onto his shoulders. The lord high protector wondered at the audacity required to disturb his slumber on the morning after conclave. "What, Boban? Out with it before I lose patience."

"Your Eminence, you must come with me immediately."

"I must?"

The familiar cloak of anger settled over the high priest as he swung his legs off the bed, reaching for the black robe hanging on the wooden peg by the headboard.

The other man wailed and cowered on the floor, the shock of realizing what he had just said draining the blood from his face. "Forgive me, master . . . my state of mind, the urgency of my desire for your guidance, has caused me to blunder in my words."

Jorthain finished fastening his robe and moved to stand over the body of his prostrate aide. He let the silence linger after the other man's babbling subsided. What could have driven this fool to disturb his rest?

He knew he would find out very shortly and that it would undoubtedly stoke his rage further.

The high priest strode to the balcony that looked out over the city below and dominated the terrain for leagues around. Only the upper spire of the monastery, directly behind his room and up the stairs to the north, commanded a better view of the plains to the south. His attention was immediately drawn to the commotion in the camp outside the city walls. The entire military seemed to be in motion, milling about in wild and frenzied fashion. Yesterday, Krylzygool had delivered a harsh message to the army of the protectors. And yet, as Jorthain looked out over that landscape on this new dawn, disorder reigned supreme.

Jorthain grabbed the far-glass sitting on the stand by the balcony and trained it on the scene below. He scanned rapidly across the encampments, observing the melee as men and vorgs roiled, some rushing toward the circle and some running away. Fights were breaking out as some struggled to free horses under guard at numerous rope corrals. Some of the corrals had actually been broken, allowing horses to run free amidst the gathering chaos.

"Your Eminence, I . . ."

"Quiet. I will get answers when I ask for them. Until then, silence is all I expect."

The high priest snapped the far-glass to the center of the maelstrom, the circle itself. No one moved onto or off the site. Although the circle was surrounded by hundreds of onlookers, it appeared to be no different than when he had strode from the area the day before. The poles stood with the putrefied remains of their victims and nothing else, except . . .

He adjusted the focus on the glass with small turns. At the base of each of the thirteen poles stood thirteen priests, the hoods of their cloaks pulled low over their heads. Then he saw it. As he moved the glass across the distant forms, one of the cloaks blew back in the morning breeze. There was no body, just the head of a priest atop a spear embedded in the ground, a head that wore the priestly cowl stained a darker shade with blood.

Jorthain scanned rapidly back around the circle of priests, this time spotting the stains on each robe, the lack of fullness to the shapes. His thoughts froze.

It was incomprehensible that someone in the mass of offal below had dared to defy him after yesterday's display. But there was no denying what his eyes now beheld just beyond the city walls. What was worse, this blasphemous attack on his priesthood had been seen, and the rumor of it spread like wildfire. The city walls were now teeming with curious onlookers, some still in their nightshirts.

Clearly someone had dared to challenge his power, and the consequences of that challenge were yet to be sorted out. A large portion of the army had apparently convinced themselves that circumstances were about to get worse than what they had seen the day before and were in the process of getting away before they could get caught up in the inevitable cataclysm. Many soldiers were being engaged by disciplined veterans, determined to thwart the mass desertions. Commanders stumbled around yelling, trying to make sense of the disorder, while combat raged all around.

Jorthain turned abruptly and strode back into the bedroom. "Boban. On your feet now."

The other man scrambled to comply.

"I want the Conclave of the Nine convened within the hour. I will lead it. Pick a woman that will be certain to please our master. We will perform the ceremony in my personal chambers. Now, be gone."

The other man bowed, then spun on his heel and swept from the room.

—∿—

By the time the high priest arrived at the stairwell leading down into his ceremonial chamber, all of the others were already within. The muffled cries that arose from below lent anticipation to the old man's steps.

While the occasion of this summoning was infuriating, he still felt the same enjoyable racing of the heart that he had felt as a young priest at his first such ceremony. The pleasure that it gave the ancient one was returned in measure to those who conducted the ritual.

As he stepped through the oblong portal at the base of the stairs and emerged behind the altar, the eight elder priests raised their arms in unison, palms upward, the mouth and eyes of the serpentine bands that encircled their ring fingers turned to face upward with their palms. A soft chant rose and fell in a pulsing rhythm, timed to pace Jorthain's steps up the dais to his place atop the altar.

The woman tied facedown was bent forward across a great ball that formed the altar's center, two paces in diameter, her hands and feet bound in leather straps to hoops of steel embedded in the altar's base. Jorthain reached forward, grabbing her blonde hair and pulling her head back so that he could look into her face.

She was in her early twenties, with light blue eyes, now distended in fright. She moaned behind her gag, shaking in spasms of fear. The high priest gazed at her for several seconds before turning to grab the pearl-handled ceremonial dagger from its mounting place on the wall behind the altar.

The chant picked up in pace and rose in volume, a beat that sounded more and more like Jorthain's pounding heart. He raised the dagger before him, laid out on his own upstretched palms, revealing the same jewel-eyed serpent entwined in the handle that formed the loops of the priestly rings. Slowly his fingers closed around the handle. Then Jorthain stepped forward and slit her throat from ear to ear.

Blood arced outward in long twin spurts, then gushed again in rapidly diminishing arcs into the large basin surrounding the round marble stone. Jorthain laid the dagger aside on a pedestal, then spread his arms wide, as if the bloody stone was an altar.

"Krylzygool . . . hear me." His voice rose in a high-pitched shriek. "Accept this offering most pure and grant us your vision, oh ancient one."

The marble stone, now stained in sheets of red on one side, had taken on a sickly yellow cast.

"Let the pure blood feed the ancient heart. Let the terror of the innocent salve your immortal desires. Let the devotion of your servants stoke your mighty presence."

The stone's color changed to purple, then it pulsed and deepened to scarlet, as a wave of pleasure brought moans to the swaying priests.

"Master, reveal to us now that which we need to see in order to serve you. Show us the source of defiance that has been thrust at your priesthood, nay, even thrust at you. Show us the one who sneers at your power and strives to drive doubts into the minds of those you dominate."

A brown aura pulsed from the stone, bringing gasps of terror from the assemblage. The darkness deepened, the feeling of rage rising, growing, reaching outward. Jorthain felt his muscles cramp and tighten as he fell prostrate on the altar, unable to breathe as his chest bound up on itself. Just as he felt his consciousness fade to the smallest pinprick of light, the darkness yielded, replaced with a deep sense of frustration. Then that, too, was gone.

The high priest gasped, struggling to draw breath. His blood beat painfully in his temples, and as he rolled to his knees, he thought that he might yet lose consciousness. He managed to raise his head to see that several of the other priests were also struggling to rise. Others had succumbed and lay curled where they had fallen.

"What?" Norel, one of the elder priests, managed to gasp. "What can it mean? Krylzygool showed us nothing."

Jorthain pulled himself erect, although the effort cost him dearly. "I must contemplate what I have just witnessed. I will call for you all to convene with me once I have meditated on this. Restore yourselves and assist the others. You will await my summons."

With that, the high priest turned and slowly made his way back to his quarters, where he collapsed, exhausted, into his bed. When he awakened, most of the day had passed so that the late-evening rays of the sun slanted over his balcony. Jorthain sat up, leaning over to splash water from his bedside basin on his face and neck.

No response. Never in all his years had he seen anything like it. A perfect sacrifice resulting in no reward other than the initial pleasure. What had Norel said?

Jorthain walked to the balcony and gazed out beyond the city walls once more. If anything, the situation was worse this evening. Veterans fought to prevent less-disciplined troops from large-scale desertion. Their efforts were unsuccessful. Commanders were trying to reorganize the remainder of their troops but with great difficulty. He could imagine why. Despite the murder of thirteen priests, there had been no response from the temple in over twelve hours.

And why not? Because unbeknownst to the horde beyond the city walls, the most powerful of the protectors had failed in communion with their Krylzygool. Or had their god failed them? Jorthain quailed, lambasting himself for the blasphemous thought.

Jorthain had a very good idea what that failure meant. The witch. The one who had killed his priests sent to collect the annual tribute from the flock in the mountains. She had somehow reached out and set a mark on their very door, a warning meant to intimidate and frighten. Somehow she had managed to place wards that blocked even the perceptive powers of the ancient one.

And now Jorthain himself had aided her by collapsing in exhaustion after the dark calling so that an entire day was lost in restoring control of the army. The old man's head pounded as the blood beat against his temples, rage turning his face a deep shade of purple. He moved across the room, bumping the oblong nightstand hard enough to bring a bruise to his thigh. Cursing under his breath, he pulled on the bell cord that dangled near the headboard of his bed. Within seconds Boban appeared in the doorway.

"Yes, Your Eminence?" he said.

"Send out word to the commander of the guard. I want a full city search conducted immediately. Anyone who cannot be proven to be a member of the army or a citizen is to be arrested and held for inquisition. Also, I want all commanders in that rabble of an army beyond our gates to conduct a head count and personally vouch for the identity of all their men.

"I want a list of all who are unaccounted for delivered to me by midmorning tomorrow. Finally, I want all priests to report to their parish masters and account for their whereabouts for the last twenty-four hours in detail. Once the masters have been satisfied that they have heard from their charges, I want them to schedule time with me personally so that I may review the matter. Do you understand exactly what I want?"

"Yes, master," said Boban.

"Good, then you may go," the high priest said. Then he paused. "One thing more. Alert all who participated in the Conclave of the Nine this morning that they are to come to my chambers immediately."

"As you wish." Boban scurried out the door.

Jorthain paced. There was no doubt that the witch of whom mighty Kragan had warned them was behind this disastrous sequence of events. He could see her in the images that Kragan had revealed in Jorthain's scrying vase. She exuded an attraction that befitted one marked by elemental kind. The witch of prophecy had now attacked Jorthain. The high priest gritted his teeth. Would that he had readied his army more quickly.

As the eight elder priests began arriving, Jorthain ushered them to chairs in his audience chamber. When all were present, he spoke. "As most of you have probably come to understand, our enemy has moved against us. There can be no doubt that the one we have to blame for this blasphemy is the witch whom we seek to destroy."

A sharp intake of breath indicated that not all the priests had arrived at this conclusion. The fact that his god had failed to identify the killer led Jorthain to speculate on the assassin's nature. Only someone in possession of powerful wards could have accomplished this. The thought of the witch who had defeated a half dozen of his protectors flashed to the forefront of his mind.

"She has managed to insert an agent in our midst, an agent warded with magical protections against discovery. I want this person found quickly. I have already issued orders for the search to commence, but I want each of you to organize the brethren in a search of every part of the city and the surrounding countryside.

"Leave no stone unturned. Anyone who cannot find others to vouch for his identity is to be taken and imprisoned for further interrogation. Any who resist are to be killed immediately. No priests are to travel in groups numbering less than three. We cannot underestimate the capabilities of the witch's agent. He has already killed at least thirteen of our brothers under our very noses. I will not let him go unpunished."

Norel raised his voice. "And if we don't find him? What then?"

"You will find him. Let no doubt enter your mind. No one violates our holy place to commit such atrocities and leaves unpunished. The assassin is running by now, probably trying to blend in with the deserters, so ensure you send out enough hunting parties to cut off escape. He will head to the east, up into the mountains, so get our scouts out in front of him. He won't be a vorg, so bring me only human suspects."

As the priests stood to go, Jorthain raised his hand. "Please, do not disappoint me. I would dearly hate to lose any of you in whom I have placed such trust."

As one, the assemblage bowed and made their way swiftly from the room. As Jorthain watched them depart, he examined the fear that had been growing within him. If the witch in the Glacier Mountains, southeast of Mo'Lier, could block the powers granted to the protectors by Krylzygool, she posed a greater danger than he had thought. A new worry sprang to mind. What would Kragan do to him if he failed in his mission to kill her and her family?

27

Areana's Vale
YOR 414, Early Autumn

Wearing a mostly white apron, Rolf Grombit scurried through the crowded Flowing Ale Tavern; the crowd had not yet reached its peak. That would happen at the guard shift change. His jovial nature allowed him to harangue his waitresses and cooks without offense being taken.

Jason and his priests had not been idle these last several months, identifying several plants in Areana's Vale that lent themselves quite nicely to the fermentation process. Thus the kegs inside the Flowing Ale never ran dry.

While the priesthood had all the stodginess associated with most religious orders, Jason ran this one like a tight ship. In fact, the priesthood had been a key factor in establishing an orderly marketplace within the vale, beginning with the minting of money, carved quite expertly from trees that grew only in the Chasm of Eternity, an area under their sole control. The money had quickly been adopted for trade, as the priests accepted the currency in exchange for their distilled spirits.

Jason had worked out all the details with Rafel, who immediately recognized and authorized the ingenious nature of the plan. Thus the priesthood grew wealthy, while the citizens were rewarded with a very effective monetary system. Yes, the money of Areana's Vale was backed with liquid gold—ale.

So, in an interesting way, Colindale, the village closest to the main fortress, had become home for what amounted to the central bank, the Flowing Ale Tavern.

Tonight Rolf was in fine form, slapping customers on their backs while whistling for serving girls to hurry up with their orders. He liked to meet each new arrival at the door, greeting every last one of them with a "Well, hello there, beauty!" or "Good to see you, stud!" depending on the customer's gender.

It didn't matter whether he knew their real names or not. Each and every one of Rolf's customers regarded him as their lifelong friend, a sentiment he returned.

The shift at the fort was due to change soon. A flood of thirsty guardsmen would wash into the tavern shortly after that. Although this was a nightly occurrence, the combination of shift change and weekend celebration meant that Rolf would soon have great difficulty moving his massive form back and forth among the crowd. For the thousandth time, he wished he had built a bigger place. May the gods bless those priests.

"Beauty! So good to see you. You too, stud. How've you been? Here, let me find you two a special table." Rolf jammed the couple into a table at the end of the bar, but they were glad to have it. "You want the usual?"

When the new arrivals nodded, Rolf put two fingers to his lips, blasting out an earsplitting whistle. "Ruthy! Two ales over here, quick as you can."

A song broke out at the far end of the bar. Lord Alan was entertaining a group of rangers with a bawdy ballad, somewhat slurred. He was well into his cups early this evening. Regardless, the lad had personality, and the rangers snickered appreciatively at his rendition. Rolf noticed that some of the women drifted away from that end of the tavern, ears burning red, while others managed to steal a look at the strapping son of High Lord Rafel.

The barbarian, Ty, appeared in the doorway, bare-chested as was his norm, huge ax slung across his back, tresses falling across his shoulders. He ignored Rolf completely as he strode to the bar and ordered a tall ale.

His bare upper torso brought gasps from several of the young women, which obviously annoyed Lord Alan to no small degree.

"Well, would you look at that," said Alan in an overly loud voice. "Our reputed Dread Lord has decided that he is just too good to wear civilized clothes."

Several of the rangers turned to look at the Kanjari, but Ty ignored the comment.

Rolf started to make his way across the tavern in order to tell Alan that he didn't need any of that kind of talk in here, but he was suddenly overwhelmed by a mob of guardsmen entering the venue. Shift change.

As the crowd of new arrivals surged through the door, Rolf gave up on trying to seat them, endeavoring to merely direct the soldiers toward the bar in the most efficient fashion possible. The crowd swelled so that it became elbow room only. Arms were raised in unison, trying to get the attention of the serving girls so that money could be exchanged for ale.

Lord Alan broke into another bellowing song on the far side of the bar. "Oh, I knew a Kanjari from the town of Traborg. He was so damned ugly, you'd a thought he was vorg . . ."

Ty continued drinking, although he was now on his second flagon of ale. Rolf thought that he detected tension across Ty's back, although that could have been his imagination.

Lord Alan elbowed his way through the crowd to stand at the bar beside the Kanjari. The crowd made room for them.

Rolf felt that he should rush over and do something but was completely blocked by the mass of humanity known as his customers.

Lord Alan turned so that he leaned sideways against the bar, his face staring up at the side of Ty's head. "So, what do you say, Dread Lord? Have you decided yet?"

Ty finished his ale and slowly turned toward the young lord. "Decided what?"

"Why, decided if you're a savage or just a man like the rest of us?"

A murmur flitted through the crowd.

"I'm sorry," said Ty.

"Sorry for what?"

"Sorry that your mommy isn't around to give you this ass whipping instead of me."

Lord Alan swung his beefy right hand, but it failed to connect with the barbarian's face. Instead, a massive blow from the mug in Ty's right hand hammered Alan in the side of the head, dropping him to the floor.

The rangers jumped to their feet in unison, rushing to the aid of their young comrade. Ty spun to face this new challenge, but they merely reached down and hauled the semiconscious lord back to his feet, blood dripping from the side of his head.

"Carry him back to the fort," Derek Scot said. "Put him in a bed to sleep it off."

He gave Ty a nod, then turned and followed the rangers carrying Lord Alan through the parting crowd and out the door. Rolf understood the gesture. As far as he knew, nobody had ever beaten the young lord in a fight.

"A round of drinks on the house," an anxious Rolf yelled, his booming voice filling the momentary silence.

He was rewarded with the sound of a rousing cheer, immediately restoring the tavern's boisterous atmosphere.

—∞—

A bruised ego is a difficult thing to heal, and Alan found that his own ego was no exception. He was not stupid, having lived a life of military training since he was just a boy. He also had no excuses for his behavior in provoking Ty on that night in the Flowing Ale. He had simply been drunk and trying to impress the rangers at his table.

Instead, he had embarrassed himself by getting beaten down in near record time and alienating someone who could teach him a thing or two about what it meant to be a warrior. And being a warrior was what Alan wanted to be. Not just a warrior. Alan wanted to be a legend, like his father.

Jared Rafel had built an early reputation as the most fearsome combatant in the army of Tal. He quickly rose through the ranks, showing that his prowess as a fighter was surpassed only by his ability to lead men into battle. By the time Rafel was twenty-eight years old, the king chose him to lead the armies of Tal against the vorg hordes.

His men said that wherever the high lord went on the battlefield, the soldiers who saw him riding past were given strength and courage, with fear and fatigue dispelled. Rafel drove himself relentlessly, arriving at key places at the right times, lending renewed vigor to combat forces. To this day, Jared Rafel had never been defeated on the field of battle. His soldiers loved him, and for good reason.

Growing up, Alan had pushed himself harder than any boy his age. He had trained his body in battle and was undefeated in any contest of arms. Moreover, Alan had fought alongside the high lord's soldiers in numerous engagements with vorgs and brigands.

Still, his father was not pleased with his progress. For that matter, neither was Gaar. Worse yet, Alan understood their reasoning. He was reckless.

When his blood rose, Alan found himself descending into a rage, where he could only think of destroying the enemy. In that state, no pain slowed him, and no one could stand before him. His rage made him unstoppable but also robbed him of the ability to think beyond his immediate fight.

He had been unable to overcome what he perceived as a monstrous weakness. Giving in to battle fury was fine for someone who would become a mighty soldier, but it was the death knell for a career as a leader of men.

Alan cursed himself as he worked, assisting in securing one of the forts. He had lost a fight for the first time in his life. By the deep, it was not even a fight.

Rafel had been none too pleased to find out that Alan had started a brawl. His son had once again displayed a lack of maturity, which meant he would receive no leadership positions for the foreseeable future. In contrast, the quick rise of Gaar's son, Hanibal, through the ranks greatly annoyed Alan. He had defeated Hanibal in every training encounter where they had been pitted against each other.

But Hanibal maintained control of himself and control of those around him. Although Alan had learned strategic thinking from his father and Gaar, the rage that filled him during battle temporarily wiped such wisdom from his mind.

Alan knew the only thing that helped him throw off a bad mood, like the one that afflicted him now, was to work. He lost himself in the effort of lifting the logs that would bolster the main fort's defenses, holding them in place as others scurried about, securing them in their final positions. The more tiredness assaulted him, the less he thought about his problems, and the better he felt.

The day passed by, and he took no notice of the hour, not stopping for lunch, only pausing for a periodic drink from the water jug to replace the sweat that soaked his body, forming a sheen on the outer layer of his clothes. As the afternoon light faded, a boy tugged urgently at his sleeve.

"Lord Alan," the boy said, "High Lord Rafel sent me to bid you come. He is waiting for you in his council chambers."

Alan mopped his brow with his sleeve, an effort completely wasted since the sleeve itself was soaked with sweat. He recognized the boy as one of the lucky few who had been chosen to train as squires to the company commanders. "What is your name?" Alan asked.

"Brad, my lord," the boy said.

"Well, Brad My Lord," Alan said, "run back and tell my father I am on my way."

"Yes, sir." The boy turned and disappeared back up the street.

Alan walked toward his father's council chambers at a leisurely pace, wondering all the way there about the purpose of the meeting. When he entered, a blazing fire roared on the hearth, and Rafel stood near it. Alan moved up beside his father.

Rafel placed an arm around Alan's shoulder. "I want to talk to you, son."

Alan said nothing.

"I keep hoping that you will become a bit more like Carol and use that head sitting on your shoulders. You are far from stupid, but I expect you to exercise more self-discipline."

When Alan still did not respond, Rafel continued. "Leadership is one of those things you have to find on your own. I try to place you in situations that I think will help you develop and exercise the will to lead. But until you prove to me that you can keep your head and see the whole of battle, I will give you no command."

Alan stared at his father. "I take it that this means you are about to send me on a bad assignment."

"Yes," said Rafel. "I am sending Derek Scot and a small group of rangers out to set up a ranger camp in the Endless Valley. Their mission will be to conduct long-range reconnaissance, trying to get a feel for our enemies' movements. The rangers are to observe the enemy and avoid getting engaged in battle if at all possible. I want you to accompany them."

Alan kept his face serious, but far from being disappointed, the thought of this mission sent a thrill through him. It carried with it the promise of danger. "I understand."

"Maybe," High Lord Rafel said, his face serious. "But you will be under the command of Derek Scot. I expect you to take orders from him and to listen to any advice he has for you along the way. Watch how he leads his men and, for the sake of the gods, learn from him."

"How soon do we leave?" asked Alan.

"Derek wants to depart tonight. Pack your things and saddle up."

Alan gripped his father's hand, his gaze meeting the high lord's. Alan vowed to himself that the next time he looked into those gray eyes, they would not be filled with disappointment.

28

Areana's Vale
YOR 414, Early Autumn

Carol awoke to find herself huddled and quivering in the corner of her room, tears streaming down her face though she could not remember why. She had dragged her blankets from the bed, stuffed one around the crack where the cabin door met the floor, and draped the others across the windows. Thin shafts of daylight bled through slots that the blankets missed.

She gasped, stunned at what she had done in her sleep. What nightmare had so frightened her that she had tried to block every crevice or portal into the cabin? And why use blankets? Why not something more substantial, like tables and chairs?

She stumbled to her feet, moving quickly to remove the coverings before anyone could come along and discover what she had done. Having deposited the blankets back on her bed, she made a quick survey of the cabin, but nothing else appeared out of place.

Sleepwalking was something she had heard about but had never before experienced herself. Gods. Was this yet another side effect of her kata practice?

Of course, it was also possible that she had just been up too late repeating the experiment. Perhaps sleepwalking was the result of the agitated state she had worked herself into rather than anything directly related to the kata. She certainly hoped so.

Carol made herself a hearty breakfast of scrambled eggs and salted bacon, compliments of Mary Beth Abercrombie, and a steaming cup of hot tea. She didn't want to think about the unnerving aspects of her activities, so she decided not to, preparing herself for an outing to the main fort instead.

The wind had died away to a pleasant breeze by the time Carol made her way down the path toward the upper fortress. The sun shone in that clear way that only comes on early-autumn days, lending golden colors to all that its rays caressed. Carol felt that she should be reveling in the morning, but she could not.

She was worried. She felt unidentifiably different. Thoughts and feelings eddied at the corners of her mind, disappearing when she tried to focus on them.

Her senses seemed odd as well, somehow sharpened. She sniffed, trying to pick up subtle smells on the breeze. Nothing. The same when she paused to listen. She could hear or smell nothing out of the ordinary. Yet as she walked, she occasionally caught a strange scent or sound.

A flock of fluffy winter birds took flight as she approached, flapping off hard toward the west. The normal animals that were abundant throughout the valley were nowhere to be seen, almost as if avoiding her. The notion was laughable, but in her current mood, she couldn't bring herself to see the humor in the idea.

The people she passed along the road were cheerful enough, although Carol thought she detected some puzzled expressions as they looked at her. Had she forgotten to brush her hair or wash up?

Glancing down at herself, she was horrified to discover that she had not changed out of her nightgown. She stopped in her tracks.

What . . . ?

She was certain she had started to get dressed. She had made breakfast, washed, combed her hair, and then gone to the dresser to lay out her clothes. Then what? She remembered leaving the house and walking down the road through Longsford Watch and on down the valley, waving to those she passed.

Carol felt the blood rush to her face. Moving quickly, she departed the road and moved into the woods, choosing a course that led back to her cabin but kept her out of sight. She was mortified. How could she possibly allow herself to become distracted to the point of failing to get dressed?

Thank the gods she was wearing a nightgown. If the cold wind of last night had been blowing, there would have been no way she would have made this blunder, but it had been warm this morning. She turned the thoughts over in her mind, searching for an explanation, an excuse even, but none came.

Arriving at her cabin, Carol fell onto her bed. She was consumed by a sudden, uncontrollable fit of sobbing, tears dampening the pillow she hugged tightly to her chest. She gradually sank back, drifting into another dream-filled sleep.

She awoke at night and suffered an instant of panic, unable to remember her location. Feeling around, her fingers found the headboard of her bed, and relief flooded over her. She was still in her bed. There had apparently been no desperate wanderings around the cabin, stuffing blankets into the cracks of doors and windows.

Despite having slept the day away, she was not hungry. Thirst, however, was another matter. Her mouth felt like she had been licking a handful of dirt. She went to the pitcher on her night table and found it empty. She had forgotten to refill it. Of course she had.

Returning from the stream with a full pitcher, she poured herself a glass of water, gulped it down unselfconsciously, and then refilled it. Halfway through the second glass, she paused for air, feeling less like she had just crawled out of the desert. Deciding that the time had come to act more like a wielder of powerful magics, Carol moved to her desk and took up the book once again.

With a thought, she set the candles to burning, noting that she would have to bring out two new ones after tonight.

The key seemingly lay in working through the points in the kata where she was startled out of her meditative state. Based on her lingering side effects, those occurrences left her mentally tied to the exercise, as if her connection to the dreamworld continued long after it should have been broken.

At least that gave her a working theory. The startling aspects of the exercise came from the tremendous variety of sights, sounds, and feelings that assaulted her senses, even when she had narrowed her focus to include a relatively small area around her visualized form.

She needed to come up with an idea that would enable her to deal with these alien sensations and get to the next level. Carol read the description of the exercise once more, mulling its references to filtering and blocking carefully, putting them in context with what else was happening in the kata. She thought she was beginning to understand what might be happening. The exercise was apparently providing insight on how certain elemental forces were perceiving the real world.

This opening of her mind incurred a significant degree of risk. The process was different from the type of magic she had learned from Hawthorne since it did not involve taking direct control of an elemental. The unknown ancient wielder had apparently gone mad while working on the techniques described in the manuscript, but she pushed that sentiment into the background. She had no intent of progressing toward more difficult katas until she had established a sense of mastery over the first one.

Kim had urged Carol to allow her to be present, assisting her if she got in trouble during an exercise and providing strength through her life-shifting magic. This Carol could not permit. Since they shared a mental bond, the prospect of placing her Endarian sister at risk was intolerable.

What she needed now was a strategy that would allow her to remain in meditation long enough to try sending out impressions.

Perhaps she could pick a particular disturbance in the void to focus on, letting the other ripples of sight, sound, and feeling pass her by, barely observed.

Carol moved into deep meditation eagerly, performing the initial steps of the kata with an improved alacrity, allowing the rippling orbs filled with competing visions of terror, hunger, rage, and peace to wash over her.

Suddenly she selected a single expanding sphere to focus on. The act of moving her point of view closer to that source had the effect of increasing its intensity while reducing other sensations.

As she shifted her focus from one glowing orb to another, the resulting visions were worlds unto themselves, filled with sights and sounds in abundance that coursed by so fast she failed to understand them, merely glimpses of disjointed places, things half-seen, half-heard, half-felt. Thoughts whispered at the edges of her own, an abundance of associations that she could not fully discern.

A feeling of freedom, then hunger, a terrible gnawing hunger that overrode all other desires. She paused, a sense of loss and deep confusion settling over her. What was missing? Something else seemed important, something that tickled at the edge of her mind. Then she saw it, a dim light, making its way ever so tenuously through the bright ocean of sensation in which she swam. The body and face were so familiar.

The realization suddenly pulled her back to consciousness. It was her own self . . . and she had almost lost it—again. Carol opened her eyes and then immediately closed them.

Once again, she centered, self-confidence flooding her thoughts before she stilled them. This time she made her way through the visualizations of the kata in rapid sequence. The feelings were penetrating, but she ignored the bulk of them, focusing her intent on a new target, one of the simpler orbs.

Its sensations passed over her, a disconnected chorus of snippets. Flashes of texture quickly disappeared as another wave from another source swept over her. But as she continued, she could feel her control improving. It was helpful to try to maintain focus on that little vibrating pinprick in the void while keeping her own image in sight, visualizing a connection between the two, a thin gossamer strand that stretched and eddied but held together.

As she worked to steady the connecting strand that tethered her to the little vibrational source, the feelings she was picking up became stronger. She had several clear images of trees rising in the forest, strong smells, and an awareness of being watched. She backed off, intentionally weakening the bond that tethered her to her target. She was not ready to be startled out of her visualization just yet.

Now it was time to send out a single image. She thought of a bell tolling in the tower back at Hannington Castle, the image and associated sound strong and clear. She saw the ripple spread out before her, vibrating the ropelike tether and then continuing toward the other pinpoints that surrounded her.

As her sending reached its primary target, Carol's stomach contracted in sheer terror, and she severed the strand, working with desperation to try to keep the storm of sensations from knocking her out of the meditation. Ripples of color formed everywhere, small reflections of the wave she had broadcast. They returned to her from multiple places, like echoes of a yell among distant canyon walls. Some were strong enough to be startling, others merely weak little whispers.

She let them all pass across her body, and though she bobbed like a cork in a lake whipped by the winds of a storm, she maintained her concentration. As the waves subsided, Carol backed off. Then with a firm purpose, she zoomed her viewpoint back in toward her floating image until it filled her mind. She raised her hands before thumping them down onto the table, ending the kata.

Her eyes sprang open, and as they did, she leapt to her feet, thrusting her arms skyward and letting out a wild yell. "Yes!"

The yell of exultation rang within the cabin. She had done it! She felt like running naked through the valley. Then again, if you counted the nightgown episode, she had already done so.

Carol walked out on her porch, threw back her head, and laughed, a sound that echoed across the valley.

—∞—

All around Longsford Watch, people stopped in their work or came out of their houses to stare up the valley toward Carol's cabin. The murmurings among the families gave testament to the collective fear inspired by the maniacal laughter.

29

Areana's Vale
YOR 414, Early Autumn

Jason's white robes swirled about his slender form as he strode up the steps leading to the High Chapel, his staff aiding him in his purposeful ascent. The news he had just received confirmed the rumors he had been hearing for weeks.

The tall ceiling of the High Chapel arched to a peak, supported by massive beams formed from the trunks of great pines that parishioners had chopped in the valley and dragged up the slope using teams of oxen. The final work had required blood and sweat supplemented with block and tackle. Fortunately, there had been no deaths.

Both ends of the High Chapel stood open to the elements, providing magnificent views up and down this offshoot of the vale that Jason had named the Chasm of Eternity. He habitually paused at the open entrance to gaze over the majesty of what he regarded as the most incredible vista in the known world. But not today.

Today he swept into the High Chapel with storm clouds in tow. His three bishops stood as he approached the flaming altar that dominated the center of the building.

"Eminence," they said, bending their heads ever so slightly in acknowledgment as he reached the inner bench, a circular affair that surrounded the central altar.

"You have all been briefed." His was a confirmatory statement, not a question.

"We have," said Bishop Williams, a rotund fellow of godly bearing. "It is as we have all feared."

Murmurs of assent rose from Bishops Smaith and Forston, the former of average build and description in every facet save for an unfortunate inward turn to his left foot. Smaith was going gray at the temples, and his brown eyes had all the sharpness of an owl's.

Bishop Forston, on the other hand, was young for an elder of the church. He had more the air of a warrior than that of a priest. Short-cropped hair framed a square face with inquisitive eyes. The man's arms ended in large hands that now gripped the crooked staff of the priesthood.

Jason had no doubt that those powerful hands could snap the spines of most men if the good bishop chose to do so. He imagined a battle of titans should the bishop contest against Rafel's son, Alan. He cleared his head of such thoughts.

He motioned to the benches, and the three bishops seated themselves. Jason remained standing before them.

"We are rapidly approaching the time when we will have to act," he began. "We have let this evil go on for far too long after the signs began to show that Carol had turned, taking up company with the dark powers.

"I have delayed because of my affection for her and for High Lord Rafel. I waited when the people of Longsford Watch began coming to us with the stories of her strange activities. I stayed my hand when people throughout the valley began to report horses that were terrified in her presence. Even her own mare will not allow her to come near it."

"What about the dreams we have all shared?" asked Forston. "And at the edge of those dreams stands Carol, clad in robes of black, arms outstretched, with that vacant expression in her eyes."

"But her expression never stays completely vacant, does it?" asked Smaith. "In the dream her eyes often burn with mad desires or her lips curl in fear or anger. Moreover, what about her actions?"

Jason said, "Have we not set a watch upon her this last fortnight? Does she not cry out wildly at times or walk about in a disheveled state, waking or asleep? She even forgets to bathe, to sleep, to eat. She immerses herself in arcane rituals, the like of which I cannot imagine, for they appear to be only in her head."

Jason paused, gazing into the eyes of each bishop in turn, seeing there only complete agreement with all that he was saying.

"We have always warned that to consort with elementals, as wielders do, is an abomination," said Forston.

Williams nodded in agreement. "It is a thing of blasphemy, a sin before the gods. And yet, with the arrogance of man, good men and women are seduced into elemental practices so that they are ultimately corrupted or destroyed."

"I warned High Lord Rafel of this years ago," said Jason, "when that ancient idiot Hawthorne first began providing Carol with instruction. Those warnings fell on the deaf ears of an old soldier who had grown to rely on wielders for their help in making war."

"And she is such a good child," Smaith said. "Such a lovely young lady in every way."

"That is precisely what makes it such a tragedy," said Jason. "Woe be it that the young and innocent should succumb to the darkest of powers. Even now I fear that it may be too late to save her."

"But how can we even try without the blessing of her father?" Forston asked. "High Lord Rafel is not a man who will take kindly to anyone suggesting that his daughter is not in her right mind."

"True enough," Jason said. "But even the old warlord has been getting reports of the bizarre goings-on all about her. And he must also be experiencing the dreams that have been affecting everyone in the valley."

"Then there is her appearance," said Forston.

"I daresay," said Jason, "that with the right presentation, we can convince the high lord to consider that certain steps should be taken to safeguard Carol's well-being, along with that of his people. Some things are hard, but I have never met a more decisive leader than Jared Rafel. He will eventually do what is right."

"Let us all hope that eventuality comes before tragedy," Smaith said.

"The gods give hope to man for a reason," Jason continued. "Let us all pray that in the coming days, they will grant our warrior lord the courage to do what needs to be done. It is best that we aid him in making the right choice.

"I want each of you to begin providing suggestive counseling to key leaders in the communities. It is vitally important that the people make High Lord Rafel more aware of their concerns so that he becomes pliable by the time I take counsel with him directly.

"Have a care to be thoughtful in your ministrations. I do not want things stirred up so that someone gets hurt. We are here to care for our people, not to incite riots."

"What about Gaar?" Forston asked.

"No," said Jason. "Leave that old warhorse alone. However, his son is of a mind that is open to the light of the church. I think it would be well worth your time to provide Hanibal with gentle guidance."

Jason turned his back and walked away. As the bishops stood to watch the high priest stride the steps along the Chasm of Eternity, the sunset bathed the rim of the valley in red.

30

Areana's Vale
YOR 414, Early Autumn

Carol sat on the edge of her bed and pressed her palms against her eyes, as if that would take away the feeling that she had been rubbing them with a wire brush. She was tired beyond any experience she had ever endured. She started to wonder whether she had been wise to isolate herself so completely.

The two weeks since her first success with the kata had been almost too much for her to bear. After the initial thrill of having completed the exercise, she discovered that the side effects she had been experiencing from her earlier attempts had gotten worse. Much worse.

It had started with the dreams where she was back in the kata once again, engulfed in the void. That blackness rippled with waves that buffeted her with sensations from all sides, sensations that thrilled, calmed, frightened, or angered, but which came in such chaotic and rapid sequence that she awakened shortly after falling asleep. She felt rage, panic, hunger, and lust, smelled and tasted blood, grass, flowers, flesh. Images of the woods and Longsford Watch as seen from the air left her gasping.

The deprivation of sleep gradually robbed her of the ability to think clearly. She began half dreaming while she was awake, nodding off in the midst of whatever she was doing, even if she were standing. Immediately after Carol lapsed out of consciousness, the dreams began again.

Sometimes she found that she had walked in her sleep, far from her cabin, or perhaps she had walked from the cabin in near delirium and then dosed off. Often she would come to her senses to find people huddled nearby in conversation, pointing and turning away as she became aware of them.

Yesterday she had succumbed to a fit of anger in her embarrassment upon awakening to discover a group of people staring at her from the trees as if she were some freak in a sideshow. She stood suddenly erect, reaching out with her mind to grab Golgorath, an elemental of storms.

Her eyes flashed daggers, her robe whipping around her as lightning flashed from the sky in jagged spikes to gather itself in a glowing orb of energy just above her upraised hands. She summoned her will, and the ball of lightning shot upward into the gathering wall cloud, the thunder so loud that she thought her eardrums would shatter.

Then the rain began, pouring down in a torrent as if it could wash away her pain and frustration along with the pitiful fools who now lay prostrate before her, crying and begging as they squirmed on their bellies. She had left them in the mud, striding back to her cabin, trembling in a white rage.

Kim had stopped by that afternoon, appearing silently in the doorway, moving as only an Endarian can move. She had approached Carol, taking her sister in her arms as one would comfort a child, and the dam of tears had broken. How long she had cried there in Kim's arms she could not quite remember, just that it had felt good to have a sister who cared and who loved her back, uninfluenced by what other people were thinking or feeling.

Kim had stayed all afternoon, talking, cajoling Carol to let her help, reminding her that Endarian magic could lend her strength in working through whatever ailed her.

But Carol could not bring herself to involve her sister. Her fear that somehow, through their mental link, through their bond of kinship, she would transmit her madness to Kim had grown into a certainty.

Madness? That was how she had come to think of her current state, although she only now allowed the thought into her head. Something in the kata had damaged a part of her mind, opening her to elemental influences bombarding her with thoughts and feelings, some animal in nature, but others all too human.

Was she being possessed by some unknown elemental or elementals? She had rejected the idea at first since she could still easily control the elementals she used in normal spellwork.

But what if there were other entities that she did not know about, elementals who stayed out of her direct awareness, merely playing at the corners of her mind? Perhaps these beings were smart enough to avoid a direct confrontation and merely intent on driving her mad with their constant distractions.

Carol stood and walked across her bedroom, pausing before the mirror to examine herself. She still wore her dark gray robe, now filthy with dried mud that she had splashed on herself stomping about in the storm.

Her face was thin and pale, almost a deathly white, into which her eyes had sunk amidst deep blue circles. Her dark hair hung limply in thick matted strands that draped across her shoulders like small snakes.

Carol cackled. Now this was an appearance that finally fit in with the glowing elemental mark on her shoulder.

A sudden knock on the door caused her to spin around. There, towering in the doorway, was her father. The hawkish visage of Jason hovered just beyond, a sympathetic smile splitting his face.

The sympathy did not extend to his eyes.

31

Areana's Vale
YOR 414, Early Autumn

Arn sat atop the big bay mare he had stolen, gazing up at the roiling clouds above the distant mountains. Buried in those heights lay Areana's Vale. The worry that had troubled him these last two weeks had become a conviction that he was needed at home.

It was funny that word came to mind when he thought of the vale. He had never thought of Hannington Castle as home, nor Rafel's Keep. Although he had only resided in the vale for a short time, it had claimed him. Maybe the feeling was just the association between the stunning valley and Carol, his wife-to-be.

Arn urged his mount onward. When he had begun getting the nagging feeling that Carol needed him, he had stolen a horse and started riding hard for high country. The delays and disruption he had inflicted on the army gathered outside Mo'Lier would have to be enough. Whatever the risk, he would not stay away any longer.

Sweeping upward through the ancient forest of giants that guarded the lower entrance to the gorge that led to the vale, he felt the same sense of awe as when he had first seen the trees.

As night fell, he made his camp next to a small brook. He dined on hardtack, washed down with mountain spring water. Then he crawled into his bedroll and fell into a troubled sleep. Dawn found him on his way once more.

By noon, the Great Forest gave way to the expanse of broad valley that led into Areana's Gorge. As he rode across the lush grassland, he soon saw a familiar trio of riders making their way toward him.

He pulled the bay to a halt as Ty's stallion slid to a stop nearby. John and Kim loped up beside Arn, the Endarian leaning gracefully across her horse's neck to hug him.

He shook hands with John and Ty in turn.

"The rangers said you were on your way in," John said. "So we thought we'd ride out to give you a proper welcome. We were a bit worried when Ax showed up a couple of weeks ago without you."

Despite the reunion, Ty's eyes held little mirth. Arn surveyed their faces, all tense. Kim's features were particularly etched with concern.

"All right, out with it. What is wrong?"

"I'll let the two chatterboxes tell you while we ride," said Ty. "We're glad to see you back, though."

Kim spoke next. "It's Carol. I'm so concerned about her, I don't know quite what to say."

"Just tell me," said Arn, his throat tightening.

"It began shortly after you left. Carol isolated herself in study. We all thought she was preparing for the upcoming battles with the protectors, and she may have been. Our father left strict instructions that Carol was to be left alone so she could concentrate and make whatever magical preparations she felt were needed. So we busied ourselves, helping in our own way to facilitate the plans he had laid out.

"But as the weeks went by, very strange things started happening. First, we began hearing about animals acting oddly when Carol was around. I saw it myself. One day I was down at the stables when she came in to see her mare. The horses went mad.

"I feared that Carol's mare would hurt itself kicking the stall. I tried repeatedly to convince my sister to let me help, but she refused to discuss her problems with me."

"And it wasn't just the horses, either," said John. "People started gathering around and whispering about how the birds would all go quiet whenever she was around. One would talk about pigs getting scared or how hens had quit laying eggs for two days after she happened by. I thought it was just gossip. You know how folks like to get on a subject and beat it to death in a mean sort of way.

"Then the dreams started, frightening, nonsensical dreams. And Carol was in all of them. I had different dreams every night. In those dreams, she often floated in a chaotic black sea, and each wave that crested over her revealed vivid sights and sounds from around the vale. In those dreams, I took the form of one animal after another, experiencing the hunger of the predator and the fear of its prey, along with smells so intense that they almost hurt my nose. Madness."

"That was not the worst," said Kim, wiping tears from her eyes. "Everybody began having the same nightmares. And as they discussed their dreams, the more terrified people became."

John raised his eyebrows in acknowledgment of the statement. "You can guess what kind of effect it started to have on morale," he said. "Gaar practically had to whip his guards to keep them on their toes instead of gathering around talking to each other like a bunch of old biddies. The other day I heard heated voices coming from a room where he and Rafel were in discussion. That was a new one to me. I had never heard the boss lose his temper before. I wasn't close enough to hear what they were arguing about, and I didn't have any inclination to get closer, let me tell you. But I can imagine."

"Then the priests started stirring the pot," said Kim. "Jason and his bishops put out the word that all of this was what they had been warning against when it came to wielders and elemental magic. Church attendance shot up like the end of the world was at hand. John and I attended one gathering, and that young firebrand, Bishop Forston, worked the people into a frenzy with his talk about the dangers of consorting with elementals and how the best of us could easily fall under the seductive influence of the primordials."

"To his credit," said John, "Forston did stomp down hard when some fool started shouting that they should all head up the valley, tie the witch to a stake, and burn out the elementals before they destroyed everyone. But he was stirring the pot, keeping it just below the boiling point. And Jason started meeting with Rafel. The speculation is that he was pressing him to talk Carol into putting herself under the watchful graces of his glorious eminence. That continued until last week."

"And there's more. I believe Carol lost her temper with some locals who were harassing her," Kim said. "She called forth a thunderstorm that dropped them to their knees. That was just too much for our father. He confronted Carol with Jason in tow and convinced her that she needed help. The kind of help that only the priesthood could provide. Since that day, she has been living in the monastery. She is being treated with a plant extract that soothes the mind." A soft sob escaped Kim's lips. "I managed to get in to see her yesterday. She didn't recognize me."

Arn said nothing, but he felt Slaken's heat radiate through him, stoking the flames of his rage.

The riders made their way up through Areana's Gorge, passing through the open gates of the two smaller forts and finally into the main fortress itself. They dismounted inside the gates and tossed their reins to a pair of waiting grooms who led the horses off toward the stables. As his companions started to follow him toward Rafel's meeting hall, Arn turned to them.

"My friends, I want to thank you for coming out to meet me and for being there when I learned this foul news. But what I have to say now is for Rafel's ears alone. I am sorry."

He turned on his heel, picking up a pace that carried him rapidly away from them and into Rafel's audience chamber.

—~—

When the warlord saw Arn, he came forward and threw his arms around the younger man's shoulders. The experience was like hugging a block of black ice.

Stunned, Rafel staggered backward, sudden realization dawning. The look he now saw in the younger man's face made him think of the hundreds of others who must have seen that gaze as the life's blood drained from their bodies.

"How could you turn her over to those religious fools?" Arn stared hard at Rafel, struggling to contain himself. "Leaving her to be drugged and indoctrinated? How could you?"

"Arn . . ." High Lord Rafel's strength of spirit returned to him. "You weren't here. Gods help me, I tried to let Carol deal with whatever she had gotten herself into. I even put up with all the muttering and moaning of the frightened people, the damage to discipline, and the weird happenings.

"But, Arn, she was dying. She quit eating, quit bathing, quit sleeping. I had to do something. Only Jason and the priesthood offered any hope. Even Carol came to recognize it. She went willingly in the end."

"Mark my words, I won't leave her to the drugs and the mindwashing that those so-called priests will give her."

Rafel's voice rang out in full command. "You will do what I determine is best for her. You will do as you are ordered!"

Arn's brown eyes took on the sheen of molten metal, and once again the warlord felt as though he heard the distant cry of a slorg, a summoned abomination of primal hunger. "Believe me when I tell you that you don't want me here in this valley. Now hear me and hear me well. I am going to go for Carol and take her out of the vale, and no one had better try to stop me.

"I know you love her as much as I do, but your judgment in this matter is dead wrong. If she doesn't die under the careful ministries of those priests, she will linger on worse than dead, addicted to plant extracts and broken in spirit.

"Listen to your heart and you will know that what I am saying is the truth. Your daughter has a beauty of spirit that is worth dying to save. To save that soul, I will kill everyone who gets in my way, and that includes you, the man I love as my father, if that is what it takes."

For the first time in his adult life, Rafel felt his knees buckle, and he dropped onto a chair, taking his head in his hands.

"I am going to go for Carol. I will take her into the high mountains where I can care for her, giving her all the support I can until she finds a way of controlling the forces with which she finds herself contending. For your part, you will say that you have ordered me to take her away from the vale so that she can bring no harm to anyone living here."

"But you can't help her," Rafel said, his desperation putting a tremor in his hands. "She will destroy you in her madness."

"You forget . . ." Arn tapped Slaken at his side. "Her magic will not harm me."

A sudden look of hope spread across Rafel's features. Arn's hand rested on the hilt of the black knife that he had named Slaken. The runes that covered that haft bound powerful elementals within it. Together, they protected the one with whom this blade had made its blood-bond from all elemental and psychic forms of magic. And only Arn could wield it. "I had forgotten. Gods. I've been so heartsick I can't think straight."

The high lord rose once again and placed a hand on Arn's shoulder. "You'll look after her? You'll help her get better?"

"I will, or we will die together out in those mountains. I can't guarantee you she will get better, but I know her. She has a strength of will that I believe has not been seen on this world for thousands of years. She just needs a chance and someone to lean on who won't be hurt by her powers.

"What I can guarantee is that no living soul will survive any attempt to hurt her. If you see us again, you will know that she has made it through this victorious. She will get her chance to heal, to fight. And if she wins, as I believe she will, I can guarantee that I will bring her back to you."

Rafel staggered forward to throw his arms once more around Arn. This time the embrace was returned.

32

Areana's Vale
YOR 414, Early Autumn

Jason awoke in the semidarkness of his room to find the sharp edge of a cold blade pressing against his throat. A strong hand clamped his mouth shut.

"Good evening, Priest."

The voice was one that sent chills of recognition up his spine.

"We are going to have a conversation, you and I. Actually, I'm going to do all the talking, and you're simply going to nod your head when I ask you a question. Do we understand each other?"

Jason nodded, still struggling to clear the sleep from his head, but felt Blade lift his hand from his mouth. The touch of the runed knife on his throat filled the high priest with horror. It felt like an abomination in the hand of a deep spawn. This was not the young man whom Jason had come to know within Rafel's Keep. This was the assassin who had earned the name Blade.

"Good. I want to speak a little of my dilemma. I arrived back in Areana's Vale this very day. And upon arriving I discovered that the one love of my life has been taken by your priesthood, drugged, and indoctrinated."

Unable to contain himself, Jason's lips moved before he could stifle the impulse to speak. "But she is possessed. She bears the mark of the elemental. I have seen it!"

It was just a flicker at the corner of the priest's eye. He would have almost thought that he had imagined Blade's movement had it not been for the sight of his ring, the one bearing the holy signet of the church, rolling slowly across the floor, his finger still encircled by the golden band. That and the accompanying explosion of pain and blood from his left hand.

The scream that bubbled to Jason's lips was cut short before it began by the increasing pressure of the black blade against his throat.

"As I said, I will be the only one to speak here. Do you understand?"

Jason nodded.

"Good. Now, you are probably thinking that you would like to tell me how it was for the protection of the people, including, no doubt, Carol herself. Well, believe me when I tell you that you have placed your beloved flock in more danger than you can imagine."

Blade leaned forward until Jason could feel his breath on his face. There was just enough light in the room that the high priest could see the dark glitter of the killer's eyes.

"You are going to call your bishops from their sleeping chambers. You are going to tell them that you have had a revelation and that you have asked High Lord Rafel to exile Carol from Areana's Vale and that he has sent me to take her away. Thus you will maintain your precious priestly authority, High Lord Rafel will maintain his authority, and I don't have to get unpleasant.

"But if you try anything even slightly different from what I just described, by the time I am done with you, you will be praying to every god you know to let you die. Then I will take Carol away from here anyway."

Jason's eyes shifted to the hellish black knife that the assassin gripped. For a moment, it seemed to him that the veins in Blade's right hand pulsed with a rhythm that crept through the runes carved into the knife's haft.

"You know me," Blade continued, his voice pulling Jason's gaze back to his. "There should be no doubt in your mind that I will do as I say."

Blade paused, his glance traveling to where the finger still twitched with involuntary spasms on the floor. The unnatural motion amplified Jason's revulsion for the enchanted knife at his throat.

"Consider that a sign from your gods of what will happen to all you hold dear should you disappoint me," said Blade. "Do I make myself understood?"

Jason nodded vigorously as Blade's eyes locked with his own. Although he was certain that Rafel's daughter was indeed possessed, he was even more convinced that he now gazed directly into the icy orbs of the primordial itself.

"Good. Get dressed and go gather the bishops. You have some talking to do. I'll bring two horses into the courtyard and be waiting."

Jason fell from the bed as Blade released the iron grip that had held him. By the time he managed to struggle back to his knees, the assassin was gone.

Wrapping a cloth around his injured hand, Jason rushed from his room.

The bishops, alarmed by the bloody cloth, initially objected to his instructions, but he was adamant. The gods had revealed to him that Carol should be sent into exile from Areana's Vale this very night. He had already arranged for Rafel to send Blade to accompany her and ensure that she did not return.

So it was that they delivered the vacant-eyed woman, in her newly acquired white robes of purity, to the waiting killer on the ugly black horse. Having packed all her belongings, including her spell books, the priests secured them to the other horse.

—w—

Thus, in the predawn darkness, Blade found himself riding slowly out of the majestic valley. Rafel awaited them at the upper fort's drawbridge. Blade gently handed the unconscious Carol down to him and waited while the warlord rocked his daughter in his arms, smoothing her hair and kissing her on the cheeks and forehead as tears cascaded down his battle-scarred face.

Eventually Rafel carried her back up to Blade, who was quietly crying as well. "Thank you."

That was all Rafel could say. He turned and yelled for the guards to lower the bridge. Two riders trotted out, one with two fully laden packhorses in tow.

Blade paused while he secured the lead rope to the pack swivel of the other horse. The escort riders then trotted through the gate, giving instructions at the middle and lower forts to let them pass.

And pass they did, out into the Great Forest, before turning in a wide southern loop up into the high Glacier Mountains to the east.

PART III

From across the great sea, he has come to end me.

—From the *Scroll of Landrel*

33

Misty Hollow
YOR 414, Early Autumn

As Arn worked his way steadily higher, the pine forest thickened, and a spongy mat of pine needles deadened the sound of the horses' hooves. By midmorning the first flakes of snow began to drift down through the still air, one landing on Carol's nose as she slept. Her eyelids fluttered open as he watched, but she was still groggy from the drugs and had difficulty focusing, jerking in his arms as she tried to orient herself.

"I've got you, sweetheart," Arn said, holding her gently but firmly. "You're safe."

As she looked up at him, her eyes cleared. "Arn? But how? Where am I?"

He smiled down at her. "I'm taking you where you won't have to worry about hurting anybody, because only you and I will be there. I'll tell you all the details, but for now you need to eat something while we take a lunch break. Can you stand if I set you down?"

Carol paused. "I think so."

"I'll hang on to your hand until you're sure."

Arn lifted her gently from his lap in the saddle and leaned over to let Carol slide down Ax's side until her feet touched the ground. For a moment he thought her legs would buckle, but she righted herself. He slipped out of the saddle to stand beside her. "If you feel strong enough to stand, I'll tie up the horses and break out lunch for us."

"I can manage. I am starving. I can't even remember the last time I ate, or much else for that matter. And if I don't go find a bush to pee in immediately, you'll have to start unpacking some clothes, too."

"Well, get to it then."

Arn found that Rafel had been his usual hyperefficient self in arranging for the supplies on the packhorses. There was tentage and bedding materials, warm clothes, lots of dried jerky, beans, flour, fishing lines, pots and pans, waterskins, and grain for the horses.

And those were just the obvious things Arn saw as he examined the packs. He tied the animals to a tree, grabbed some dried jerky, a couple of biscuits, and a water jug, and went to meet Carol, who was making her way back from the privy of convenience.

They sat together cross-legged on the ground and ate. Carol's face clouded with worry.

"Out with it," Arn said. "What's bothering you?"

"Now I am remembering things. I can't go with you. I failed miserably in my study of the spell book you gave me. I began hurting the people around me in the vale, and no one could help me. I'm so afraid that I will hurt you in the same way."

"I would have rescued you no matter what, but the only reason Rafel didn't try to stop me is because he knows that no wielder has any power over me. All because of this."

Arn pulled Slaken from its sheath, the dull nonreflectivity of the blade's surface making it seem like a hole torn in the fabric of the daylight.

Carol's face lightened. "I had forgotten. Nevertheless, it's not going to solve my problems. I'm rested now, but if the past several weeks are any indication, I won't be for long. And if I spiral down and sink into madness on you, then what have you accomplished?"

"If that happens, then I have given you another chance. I have given myself a chance to help you. And I will have loved you until the end of your days, without letting you rot in a drug-induced haze. But I don't believe in such a fate. You're going to figure out how to beat this thing, whatever it is.

"When we find a place to set up our home for the winter, you're going to get busy again. I had all your books packed, and this time I will be here to listen to your ideas, discuss options and plans of attack, and hold you on bad-dream nights instead of letting you wander the valley in a daze."

Carol leaned over and wrapped her arms around Arn's neck, kissing him. The softness of her slightly parted lips lingered on his after she gently pulled away.

"I've missed that," Carol said.

"You've missed it? Gods, I would kill an army just for that one kiss."

She snickered, suddenly overcome by a fit of laughter.

"What?" he asked, although he started picking up the giddy desire to giggle himself.

"Oh, my love," she gasped. "We are going to have to work on your romantic responses. A vow of mass homicide isn't commonly considered poetic crooning."

Arn failed to hide his distress at the comment, but Carol smiled and leaned forward, taking his face between her hands. "But, my love, the feeling is there, and that works for me."

Then she kissed him, deep and long, such that had they not felt a pressing need to be at a better place before nightfall, they would have passed the afternoon in the same spot, on the pine needles, beneath the trees.

Carol said she felt that she could ride her own horse, although she was a bit worried that the animals would go wild around her now that she was awake. That fear did not materialize, so they mounted up and began a steady climb up the slopes into the high country beyond.

The clouds continued to spit a few flakes of snow all afternoon, but nothing more. By late evening, the temperature had dropped to the point that Arn decided it was time to set up camp for the night.

They stopped by a stream, and he unpacked the animals. He led them a short distance away and took the dual precautions of tethering them to a long rope tied between trees and hobbling them. Each was given an ideal spot to graze on the abundant grass.

By the time he returned to Carol, she had already gotten a fire blazing, preparing beans for dinner. Arn unpacked the bedrolls and laid them out side by side on a tarp he spread across the ground. He added some shelter from the wind by staking another tarp and tying it to a branch to form a modified lean-to.

After dinner Arn found some tea in a bag and brewed up a small kettle. The two sat together late into the evening, sipping tea and talking as the fire reflected off their faces and the wind sighed in the treetops. As good as he felt to be reunited with his betrothed, she seemed shaken by her ordeal. For the first time since he had known her, Carol seemed to doubt herself.

She was worried about falling asleep, but her nervousness abated as she crawled into the blankets beside Arn, and he wrapped himself around her, her head resting on his chest. She fell asleep to the steady thumping of his heartbeat.

Dawn found Carol in much the same position but with the arm that she had been lying on fast asleep so that she had to swing it about limply until the blood began circulating again.

Arn chuckled softly as he watched her. "That's a graceful little dance."

"You're not winning any sympathy points this morning. By the way, I don't remember any dreams last night. Did I do anything?"

"Not much. You got a little restless, but I just talked to you softly and held you, and you settled right back down."

The relief on her face revealed how she felt about this bit of news.

They had a quick breakfast, packed the horses, and headed out once again. The day passed much like the day before as they worked their way higher into the mountains. That night, she had a nightmare that awakened them both. He listened to her vision of ripping a young doe's throat out with her teeth and the thrill the kill had given her. Arn put his arm around her shoulders, his touch gradually calming her. They rebuilt the fire and sat cuddled together while he told her funny stories of his travels with John, Ty, and Kim. When he described how he and Ty had been forced to hog-tie the bewitched John, Carol laughed aloud. Then, wrapped in his arms, she drifted off into a sleep that lasted until dawn.

At noon on the fifth day, steam rising from a small canyon on the south side of a ridge drew Arn's attention. He led them winding down the steep cliff wall on a trail made by deer or mountain sheep until they reached a flat meadow covered in thigh-deep grass.

The sun broke through the clouds of steam that rose from several spots around the meadow to paint little rainbows against the far slope. A stream meandered through the center of the meadow, and Arn was rewarded with the sight of pools filled with trout of all sizes. They dropped the packs, hobbled the horses, and turned them loose, although he had no doubt that they would stay put.

The meadow formed the bottom of what turned out to be a hollow carved out of the mountains by glacial forces millennia ago. Mists rose from a half dozen hot springs and three geysers that went off several times an hour, spraying great shoots of steam.

The net effect of all the subterranean activity was to keep the hollow humid and the temperature above freezing. The surrounding cliff walls rose several hundred paces instead of the thousands back in Areana's Vale.

"I love it!" Carol said after they had made their circuit. "I absolutely love it."

"Sold."

They spent the rest of the afternoon selecting a place where they would set up their dwelling. The spot they picked was at the base of a cliff that had a broad overhang ten paces above the ground. The location was on the east end of the hollow so that the late-afternoon sun angled under the eve, which was what Carol called the overhanging ledge, giving them a stunning view of the sunset.

They rolled out tarps on the ground, and Carol began unpacking. She placed the contents in an organized fashion along the walls, protected from dampness by smaller tarps.

Arn performed a miraculous inverted climb along the cliff wall, where he fastened the corners of the tent, allowing it to drape down to be secured to the ground. It formed a sheltered bedroom that blocked any wind, rain, or snow that might blow underneath the ledge but left them the ability to see out from the bulk of their living area.

By sundown, they had the elements of a rudimentary shelter in place. Arn and Carol began exploring along the streams that emerged from springs, both hot and cold, around the cliff wall. The closest was a hot spring far too warm to swim in.

"Let's start a fire," Carol said, leading the way back toward their new home.

They each grabbed dry branches on the way, and Arn used the small hatchet Rafel had provided to chop them into bits just right for the fire. Piling the sticks up on a large flat stone just outside their shelter, Arn was getting ready to pull out his kindling when Carol magically brought forth a full blaze.

Carol cooked a pot of beans over the fire, and they ate, settling down afterward to sip tea in the fading light. As night fell, the mists rose from the hollow, effectively hiding all but a couple of the brightest stars from view on the moonless night.

Arn held the metal cup between both his hands, letting the warmth of the hot tea spread through his palms and into his fingers. He sat beside Carol so that their shoulders and legs touched as they faced the fire.

"I want you to tell me about your studies of the book I gave you." As she started to object, he continued. "I know that I have no magical training. But just bouncing ideas off another person, even if untrained, gives a fresh perspective."

She leaned back, thinking. "That sounds logical."

"What have you discovered about the manuscript so far? What are you trying to accomplish?"

Late into the evening, Arn listened as Carol explained how she had carefully examined the book for days before actually starting to read the pages. She talked about how the writing, which was so legible and clear for the beginning exercises, digressed to the point of wild scrawling for the most advanced lessons at the end. She believed the author had gone mad.

Arn looked at her intently. "I think that in the morning you should unpack the book and start again."

Carol gasped.

"Only this time," he said, "you're going to have me here as a silent observer. If something seems awry, I'll interrupt the session."

"That may not be good. I should bring each exercise to a close in a controlled fashion."

"And unless I feel that you're in danger, I agree that's what you should do. But I have a couple of questions."

"Okay."

"When you described your experiences during the kata, it sounded like you were picking up sensations from external sources."

"Yes. I believe that it opened my mind to elementals that emotionally influence nearby animals and people. I think that those elementals were consciously working to overwhelm my resistance so that they could directly possess my mind."

"Perhaps there's a more direct explanation."

"Such as?"

"Perhaps the kata was opening your mind to directly receive feelings and impressions of the living things around you. Perhaps no elementals were involved at all."

"What?"

"The sensations you were describing sounded a lot like the normal thoughts and feelings of people or animals. Perhaps the magic described in that book may work completely differently from what you studied under Hawthorne."

"Right . . . I guess it's a possibility."

"And what if the wielder who wrote that book was already mad when he started writing it?" Arn asked.

"If that's true, I'm sunk."

"Not necessarily. Just because someone is mad doesn't mean that they aren't smart. What if, paranoid, he was protecting his discoveries from prying eyes?

"You said that the handwriting got wild and hard to read toward the end of the book, and if not for that, the last exercises would have been much shorter than the first ones. What if the crazed old fool wanted to make anyone who found his work think that he went insane trying to master more and more difficult exercises? What if he wanted potential usurpers to try the most dangerous exercise first?"

Arn saw her eyes widen as she weighed the meaning of his words.

"That's it! The deep spawn wrote his book backward!"

"I think so," said Arn. "The only reason you survived the experience is because you're so powerful. Tomorrow you should reexamine the book."

"I want to start right now."

Arn reached out and gently grabbed her arm as she tried to rise. "Tomorrow. You need to be well rested. We should start in the daylight."

She started to argue, then paused, took several deep breaths, and looked up into his eyes, her face shining with warmth in the firelight. "You amaze me. In one evening, you see a possibility that I didn't consider during my weeks of studying the manuscript."

"Sometimes you can be too close to a problem to see all the angles," said Arn.

"I don't know if I'll be able to get to sleep now. I can't wait for morning."

"Fine. Sleep wasn't really at the top of my agenda anyway."

—∾—

When at last they both roused themselves, Arn brought up wood for a fire, and the couple cooked a simple breakfast of beans and dried bread. After that, he rigged a setline across a deep pool in the stream where the shadows of many mountain trout darted about. After he baited all the hooks, he took the hatchet and set about the work of gathering stacks of dead logs and branches. That done, he used one of the horses to drag them beneath the overhang.

Carol greeted him with a smile and a wave on his first trip back, holding up a piece of paper, her face flushed with joy. "Look what I found inside one of the packs," she said. "It's a letter from Father. He put the note where I would find it once I started unpacking."

"Good man."

"He said he loves me and he has faith that I will overcome this challenge. Gods, but I hope that I can live up to his expectations."

Arn lifted her chin and looked into her brown eyes. "In that, I have complete confidence."

"I wish I did."

"Think about it. I slept without my knife after we made love last night. If you had any bad dreams, they were too mild to wake me. I think your mind is healing from the damage it endured. Your psyche seems to be rebuilding itself stronger than before."

"Promise me you'll wear Slaken constantly when I start trying the exercises again. At least until we're sure that I'm capably handling the spellwork."

"So long as you don't mind us making love while I'm wearing it."

"I knew you'd say something like that," she said. "Seriously, I need to read through the exercises at the end of the manuscript to see if we're right about its true organization. I'll let you know before I try any of the katas."

"Good plan," Arn said as he headed back out to gather more wood.

By the time he returned with the next load, Carol had propped herself up against a fallen tree, immersed in her study of the manuscript. Arn left her alone in concentration and went to check the setline.

He was pleased to discover he had hooked three good-size trout. He cleaned the fish and, upon returning to their camp, set about cooking lunch. By the time the catch was fried a golden brown, Carol had been drawn away from her studies by the mouthwatering smell.

"Oh my, that smells so good," she said, holding her nose out over the pan. "It sure is great to have something besides beans and hardtack bread or jerky."

As they ate, she told Arn what she had discovered so far in her reading of the last exercises. The last two had been a variation of a simple meditation technique that she already used. However, the third from the end appeared to be the blocking technique referred to in the first kata she had attempted.

Snowfall began late that afternoon, the flakes large and fluffy. As night fell, the wind howled in the heights. The storm lasted for three days, and both Arn and Carol were pleasantly surprised at how dry their shelter under the ledge remained. Although only a few inches of snow piled up in their hollow, the trail that led out was completely blocked.

"It looks like you're stuck here with me for the next few months," Arn said.

"That sounds very nice." Carol smiled up at him from where she sat beside the fire, reading.

"Yes, it does."

But as Arn spoke those three words, a sudden gust lifted Carol's left sleeve, briefly revealing the fiery brand on her shoulder. Even though he'd seen the mark many times before, tonight it washed him in a wave of dread.

34

Areana's Vale
YOR 414, Mid-Autumn

The autumn snowstorm arrived with a fury that took the people of Areana's Vale by surprise. It had been mild, a few high clouds, but no sign of what was to come. The first indications of bad weather came late in the day as the wind picked up and the temperature plummeted. The soldiers shivered atop their outposts as sharp pellets of sleet stung their exposed faces. John finished his archery class, noting the uneasiness with which the men he was training regarded the worsening weather. Considering the horrible experiences Carol had related from last winter, their worries were understandable.

He made his way to his preplanned rendezvous with Kim a league up the valley, where a bend in the stream formed a small waterfall, the sound of which they both loved. He spotted her silhouetted against the pearly-white face of the cliff, the mists of the falls rising around her, unbothered by the cold of the storm.

John stopped short. He could not get over how he had become this most fortunate of men, to love and be loved in return by this Endarian princess. But she had changed. She had grown less formal in her speech and interactions with the people of Areana's Vale. And High Lord Rafel had chosen to treat John as a son because Kim was his wife.

Queen Elan had sent Kim to inform her sister and their father that Kragan still lived and was hunting Carol. Kim had accomplished her mission but chose to stay in the vale, even after Arn had taken Carol away. She was convinced that, given time, he would help her sister recover.

"Hello, dear heart," John called as he walked toward her.

Her smile spread across her face as the sunrise moved across the early-morning sky. "You're late," she said. "You know, it's not a good thing to keep a woman waiting in bad weather."

"It's not a good thing to keep you waiting in any weather. I was dealing with some overeager students."

Kim kissed him lightly, letting her fingers linger in his hair. "Ah yes, and how do the lessons progress?"

John took her by the hand and guided her to an outcropping that provided shelter from the wind. "Surprisingly well. Some of the guards have taken to true bowmanship as if they've been awaiting a proper course of instruction all their lives."

"I bet Gaar wouldn't take too kindly to a statement like that."

"You know what I mean," John said. "The standard military training consists only of the basics. Here is how you grip the bow. Here is how you nock the arrow. That sort of thing. Once these lads have a chance to see it for the art form it truly is, their progress is magical."

He stared up at the darkening sky, the sleet having changed to snowflakes that stuck to his eyelashes. "We better get inside the cabin."

Rafel had given Kim, and by way of their marriage, John, a cabin in a secluded part of the vale. John felt that he was merely the lucky recipient of the graces bestowed upon him by Kim, the cabin being the smallest of these. It had just two rooms but was very cozy, with a broad hearth and a solid stone chimney.

John grabbed a large armload of wood. They were soon bundled together in a blanket before the roaring fire, looking out through the window at huge snowflakes. Darkness was closing in on the vale so that soon the only indication they would have of the continuing snowfall was the occasional hiss of moisture that made its way down the chimney to fall into the fire.

Throughout the evening, the intensity of the storm climbed, accompanied by a howling wind and heavy snow.

In the deep canyon of the vale, that fury was nothing compared to the ferocity of the winds outside the valley. But here inside their cabin, the protection offered by the thick logs was complete, as was the comfort of the couple passing the evening entwined in each other's arms.

As they finally drifted off to sleep, John was only dimly aware of the low moan of the wind in the rafters.

35

Mo'Lier
YOR 414, Mid-Autumn

Deep within the dungeons of Mo'Lier, the steady drip of water from the ceiling of the cell splashed into a small puddle on the floor. The lone occupant worked to keep that puddle separate from the stinking sewage on the far side of the cell. That water and a steady supply of roaches provided most of the sustenance that kept the mind housed within the protector's body alive, a mind that belonged within the body of Jaradin Scot.

After the mind swap that had placed him in this form, a group of four protectors had taken Jaradin prisoner and brought him back to the dungeon, where he had been held ever since.

Every day since the transference, Jaradin found himself wishing that he had died during the round of torture the protectors had inflicted upon him before they had forced his mind from its body to swap places with that of the evil priest, who must even now be striding among the people of the vale. What kept him going was a lifetime of training as a ranger.

This deep in the dungeon, even the screams from the upper levels barely penetrated. He was trapped in silence and shadow. He had learned the inside of the cell by smell, touch, and taste. The walls were stone, as was the floor. Jaradin thought that this dungeon was probably an ancient cave system with some modifications added by the protectors over the centuries. One of these modifications was the set of iron bars that kept him inside the cell.

Four and a half paces wide by six paces long. He had lost track of how many times he had stepped off the dimensions of the small dark place that held him, enough times for the half a pace to be maddening. Somehow he needed the closure of touching each wall in the dark. To stop short made his skin crawl with a feeling that maybe an opening might have presented itself and he might have missed it. The nonsensical thought chided him, clinging to his mind.

Jaradin didn't really have any idea how high the ceiling was, but he guessed it must be around twice his height. The echoes of his footsteps or any other sounds he made seemed to confirm that estimate.

How long had it been? Three months? Six? Time meant nothing down here, and he had long since quit trying to count the days. It was funny how, when you couldn't see your hand in front of your face, it seemed like you were seeing things all the time, little flashes of color or items moving at the edge of your vision. The same went for silence. Sometimes when he heard the distant clank of a door or a footstep, he would wonder if it was just his imagination.

Wondering about things was something Jaradin did a lot. He wondered if he was going mad. He wondered if the protectors wanted him to go mad or if they cared whether he lived or died. Did the protector who had his body want this old one back?

From the shape the body was in, Jaradin doubted it. So why hadn't they just killed him? Did the other one need him to be alive? If so, they were doing a wretched job of worrying about his health. Once a week someone would wander down to his cell carrying a torch, peer in to see if he was alive or dead, toss a bucketful of slop through the bars, and then wander away. If that was needing him alive, he didn't want to see what not caring was like. Jaradin washed down the gruel with water that dripped from the ceiling and pooled on the floor.

It was funny how he had come to believe things that made no sense, things that had zero chance of happening. Jaradin Scot believed that his brother Derek would find him. He believed it to the depths of his soul.

If he doubted that his brother would come for him, then there was really no reason to keep on struggling to survive. There was no sense fighting through the sickness that came on from time to time due to bad water and worse food. There was no sense dreaming about seeing the trees again or hearing the sound of a mountain stream as it bubbled over rocks on its way to a cold, clear pool.

He felt a roach crawl rapidly over his bare foot, and quick as a cat, he scooped it up. Grabbing it by the legs, he quickly stripped off the wings and popped it in his mouth. Funny thing, that. He had grown used to the disgusting crunch with its accompanying gush of goo, but he couldn't tolerate the feel of the wings in his teeth.

A low chuckle built inside him until it burst out, echoing off the walls within the passages. He laughed for a long, long time.

36

Areana's Vale
YOR 414, Mid-Autumn

Angloc, wearing the body of Jaradin Scot, sat at the back of Jared Rafel's audience chamber, his feet propped on an adjacent bench, watching through his remaining eye the small group of men who gathered around the high lord, deep in animated discussion. Derek glanced disapprovingly in Angloc's direction.

He redirected his attention to Rafel's words. From where he sat, Angloc could hear everything he needed to know about the defensive preparations. They never asked his opinion anyway. The only reason they let him into these meetings was his insistence that he stay close to Derek. They believed all that malarkey about how he had a feeling that something bad was going to happen to his brother and he needed to be there when it did. If everything went right, something bad would indeed happen to Derek Scot, and Angloc would definitely be there when it did.

Angloc did not care that his good brother might disapprove of him resting his tired body while they droned on endlessly. He was exhausted. Derek, and all the other rangers for that matter, had outlandish expectations of how this body of Jaradin's should have recovered and how hard he should be willing to drive it. And hadn't he driven it beyond all reason, almost keeping up with the other rangers on numerous occasions? Didn't they know how badly he had been hurt? Surely the real Jaradin would have done no better.

That damned bear of Derek's was another problem. It snarled at him whenever he passed nearby, despite Derek's scolding. Nobody else could imagine that Angloc was not really Jaradin Scot, but that animal knew.

Angloc's mission trapped him here, away from his god and among people whom he despised in every way. What they needed was to feel the master's lash and eke out the remainder of their miserable lives washing the feet of their betters. Jorthain's forces should have been here weeks ago. Angloc could not understand what had so delayed the army of the protectors. Now the early blizzard had sealed the high country, preventing the arrival of such a large horde until spring.

Well, if he was trapped here, then he would just have to make the best of it. Angloc's hand absently adjusted his eye patch. He would continue to study the state of Rafel's improving fortifications, knowing that whenever Jorthain desired to do so, the high priest could peer through the eye that had been cut from this face to see what Angloc saw.

The high lord's meeting came to a close, and Angloc stood as Derek approached.

"Well, brother," said Angloc, "have you figured out how we are going to get out to do any scouting when we're buried neck-deep in snow?"

"Actually, I want to talk to you for a bit," said Derek.

"I'm listening."

"Walk with me. I don't want to discuss this here."

Derek led the way outside. The world outside the hall was a surreal place. The snow had piled up in great mounds and drifts. The men had shoveled paths through the snow along the streets through the fort, and teams of oxen had dragged logs along the trails between villages to clear the way for people to travel about. All of this made the piles of snow beside the roads even higher, making passersby feel like they were traveling through a white maze.

Derek headed to the stalls. Seeing that no one was about but the horses, Derek turned on his brother. "All right, Jaradin. I've had it with your behavior these last several weeks. I don't know what's wrong with you, but I'm not going to tolerate any more disrespect to High Lord Rafel, Broderick, Gaar, or even myself."

Angloc held out his hands in a gesture of dismay. "Disrespect? You think I am showing disrespect?"

"Damned right I do. I've taken it easy on you because you're my brother and because of how badly you were hurt. But I'm starting to feel like you're using that as an excuse. So I want to know what in the deep is going on in your head? By the gods, you don't even sound like yourself."

Angloc stared at the ranger, adjusting his eye patch as he did so. The fool had faith in brotherly love. Fine. Angloc would use it.

"Okay. I admit it. I have been shirking my duties and trying to get out of work. I've been dragging out my injuries longer than is warranted. And I don't even have a good reason."

Angloc paused for effect. He could not count the number of times he had rehearsed this little speech, knowing that Derek would confront him about the "changes" in him since the injuries, knowing there was nothing he could do to try to imitate Jaradin Scot's behavior. And what he had come up with had just the right ring of truth. Especially since Derek wanted to believe him.

Angloc turned and smacked the log wall with the palm of his hand. Then, slowly, he lifted his gaze to face Derek.

"You want to know why I've been sneaking off at odd times? Okay then. Here it is, laid out in the open for you to ridicule as you see fit. Do you remember who it was that helped me get well, who it was that healed pieces of me that nobody else could? Rafel's half-Endarian daughter, Kimber.

"And she stayed with me for countless hours, holding my hand, even letting me lean on her when I was first learning to walk again. Now I see the light dawning in your eyes.

"The shameful truth is that I can't get her out of my head. She is in my thoughts from the moment I wake up until I go to sleep. She is in my dreams. I will go crazy because I can't tell her how I feel. She is married to another man. They are living together in a cabin just up the valley."

Angloc clenched his fists and then relaxed them. He began pacing slowly, playing the part for all he was worth.

"Do you want to know where I go when I have been sneaking off? I go to watch her. I hide in the woods like a lovesick boy and peer at her from a distance. That's as close as I'll get to holding her, but it may drive me mad."

Derek stared, his mouth open. When it snapped shut, a huge grin spread across his face. "So that is all that's been wrong? My brother is lovesick?"

Angloc let a deeply offended look settle on his face.

Derek came forward and threw his arm around his brother's shoulder. "I'm sorry to make light of your predicament. I know it is really terrible for you. But you can't imagine what other kinds of worries and thoughts have been coming into my mind to try to explain why my own brother is acting like a complete stranger."

"That's all well and good for you to say, but it does me no good at all. And you know if you tell anyone about this that it will infuriate High Lord Rafel and Kim and embarrass me throughout the vale. John would come for me, and I would kill him, whom I want to kill anyway."

"I won't tell a soul. You have my word on that."

"Worse yet, this damned snow has us trapped here in the valley so I can't even get away. And I don't want to get away. I just want to sit and hold her or watch her from a distance since I can't do that. You'd be a lot better off if you would just kill me here and now."

Angloc pulled a knife from its sheath, holding it out to Derek, handle first.

Derek shook his head. "I'll do no such thing. You, my brother, are just going to have to live through this. I know this kind of advice never helps, but you'll find another woman, and when you do, you'll be glad that this love didn't work out."

When Derek extended his open hand toward him, Angloc stared at it for several seconds, gradually allowing the tension in his face to soften. Although he did not smile, he finally gripped Derek's forearm.

"Thank you, my brother," Angloc said. "I will do everything in my power to make sure your faith in me is rewarded."

—∞—

Angloc kept to himself, brooding, even as he worked alongside the other rangers. Being snowed in meant that even the rangers were put to work building fortifications or refining those already in place. For the following two weeks, they worked, always making steady progress on the layers of fortifications along the canyon that provided the only entrance to the vale.

But despite the urgency, Rafel ordered that one day a week be set aside for minimal staffing as a day of rest and recuperation. This was the type of idiocy that drove Angloc wild, although he readily applauded the decision for his own personal reasons.

It was certainly true that the men and women of Areana's Vale practically worshipped the ground Jared Rafel walked upon, but that only pointed out his weakness. A whip across the back was all the motivation you needed to get people to work themselves to death doing whatever you wanted. If you wanted more pressure applied, threaten their families. These were tried-and-true approaches that Rafel seemed to lack the stomach for.

Walking along the meandering line of defensive outposts, working his way back up the canyon to the main fort, Angloc did marvel at the creativity of the man. Perhaps in past battles, that type of thinking had compensated for Rafel's other weaknesses. Yet the high lord's strategizing would not prevent what was to come as soon as the spring thaw made the way passable.

Today was Rest Day, and as much as Angloc desired the taste of ale, he was driven by a desire that burned deeper than his stomach. He walked into the valley above the main fort and quickly made his way through the villages of Colindale and Fernwood, turning off the road before getting to Longsford Watch.

The path through the deep snow along the route was a narrow one, traveled on a regular basis by only three pairs of feet: Kim's, John's, and his. The trail crossed a small tributary stream, and as always, Angloc turned to the east, wading through the icy water in order to hide that someone had turned off the trail between Fernwood and Kim's cabin.

After rounding a bend where the woods blocked a view of his position, Angloc followed yet another path through the snow, one that had been made by a single person, roughly paralleling the main trail to the cabin.

The way twisted and turned among the trees, terminating in a heavy thicket into which Angloc had dug a tunnel through the snow. The spy scurried inside until he arrived at the spot where he could peer out at Kim's cabin, a hundred paces down the gentle slope.

Shivering, Angloc began a low chant that spread a warm glow through his body, drying his wet clothes and chasing away the ache that had cast its leaden weight on his limbs. Then he turned back to his peephole.

A thin wisp of smoke curled skyward from the chimney that rose from the cabin roof. One good thing about people, which apparently also applied to half-Endarians, was that they were creatures of habit, taking solace in the ordered routines that gave their lives a measure of simplicity.

Angloc had only required two days of watching to learn Kim's habitual movements on Rest Day. John's habit was to lounge around the cabin half the morning and then go out with his bow, hunting. The only interest this held for Angloc was the dim hope that perhaps the archer would meet with some unfortunate hunting accident. He had even considered arranging one, but had decided that Derek would suspect him of foul play.

While the story he had come up with for Derek had worked to eliminate Derek's immediate concerns about his change in personality, it did have the downside of keeping the priest from killing John, at least for now.

Instead, he merely sat, peering out through the hole in the bushes, waiting. Fortunately, Angloc did not have to wait very long.

Kim emerged from the front door swathed in Endarian garments that looked too thin for the harsh winter weather, but that, reputedly, were as warm in winter as they were cool in summer. She paused to glance down the path and around the meadow. Her eyes passed over his hiding place, but even Endarian eyes could not see through the additional camouflage provided by his priestly art.

From the first moment he had seen the Endarian, she had captured his imagination, filling his mind with fantasies that would bring him great pleasure. Unfortunately, his duty to weaken these people from within prevented him from fulfilling those desires, at least for the time being.

In the meantime, Angloc would watch and wait.

37

Endless Valley
YOR 414, Early Winter

Alan's ranger team had been out for eight days. Ty loosely accompanied them, although he often scouted farther out, not as a part of the ranger formation. Derek had placed Alan in charge of the three-man team, the two others being Kelly Farnsworth and Greg Smith. They had journeyed down below the snow line, spending a day longer there than planned in order to follow a small vorg patrol.

The vorgs moved over the ridgeline in a careless fashion, lazy, sloppy, clearly unconcerned that anyone with hostile intent would see them. That combination set Alan in motion. He signaled to Greg and Kelly to follow, then began working his horse around the head of the draw so that he could circle around the vorgs.

"Careful now," whispered Greg.

"Don't worry," said Alan. "I've got them."

A couple of hundred paces from the vorgs, Alan spurred his horse into a dead run down the slope, his ax held at the ready.

Hearing the clamor of hooves, one of the vorgs brought a horn to his lips, sending out a low warbling honk. Alan's ax cut the sound short, the force of the blow cleaving the vorg's head from his shoulders, sending it and the horn bounding away down the slope.

Suddenly the sound of an answering horn echoed through the hills. Fierce howling behind him told Alan all he needed to know. A group of vorgs riding werebeasts topped the rise, bearing down on the rangers at a dead run. Alan had little time to contemplate his error as the remaining vorg before him charged, swinging a spiked ball at the end of a three-foot chain.

Alan whirled his mount to the side, but the chain struck the animal's rear leg, breaking it and sending both him and his horse tumbling down the slope. Greg rode forward, driving his sword through the vorg's back.

Alan rolled to his feet, having somehow managed to maintain his grip on his battle-ax. His horse floundered, trying to rise despite its broken left rear leg, but he brought the effort to a sudden end, a sweep of his blade putting the animal out of its misery. Looking up the slope, he could see more than a dozen vorgs closing fast.

"Get out of here!" he yelled at the two rangers. "You can't save me."

They ignored his command, leaping off their mounts and fitting arrows to their bows. In an instant, twin shafts arced outward toward the charging vorgs, sending two of them rolling across the rocks.

"What in the deep are you doing?" Alan yelled. "I ordered you to go on."

"Oh?" Greg said. "I must have misunderstood."

Kelly nocked another arrow.

At this point, an argument was moot. Alan lifted his ax and stepped forward, putting his whole weight into the swing. The curved blade split the head of the lead werebeast, launching its rider out in a high arc, the termination of which crushed his skull against a jagged boulder beside the trail.

The charge faltered as two of the vorgs sprouted arrows and tumbled from the backs of the beasts they rode. Alan raced forward, accelerating toward them at a ground-eating run, a familiar red film coloring his vision as he felt his heart thrum in his chest. He collided head-on with a huge werebeast and its vorg rider, Alan's ax accelerated by the impact. The vorg threw up his shield and attempted a counterswing, but the ax split the shield, driving its way through metal armor and the bony sternum of the warrior, stopping only when it lodged in the thick skull of the werebeast.

Alan rolled to his feet as he hit the ground, having pulled the ax free of the dying beast as he twisted and fell. Three more vorgs charged toward him, although one of them suddenly rolled to the ground as his mount was shot from under him.

As the unseated vorg got to his feet, Alan removed the warrior's head with his ax, sending a great red fountain spurting into the air before the body tumbled to the ground. A werebeast hit him, knocking him down and sending his ax flying away. He scrambled to his feet, pulling his sword as the next werebeast-vorg pair rushed at him.

Feinting to his right, Alan rammed his shoulder into the charging beast, driving the sword up through its neck as its jaws closed around his left arm. The rider drove his curved sword downward, but was suddenly thrust aside as Greg struck the vorg full force across the face with his battle hammer. The werebeast struggled backward, attempting to drag Alan off his feet for the kill, but he held firm to the haft of his sword, twisting with all his might, dragging the blade through bone and cartilage until it struck and severed the principal artery in the beast's neck. The light faded from its eyes, and it released its grip on his arm.

As Alan turned, Kelly's body flopped to the ground not five feet away, impaled on the end of a pike. Greg rushed the last vorg, but the clawed paw of the werebeast he rode knocked the ranger aside. Caught up in a bloody rage, Alan leapt onto the back of the beast, his arm encircling the waist of its rider, dragging the vorg to the ground as Greg attacked the werebeast with his sword.

The vorg was strong and wrapped his arms around Alan's neck, attempting to break it. But Alan had his own arms around the neck of the vorg. The two strained, the sinews within their limbs knotting so tightly that it seemed that they would pop through the skin.

With a sudden loud crack, the vorg's neck snapped. He dropped limply to the ground as Alan released the body.

Alan gasped for air, his lungs burning from exertion.

"Greg," he panted, "where are you?"

And then he saw. Greg lay bleeding a few feet from the body of the werebeast, blood spurting from the great wound in his neck. Alan ran to staunch the bleeding, tearing off his shirt and pressing it into the wound, but he could see immediately that the effort was futile. Greg opened his eyes and tried to speak but could only manage a gurgle. Then, after one last gasp, his eyes lost their focus, freezing into a distant stare. Tears dripped down Alan's nose to splash onto the face of the dead ranger in his arms.

Another horn echoed in the still air of the day as another group of vorgs crested the hill. Suddenly a wild yell from the ridgeline to the east brought the vorgs to a momentary stop as they spun to face in that direction. Ty shot down the ridge atop his stallion, the sun's light shimmering off the curved blade of his great ax.

The vorgs had barely begun their charge toward him when he struck, the force of the first blow sending a vorg rocketing off his mount into one of his comrades, both of their bodies tumbling to the ground to be trampled under the feet of the werebeasts.

Alan raced up the hill toward the fight, but it seemed as if he were walking through a tar pit, so rapidly did the action unfold above him. The barbarian was laughing now, the sound ringing out above the cries of his victims, for suddenly the vorg hunters found themselves the hunted.

With no saddle or bridle to control it, the stallion that bore Ty seemed an extension of the warrior himself. As the horse darted in and out of the milling vorgs and their hideous mounts, the Kanjari whirled his ax so fast that it sang through the air, barely slowed by the flesh it rent.

Alan stumbled to a stop as he arrived at the scene, panting heavily. The fight was over. Eight vorgs and six of their werebeast mounts lay dead atop the ridge, the two other werebeasts having run off into the canyon on the far side.

Ty rode up beside him. "You all right?"

"Fine. I am fine," Alan said, his gaze directed back down the hill where the two men under his command lay dead.

A wave of depression assaulted him, sapping his strength far more effectively than the brief battle and run up the hillside had done. Two fine young rangers lay dead because he could not wait to fully assess the situation. His foolhardiness had ended their lives. It would have been better if Ty had not arrived, if Alan, too, had fallen in battle alongside his comrades.

The thought of his father's stern words replayed themselves in Alan's mind.

Alan walked back down the hill to where the rangers' bodies lay sprawled across the rocky ground. Ty trailed along, leaving him to his silent misery. The rangers' horses had stayed close, and Ty retrieved them. Alan removed a blanket from each of the dead men's bedrolls, carefully wrapping them around the bodies. Then he and Ty slung their corpses across one of the horses, tying them firmly to the saddle.

As they readied to depart, Ty tore strips of cloth from Alan's blood-soaked shirt, binding the deep werebeast gashes across his chest and left arm. Then with Alan mounted on Greg's horse, they turned back to the east, leading the horse carrying the two bodies behind them. It was not the most direct route back to the ranger base camp, but Alan wanted to make certain that no one would be able to track them back. Thus, they splashed several leagues up the streambed, eliminating the risk of leaving a trail.

Having committed one foolish act that had cost lives, Alan could not bear the thought of making another. It seemed that Ty could sense what he was thinking, although Alan caught no hint of a reproachful stare from the warrior. Instead, he rode in silence alongside Alan's horse, satisfied to let the young man judge himself.

Though no snow appeared at this altitude, the day was chilly. As the afternoon wore on, the sky turned a dingy gray, and a biting breeze picked up. Still, Alan felt hot. He touched his arm and found it already burning with fever.

Ty called a halt to examine Alan's wound. Finding it feverish, he set about washing the injury in the cold stream. Pain burned through the young lord's arm as the Kanjari scrubbed the scabs away, opening the wounds and flushing them with cold, clear water. Then he rinsed out the makeshift bandages, scraped some moss from the shady side of a cottonwood tree, and pressed it into the wound, securing the bandages once more.

The jerky, which Alan forced himself to eat, tasted like leather in his mouth and made his stomach roil when he swallowed. Even the water in his waterskin tasted bad, though his mouth was dry and he had just refilled it from the stream. Alan forced his head to clear and concentrated on the surrounding country. Even though he was using the streambed, he was determined to ensure that he was not being followed. Ty disappeared for lengthy stretches to clear the back trail.

Afternoon gave way to night, but the two men pushed onward. The fever in Alan's arm worsened. He worried that if he stopped, the wound would continue to fester. Alan dozed in the saddle as they continued to the east, steadily working their way toward the high country.

Toward morning they paused in a grassy meadow and, after lifting the dead rangers to the ground, tied the horses to graze. This time Alan opened the wound and washed it in the cold stream. He saw no sign of the telltale greenish-blue striations that indicated blood poisoning had set in, but if he didn't take more drastic action, that would happen soon.

At low elevation, the temperature remained warm enough for flies to hatch given the right breeding environment. He began searching the grassy meadow, knowing that the abundance of food would attract large animals, and where large animals ate, they crapped.

It didn't take him long to find what he was looking for: a good-size pile of excrement. Dipping his hand into the pile, he found it still damp in the deep center, the foul odor making it obvious that one or more wild pigs had been there. As he spread the excrement pile open, a flood of relief washed over Alan. The inside of the dung pile was full of writhing white maggots.

Alan carefully scooped them out into a scrap of cloth. Then, scraping the wound open once again, he carefully spooned the maggots into the foul-smelling pus pocket. Once it had reached the limit of maggots that it could hold, he very gently wrapped a layer of cloth around the wound, ensuring that it was loose enough to preserve the larvae's air supply.

He just wanted to keep the wound warm and wet, a nice safe place for the bugs to feed. The hungry little things would eat many times their weight in rotting flesh as they matured. It was not the most palatable of treatments but had saved many a limb when no better medical treatment was available. And right now, Alan's need was desperate.

The remainder of the afternoon, Ty let Alan sleep, although his fevered dreams let him have little of what could be regarded as rest. Alan awoke deep into the night. Resaddling the horses and tying their burdens back in place, the two riders once again headed east, climbing steadily.

For Alan, time lost its meaning. There was only the feel of the saddle beneath him, the fire in his arm, and the terrible itching.

Before long he found that he could no longer eat, certain that if he did, it would not stay down. Water he drank by the skinful. Ty had retrieved the waterskins of the rangers, filling all of them, and whenever they stopped, it was because of Alan's thirst.

Night came again. Ty no longer checked the arm, since to open it up and look would potentially kill the maggots, which were Alan's only hope. Judging by the infernal itching, the squirming white larvae were at work.

At some point, the two men reached the snow line. In one of his brief lucid periods, Alan saw that the snow was over a foot deep. He checked his direction and found that they were indeed still headed east. Perhaps even now he was in some part of the valley that led eventually to the Great Forest and then to the vale. Alan slumped forward once more as dizziness drove conscious thought into retreat.

The feel of strong hands dragging him from the saddle fought to intrude upon his dreams. They were accompanied by vaguely familiar voices that urgently asked him something. Someone stripped the wrap from his arm, and then there was that voice again.

"You used the maggots. Good lad."

And then the voice was gone, lost in the dreamworld within which he now strode.

In that dream, Alan ran through the hills, strong and fast, feeling as though he could run forever. Ahead of him, his father rode his black warhorse, trotting along at an easy pace. High Lord Rafel turned, smiling back at Alan and waving for him to come forward.

Alan redoubled his efforts, sprinting ahead so that his sinews stretched taut like the strings on a lute, the ground blazing past him as he sped forward. When he looked up again, though, his father was no closer. He strained harder and harder still, but could not gain Rafel's side. If anything, he may have lost another step.

Suddenly Carol's face swam into his dream—such a sweet and caring face. Worry creased her brow as she looked at him, and he smiled at her so that she would know that everything was all right. Then she was with him, almost as if he could feel her thoughts, analyzing the truth of what he was telling her and finding it wanting. Seeing her look of horror, Alan grinned broadly, spreading his arms wide.

"I am fine, big sister. 'Tis nothing but a scratch."

Her image wavered and disappeared. The dream faded into nothingness.

38

Misty Hollow
YOR 414, Early Winter

The weeks following their arrival in Misty Hollow, as Carol had named it, had been wondrous in every sense of the word.

Sunrise and sunset, her favorite times of the day, took on a completely new ambiance in the hollow. When the morning sky glowed pink, the mists picked up the color, refracting it in a variety of rich hues so that Carol almost felt like she could breathe in color. The same was true of the dark reds and purples of the evening sky. Pure bliss. Exercise, good food, and her love at her side restored Carol's health.

The ground in the hollow always stayed above freezing throughout the bottom of the hollow so that even heavy snows melted off within a day. She looked up the cliff walls to see where the frost line began, a wandering band of icicles and snow that emerged almost a hundred paces above the floor.

Carol had completed the last part of her transcription of the contents of the ancient wielder's tome two weeks ago, having organized the manuscript in reverse order from the way it had originally been written. The first katas in her version started with the two on meditation technique. She originally thought that both were so similar to her own form of centering that she would skip the exercises. However, upon closer examination, she had discovered subtle differences that were potentially important.

The practitioner was to form a globe of indifference around herself that bled away all sensation. She certainly did a variation of this in her attainment of the meditative states she was accustomed to, the practice being critical in separating a wielder's consciousness from her own sensations.

She and Arn agreed that any time she tried an exercise from the manuscript, no matter how simple, he would sit nearby and observe, only shaking her from her meditation if he thought she was in danger. For weeks he had done this whenever she had performed a kata and had not interrupted her thus far. In that time, she had mastered the two meditations and the third exercise. In that kata, she modified the visualized globe around herself so that it solidified, blocking all external sensations.

The kata also involved the somewhat complicated mental trick of sending herself a feeling to block. This had required her to center, create the globe, and make it solid.

This exercise had taken her several attempts to accomplish, but upon achieving success, she felt exhilarated. The clear, hard surface of the visualized sphere pulsed with color when it absorbed the transmitted sensation, but her centered self felt nothing. Sensing that this technique was a crucial foundation for the work that followed, she had practiced it repeatedly.

The fourth kata made her slightly more nervous. Although much simpler than the vast visualization of the kata she had attempted in the vale, the similarity was undeniable.

This involved the visualization of only one tiny source, very small and very near to her, just beyond the clear shield that surrounded her form in the darkness. She had talked the exercise over with Arn, and he seemed comfortable with her ability to handle the process. They had both agreed that it was likely that she would be trying to establish some sort of mental awareness of the closest being open to that sort of connection. Her target had no chance of being Arn, since he wore Slaken.

She slipped into the meditation, quickly establishing the orb shield around the vision of herself floating in the void. Turning her attention just beyond the protective sphere, she looked around, spotting a small pinprick in the darkness upon which she now turned her full attention. It gradually became more distinct, giving off clear little spheres of its own that pulsed and spread in waves.

When these hit the surface of her shield, they imparted a pulsating sequence of colors that quickly died out. Readying herself, Carol weakened the shield. She weakened the shield further until she began to pick up faint sensations as if from a great distance, something she could almost believe was only in her imagination.

Ever so slowly, she continued weakening her shielding until she was able to identify what she was experiencing. She caught a glimpse of a rock, the surface of the water just above her, a distant gurgling sound. She felt no emotion, only a watchfulness along with the slight sensation of hunger. The rock moved so that she saw it now from a different angle, disappearing as other rocks, sand, and weeds slipped below her.

Carol strengthened the shield until the sensations disappeared entirely, passing around her once again. She brought the globe's surface back to a clear hard shell that again completely blocked the little ripples from the small source just beyond its boundary. Having completed all the steps, she backed out of the kata in the same controlled fashion as she had begun it.

As she thought back on the exercise she had completed a little over a week ago, she found that the warm feeling of accomplishment still lingered.

As a result of that kata and subsequent ones in which she shifted awareness from one pinprick disturbance in the void to find another, blocking out the first and concentrating on the second and so on, Carol had become convinced that Arn was correct. No elementals were involved in what she was now doing. This new form of magic trained the psychic abilities she had long used to contact and control elementals to instead connect with animals and perhaps even the people around her. She had barely come to terms with the possibilities such power might present and how it might be used to augment her wielding of elemental magic.

There was no question that over the last week, she had been picking up the sensations of nearby animals. Some of the more primitive ones, such as fish, gave off weak impressions. When she made contact with some of the larger animals, though, such as deer, strong emotions like watchful nervousness, fear, and hunger came through their link in addition to sensations associated with the five senses.

More recently, her katas added another modification to her protective shield. She created an outer layer that briefly trapped any disturbance that hit it, giving her a chance to decide if she wanted to link to the new target. She thought the technique was what the author of the original tome had called filtering, thus greatly increasing her capabilities by giving her a safe way to search for a target of interest.

Yesterday she had done her first kata in which she sent out thoughts or sensations or feelings on a link. The result had been most gratifying and odd. She had picked up a source and established a strong link. Then ever so gently, she had sent out a desire to come close to the overhanging ledge where she and Arn sat.

Shortly thereafter, she found herself seeing images of Arn and herself seated quietly in the grass. He turned toward her, or rather, toward the animal with which she had linked, and startled it, a feeling she picked up very strongly. She increased the strength of her filter so that the intensity of the experience died away without breaking her meditation.

Since then she had completed several more sessions of the same kata until Arn had finally had enough sitting and watching, telling her that he needed to get out and stretch his legs.

"You know, there will be more to learn tomorrow," he said.

"Not if I learn it all today. But I see your point. I'll be patient and relax."

"Actually, this will be great for hunting," Arn said. "You do your kata thing, find a nice deer, and then have it wander up here. That way I can kill the white-tail real easy without having to sneak around."

"I'll do no such thing!"

"There wouldn't really be much difference except that you would make my hunting a lot easier."

"I've heard enough on this topic. Go do whatever you were about to do. I'm going for a swim."

With that, she turned on her heel and headed toward the stream, briefly glimpsing the smile Arn tried to hide.

The next morning Carol collected her transcribed version of the manuscript and began preparing for the next kata.

This one interested her greatly. She would select the target for her initial link as usual, but then use it as her center to search for her next link, traveling in a leapfrog fashion designed to extend her range. She saw how this would enable her to search much farther away from her body without having to open herself wide, as was done in the first kata she had ever attempted, after Arn gave her the book.

Arn arrived carrying a stringer with two fresh trout.

"Let's have some lunch, and then we'll get down to business on the new kata," Carol said. "I'll brief you on the details while you cook."

He piled an armload of wood on their fireplace, a broad flat stone surface around which he had stacked stones, leaving one side open.

Carol quickly lit the fire, and Arn busied himself frying the trout. By the time he had finished cooking the fish and they had settled down to eat, Arn understood what she would be attempting.

"Just be careful not to leave yourself open to the kind of overload you experienced back in the vale," he said between mouthfuls of fish.

"I won't try a third link if I have any problem shielding myself on the second one. Since I'll only be doing one link at a time, it should just be a repetition of what I've already been doing."

"Be cautious."

"I will. And you'll be here to wake me up if you think I'm in trouble," she said. "But don't interrupt me just because I'm spending time in the meditation. I want to explore this one."

"I'll try to control my motherly instincts."

"Good."

They soon settled down under Carol's favorite pine for the exercise, Arn with legs crossed, sitting far enough away to avoid being a distraction. She leaned back against a deformed section of the tree that had grown out at an angle almost parallel to the ground before turning up toward the sky.

Arn began carving on a small block of wood, a habit he had started during the time she worked on her exercises. Carol was pleased with the hobby since he had already acquired considerable skill, producing a menagerie of carved animals that she placed around their ledge.

As she centered, the void closed around her in all its inky blackness, her imagined body now clothed in robes of glowing white. She took the time to circle her form, zooming in and then out as she established a more detailed image. She could see the lace on the cuffs and neck of her silken attire. Stitching over her heart formed the monogram of a dove sitting on Arn's shoulder.

Satisfied that she had complete control of her meditation, she formed the blocking globe and then added the hazy layer that let her identify minds with which she could create a link. She examined the colored patterns that froze briefly where they touched the haze. Each impression was different from the next, but Carol recognized two of them—a turtle and a doe. A new target intrigued her, and she opened a portal in the shield to form the link.

The ground of the hollow swept away below her, and Carol was thrilled to discover that she was receiving sensory impressions from a large bird, perhaps a falcon or an eagle. It flew from the hollow, giving her a clear view of the snow-covered landscape beyond. Great mountain peaks rose up into a blanket of clouds. Her vision darted here and there as the great bird looked for something to eat. Hunger drove her onward, gazing down over dunes of snow piled against rock ledges.

She established a new shield around this moving center of consciousness and once again allowed the waves in the void to impact the new orb. She picked the first source she detected and again established a connection. This turned out to be a bear, deep in hibernation, the gentle nature of its deep sleep almost causing her to fall asleep herself.

Establishing the globe once more, she spent some time strengthening it so that she felt satisfied that she was proceeding in a controlled, orderly fashion. Carol found another source and created the connection more quickly this time, receiving a variety of impressions from some other small creature in darkness. She began wasting little time between jumps, following the same detailed steps each time, the practice becoming as simple as preparing a familiar meal. Establish the connection, adjust your center to the new host, set up the shielding, modify the shield to capture nearby disturbances in the void, select one, and repeat.

As she continued with the exercise, she became more adept at the procedure, and as her skill improved, she increased the tempo of her leapfrogging. She experienced the area from numerous perspectives—from the air, from darkness belowground, scampering through the trees, swimming in a stream. Sometimes she felt the menace of a predator or the fear of its potential prey.

She made another link, but this one yielded such violent desires that they rocked her shielding. She increased the strength of her filter, trying to come to grips with the new connection she had established. Burning hatred and a savage desire to torture and kill assaulted her. This being was hunting, and its prey was nearby.

It was part of a group of creatures that Carol did not recognize. They were grotesque in appearance, looking something like a cross between a mountain lion and a man. The images and desires that came to her mind revolted her, but also raised great concern. There was a cabin set back in the woods, sheltered from much of the snow, and it was around this cabin that the graken—a word that came to her—were moving.

The smells the stalking graken was picking up told her that a lone man was inside, a man who was bleeding. They had caught him in the deep snow, and although he was an opponent whom they would not normally have risked attacking, the conditions had enabled them to inflict grievous wounds before he could fight his way back to his cabin and bar the door. He had killed several of their kind in the fight, and the graken were going to extract their revenge. They just needed to let him bleed for a while.

She strengthened her shielding around the rodent in which her consciousness was centered, but kept the link to the graken. She had to do something, and only one possibility came to mind. If Arn knew what she was about to try, he would pull her out of her deep state before she could complete her task.

Despite her disgust with what she was feeling from the graken and her urgent desire to take action, Carol spent several long moments bolstering her shielding. Suddenly she knew she was out of time. A pack of the creature's fellows had joined the graken, and they were pummeling the heavy wooden door of the cabin such that it strained at its hinges, great cracks spreading through the wood.

Carol exploded through the link, centering on the graken, throwing up the weakest form of the shield and opening herself to the other disturbances that bubbled in the void nearby. Multiple links sprang into being, pummeling her with bloodlust. One distinct link was filled with a combination of bravery and impending doom. She opened herself to that fear, receiving it and amplifying it a hundredfold so that the feeling poured outward along her connection to the various graken, engulfing them in staggering waves of terror. She immediately strengthened the shield around the graken that formed the center for her consciousness, but felt herself engulfed in terror nonetheless.

She found the link she had left open to the rodent and retreated back along it, centering on the form and throwing up a solid shield, severing all connections. The sphere around her new center glowed in cascading colors under the violent impact of emotions that bombarded it, but the shield held.

Now that she had severed the external links, she could tell that the rodent was starting to calm down, a very good thing since she had been worried that its small heart was going to burst, so hard had it been beating in the panic of the mind storm.

For a moment Carol considered trying to establish a new connection to check on the man she had tried to save, just to see if the graken had been panicked badly enough that they would not return. But she decided she had done all that she could reasonably do and had, in fact, done more than she probably should have attempted. Her feeling of success was not diminished.

Carol prepared to depart, and suddenly a new worry came crashing in on her: Where was she, and how would she find her way back?

The links she had used to get to her current location had been closed one at a time as she leapfrogged along. Because there was no sense of direction when she chose sources in the void, she didn't know how to pick sources based upon a concept of direction in the physical world. Worse, even if she were able to choose her targets by direction, she had not done so on her way here and had no idea of the way back to Misty Hollow.

That made her choices pretty clear. She could either try to identify birds that gave her a wide view or attempt a variation of the first kata she had ever tried. The kata would vastly expand her awareness to take in hundreds or thousands of sources, with the hope that she would be able to identify her own dim pattern among them. Unfortunately, her body was in a deep meditative state and would be difficult to detect from a distance. The thought was not comforting.

She made her decision and began working her way through sources in rapid leapfrogging fashion until she found a bird in flight. The scenery was not familiar. Or maybe it was. As she studied new and different views, discouragement set in. The mountains to the north and south both looked the same. The mountains to her east rose to frosty peaks, and storm clouds were closing in from the west.

Cut off from her body, Carol had no idea how to find her way home.

39

Misty Hollow
YOR 414, Early Winter

The sun was sinking toward the western horizon when Arn found that he could no longer contain his growing level of concern. Carol leaned against the tree, her face serene. She breathed deeply, and her posture remained unchanged. In fact, nothing about her appearance gave him any indication of trouble. He felt it nonetheless.

The late-afternoon sun filtered through the branches of the pines in fits and starts as intermittent high clouds made their way across the sky from the west. Gusts of wind swirled the late-afternoon mists, dropping the temperature by several degrees. Arn moved over and gently placed a blanket around Carol's shoulders.

Time's passage slowed so that it seemed that the fluttering of a leaf in the breeze took an hour. The amplification of Arn's senses continued to increase, almost as if he was detecting a nearby predator. The fear that grew upon him, though, had nothing to do with physical danger. Moving close to Carol, he could hear the sound of her breathing. It seemed that he could almost hear her heartbeat.

A strong gust of wind swirled her hair about her shoulders, bringing Arn to his feet. Having had enough of waiting and worrying, he knelt down beside Carol and placed a hand gently on her shoulder. When he received no response, he shook her gently. Her lack of response caused his heartbeat to jump. Sitting down, he took Carol in his arms, rubbing her hands and whispering in her ear.

"Carol, wake up now. Come on, darling, wake up." Arn continued talking, reaching up to squeeze her cheeks.

It was as if he wasn't there. No, he thought. She was the one who wasn't present.

"Where are you, baby? Come on back now."

The smack of his palm on her cheek sent an electric charge through his body, hurting him as if he had sliced his hand with a knife. Arn was mortified that he had hit her but was more dismayed by her lack of response to the blow.

His mind whirled. Could it be that she had been sucked in by another of the ancient wielder's traps? The uneasiness he had felt all day seemed to point to such a possibility. Why had he ignored his instinct and let her try the kata?

Carol's head lolled to one side, and he moved back in close so that it rested on his shoulder as his arms wrapped themselves around her.

Where was she? Most likely she was out in that void she had described to him, maybe too distracted to even realize that he was trying to call her back to her body. A sudden thought burned into his brain. What if she were trying to find her way back and couldn't? She might not have any recognizable beacon in the void to guide her back.

Arn tore Slaken from its scabbard, whirling the blade in his hand and then flinging it to the ground beneath an adjacent tree. Stripped naked of his magical protection, he leaned his forehead against hers.

The foolhardiness of what he was now attempting flitted across his thoughts, but he shrugged the feeling off. The only way he could imagine reaching Carol was to attempt to achieve the same state of consciousness that she had entered, knowing full well that he would be like a child dog-paddling in the sea.

"I'm here, baby. Come find me."

He closed his eyes, repeating the same thoughts, his head touching hers, doing his best to open himself. He tried to picture the void she had described with her there floating at its center and him standing beside her, holding on and calling out the same words into the darkness. Ever so gradually, the void formed around him.

—∾—

The night's search for Rafel's daughter, which had begun so typical in its fruitlessness, had suddenly attracted Kragan's complete attention. He had tested her wards so many times these last few months and with such little success that any sane man would have given up looking for an opening. But he was neither sane nor a man, not anymore. She had recently set up a fresh set of wards. Like the others, Kragan could not get a fix on them, although it seemed to him that these new protections were in a different location.

Then Kragan was suddenly handed a gift beyond his imagining. A fluctuation weakened the wards from within as a neophyte mind created an opening. It asked to be found, broadcasting the message as loudly as it could, with no corresponding understanding of any of the principles involved.

As the sendings touched his consciousness, Kragan gasped. How could his fortune be this good? The one providing the opening through Carol's wards was none other than Blade.

Kragan passed the thought directly to the mind of the primordial.

Exhilaration flooded through the elemental's being as he swept in upon the open mind of the assassin.

—∾—

One moment Arn was a beacon, calling Carol from within the void, and the next he was spiked to a stone floor within a vast cavern, hands and feet spread eagle as agony blossomed in his head. Above him towered a bronzed, iridescent figure with sharp golden eyes and taloned hands, a being from tales parents told naughty children. When the entity sneered, Arn saw that he had inch-long fangs made for rending.

The thing spoke with a sound somewhere between a growl and a purr. "Blade, welcome to my lair. I am Kaleal."

Arn cursed himself. Not only had he failed in his attempt to contact Carol, he had stripped himself of the weapon that could have shielded him from the Lord of the Third Deep that Carol had warned him of. Despite the agony in his hands and feet, Arn knew this experience was about to get far worse.

Kaleal knelt beside him and reached out a clawed hand, raking a nail down Arn's arm, peeling away flesh as if filleting a fish. Although Arn did not cry out, sweat oozed from his skin. With a grunt of focused effort, he allowed Blade to take over, to transform the pain into a searing rage. Like Carol, he had his own ways of centering, his own methods of hanging on to sanity.

40

Glacier Mountains
YOR 414, Early Winter

The darkness around Carol's center was complete. She modified the shield, reducing it to near nothingness as her visualization expanded into the void around her. Having tried the safer approach, it was now time to gamble. If only she could have recognized any of the terrain around her numerous leapfrog transitions. But that was not to be.

So she relied on her remaining option. The disturbances in the void grew in number as she moved outward from her center. They washed in upon her, impinging on her shield so that she could selectively look at each one. Already the globe glowed with bright colors as many sources impacted its surface, one bleeding into the next as she strove to examine each.

The protective sphere took on a reddish glow that changed to purple, then white, but she was still unable to fully examine any of the thousands of sensations that cascaded across her. Carol weakened the shield ever so slightly, and then, deciding she still couldn't recognize any thoughts or feelings, she diluted it yet again.

Immediately a storm of feelings almost swept her away. Anger, lust, fear, longing, and hunger were mixed together with a host of sights, sounds, tastes, smells, and pains. She concentrated, keeping the shield at this level. She endured the cacophony, searching. And as she searched, she tired.

Suddenly she heard, felt, smelled, tasted, saw the one she loved. Arn was there in the void, distant, but calling to her.

Then, as relief flooded over her, otherworldly pain racked her lover. His mind seemed as if it would burst, but he did not cry out as something swept him away. Carol modulated her shield, blocking all other sources, accepting Arn's pain, establishing a link to the source of that agony. Kaleal was here, and he was very close to the destruction of her betrothed's mind.

Carol's mental shield went white-hot as she jammed it into place, trapping the primordial inside with her and Arn. She shifted her focus, linking firmly to Kaleal. He groped for her, and she lashed out with all the anger and fear that the thought of losing Arn to this thing conjured up. She slammed into Kaleal with her psychic energies, pinning him to the inside of the shield with such force that his snarls turned to screams of agony. The primordial released his hold on Arn to address the new attack. Carol's mind lashed out again, pummeling Kaleal and forcing him to throw up a shield of his own.

Against this elemental barrier her mental attacks raged, an ethereal battering ram.

Suddenly she created a small hole in her own shielding against which she had pinned Kaleal, thrusting him outward into the void with such force that great ripples of red light cascaded away from his tumbling form. She shifted her attention, snapping the shield around herself and Arn back into place.

Arn's consciousness was faint, but it was there, and pressed up against him, she could sense her own body. The transition back to full consciousness left her gasping. Sensing that Kaleal had breached her magical wards, she reestablished and strengthened them.

Carol moved Arn's limp body off her and climbed to her feet. Then she rolled him onto the blanket that had been wrapped around her shoulders and, with considerable exertion, dragged him back over to their fireplace just under the ledge.

His chest rose and fell steadily, but his body had begun to shiver violently. She placed a hand on his forehead. It felt cold.

After covering him with blankets, she grabbed a pile of sticks and threw them onto the fireplace. Steeling herself against the memory of the mark of fire with which the elemental had branded her arm, Carol ensnared Jaa'dra, forcing him to light the blaze. Then she stripped off Arn's clothes and her own and slipped into the pile of covers with Arn, lending her body heat to that of the fire as she worked to warm him.

"I've got you, my love. I've got you," Carol whispered as she wrapped herself around him.

41

Kragan's War Camp—Eastern Tal
YOR 414, Early Winter

The force of Kaleal's expulsion knocked Kragan across the room, sending him crashing into the far wall of the house he had turned into his headquarters, as the primordial returned to his body. Kragan crawled back to his feet, having difficulty lifting the massive form within which he was encased.

His amazement at what had just happened shook him to the bone. Had Kaleal been knocked out? The concept of driving an immortal into an unconscious state was beyond the realm of imagination. And yet, here Kragan was, staggering around in the primordial's body without any perceived help from his host.

What had just occurred? Had Carol set a trap for them with Blade as the bait? That must have been it. The devious witch had come up with a plan to pull Kragan's mind away from his body so that he could be assaulted on her terms. If he hadn't given Blade over to Kaleal instead of taking the assassin for himself, the plan would have worked.

Carol had not expected the primordial, and yet she had almost destroyed him. Kragan sank down onto the stone floor, his head swimming in pain as Kaleal roused himself.

Fires sprang up around the room, spreading rapidly to the ceiling beams. The primordial was not happy.

Fine. That made two of them.

42

Misty Hollow
YOR 414, Early Winter

The deep scarlet glow of the sun, which had just sunk beneath the foreshortened horizon, bled into the mists of their hollow like the breath of a lunger. As a child, Carol had hated the term upon first hearing it, even more so once her father had explained that it referred to a mortally wounded soldier whose rattling breath misted red.

Arn's unconscious body lay next to the fire, where he'd lain unmoving since she had dragged him up the small rise to their ledge. She would not leave him out in the meadow to care for him. No. She had needed to get him home, as she now thought of their shelter.

In the moment when she had torn Arn's mind free from Kaleal's grasp, what she had seen, felt, and heard terrified her beyond reason.

It was said that a moment of elemental possession caused time to stop, as if that moment were a hundred or even a thousand years of unspeakable suffering. That was not what terrified her. As she tore Kaleal from him, something had ripped open inside Arn's mind. It had seemed like such a small injury, a bit of a tear in the fabric. Such a tiny thing.

When she was eight years old, her father had given her an intricately woven sweater that had been her mother's. Its unique pattern seemed to change with the lighting. A rosebush had snagged it, unraveling just a little spot. Such a tiny thing. She had tried so carefully to repair the sweater, but each move only made the damage worse until it seemed to fall apart before her very eyes. She rushed home, hoping Nana would do something to save the treasure.

Nana had just shaken her head and said, "Oh dear child, if you had brought it right home, I probably could have fixed it. But now . . ."

Carol had cried for days. Such a tiny thing.

Lost in the memory, she had brought Arn right home. Now he lay wrapped in her arms beneath the blankets, with his head resting on a soft pad that served as a pillow.

As she pulled him close, Carol gazed out at the lunger mist.

—w—

She had not intended to fall asleep, hadn't really thought about it at all when she had slipped under the blanket with Arn and spooned up against him. His breathing sounded regular, and the strong beat of his heart felt as it always had, a slow but powerful thumping within his chest. He didn't feel comatose, either, merely sleeping the sleep of exhaustion, something she had never heard of Arn succumbing to. It must have been while she listened to his breathing that the dark robes of sleep enfolded her, and as they did, her perspective shifted.

A strangeness crept over her as she recognized the walls that formed the lower canyon defenses to Areana's Vale. Arn moved along the top of the wall, and she moved with him, an invisible specter, seeing what he saw, hearing what he heard. The battlements were different, much farther along, although they showed signs of not yet being complete. Soldiers crammed the walls as their leaders passed behind them, shouting instructions that were lost in the din of battle. Arn looked out over the seething mass of the army of the protectors, jammed tight between the towering cliffs, struggling to carry the ladders forward along the narrow path beside the rapids.

He continued on, quickening his pace until he was practically swinging from the support railing as he moved around the soldiers struggling to hold the top of the wall. Immediately she saw his target: A group of vorgs backed by a robed priest had breached the wall, trapping her father and a handful of men against the southern cliff face. A ball of flame grew above the priest's outstretched palm.

"By the gods, hurry!" she screamed, although no sound came from her spectral mouth.

The priest paused in the midst of his cast, his eyes wide with surprise as a new mouth opened in his throat. Arn's arms worked like pistons, moving in and out with a rhythm that sounded like the beat of a drum as he carved his way toward Rafel.

Confusion swept the ranks of the nearest vorgs, who were cut to ribbons by Rafel's guard as they turned to see what was happening to their rear. In seconds the breach had been sealed. Rafel's look, however, was one of horror as he stared in the direction from which Arn had come. A group of protectors who had hidden among the vorg warriors along the north wall called forth a mighty blast at its base, bringing the section atop which Alan and his men fought tumbling outward, flinging them all into the seething mass below.

"No!" Rafel's yell sounded above the din as the dream shifted.

Again and again the battle replayed itself. Always, Arn was the anchor from which her specter observed the action, and each time he took a different course of action. Always his deeds made no difference in the outcome. Alan died, Rafel died, Carol died, Arn died, Ty died, John died, Kim died, everyone died. Over and over again, in a hundred different ways, the two lower fortresses fell, then the upper fortress fell, and then the vale itself fell to their enemies.

Carol awoke with a start, her heart pounding. Wrapped in her arms, Arn slept on, dreaming his chaotic dream, his heart still beating with the same slow, steady rhythm.

Reaching out to him, Carol caressed his face with her right hand. Gently she shook him, then more firmly. When he did not respond, she moved across the ledge, wet a rag in a pail of water, and placed the cold cloth upon his brow. Then she wet the rag again and rubbed it along his face and neck. Nothing. No response.

Carol had a desperate need to wake him, feeling as though he needed something and that need had been communicated to her in a way she did not understand. As much as she had been lost, unable to find her way back to her body, she believed that Arn was now lost and needed her to help free him from a horrible bondage.

But no matter what she tried, he would not awaken. Feeling for his thoughts with her mind, she could not find them. He seemed beyond her power.

Beyond her power. Something about that thought tweaked her mind. Beyond magical power. Of course. Slaken. The one thing that had always helped protect him from magic. He had told her about the blade, how he had mingled his own blood into its runes, how no other could grab the weapon without being consumed.

She ran to the spot where Arn had tossed Slaken aside. The thing lay there on the ground, the delicate runes in its ivory haft a dizzying sight. Slaken's black blade seemed to lie in a world where light did not exist. How could she get the weapon to him without being consumed herself?

She reached out with her mind, calling forth the elementals that would whirl the thing into the air, but although the air howled around her, the knife did not move. She strengthened her will so that the wind screamed.

In the sky overhead, great thunderheads boiled up as she increased the power of her casting, the friction of the wind producing electrical discharges that crackled and crashed in the sky above. A hundred-year-old pine broke off, crashing to the earth with a sound even louder than the howling gusts and thunder of the storm.

"By the deep," Carol said, casting the elementals away in disgust. "How stupid can I be?"

Grabbing her shawl, she tossed it over the knife, wrapped the cloth around the handle, and carried it back to where Arn lay. She set Slaken upon his chest and withdrew the shawl, then placed his right hand atop it. As she watched, his fingers twitched and grasped the magical weapon, though his eyes remained closed.

Carol stepped back to stare down at the man she loved, struggling to control her dread.

—

Far away at a ranger camp in the Great Forest, Ty staggered, stumbling to his knees as his blood boiled and pounded in his veins. Rolling onto his back, the Kanjari's body contorted in spasms as every muscle cramped. The fit passed, allowing him to stagger back to his feet, great rivers of sweat dripping from his torso. He had felt the same when Slaken had fed on the blood of his and Arn's beating hearts.

Ty pulled himself to his full height and gazed off over the high canyon walls toward the mountains in the southeast. "Brother of my blood, where are you?"

43

Southern Coastal Range
YOR 414, Early Winter

Earl Coldain looked east across his winter camp on the Endarian Continent's southwestern coast. The snowcapped peaks of the Coastal Range blocked his passage to the east until the spring thaw. He seethed with frustration at the constant delays that had confronted him and the army of Tal as he searched for High Lord Rafel and his legion. Coldain had wasted months blocked at Endar's southeastern border by Queen Elan's edict that barred his army from passage through her lands. She had sent thousands of Endarian soldiers to enforce her decision.

Although her son and emissary, Galad, had been polite during the meetings in which Coldain argued that he would make sure his soldiers passed peacefully through her territory, the queen's relayed responses had always been a terse no. Those answers had led the earl to suspect that Elan might be harboring the high lord within Endar. Three decades ago, at the beginning of the Vorg War, Rafel had been Tal's emissary to the queen and had successfully negotiated an alliance between the two kingdoms. But in answer to Coldain's query, Galad had assured him that Rafel was not within Endar nor had he been since long ago.

The Endarian's forthright manner had convinced Coldain of the truth of those words.

So the earl had been forced to make the arduous journey around the southern tip of Endar and then westward to the Gauga River. There he had been confronted with a decision: journey south through the Endless Valley or continue west to the coast and then follow it south. Rather than force his footsore army to zigzag south and then possibly back to the north, Coldain had chosen the westward path. Due to the coast's remoteness from Tal and access to the sea's abundance, Coldain considered it to be Rafel's most likely destination.

Once again, he had been proven wrong.

The stiff sea breeze ruffled Coldain's hair, its temperature pleasantly contrasting to the ice he saw in the mountains. Come spring, he would march fresh troops across the Coastal Range and turn north, knowing that he would find Rafel somewhere along the Endless Valley. Only after he performed his unpleasant duty could he go home.

Coldain tasted salt on the wind and turned his eyes back to the sea. All things considered, this was not a bad place to winter.

44

Misty Hollow
YOR 414, Early Winter

The squawking of two jays arguing over possession of the aspen nearest their porch ledge awakened Carol from a troubled sleep. The morning sun had already crested the eastern rim of the hollow, bringing with it a warmth she had not felt since early autumn. The sounds of the day carried a musical quality that she categorized as the symphony produced by numerous sources of dripping water. Faint drips and splats close at hand accompanied the sound of the nearby stream.

All of this melting glory culminated in new veils of water that plunged from numerous cliffs high above, forming streams and rivulets that joined together only to disappear underground.

A very large, fat fly buzzed around Carol's head, dodging as she swatted. A fly so big and fat this late in the year was a mystery of nature. As it continued to annoy her, Carol reached out with a flick of her mind and crisped it, leaving a small, smoky trail marking its descent to the stone below. She immediately regretted so casually imposing her will on such a tiny being whose only sin was trying to survive. A second fly swooped down, as if in revenge, inflicting a painful bite on her forearm. She immediately fried this one, too, suffering no feelings of guilt.

Arn sat up and groaned as he cradled his face in his hands.

Carol moved to sit beside him and took one of his hands in hers.

"I feel like I've been out drinking with Ty." He squinted and tried for a smile that looked more like a grimace.

She leaned over, wrapped him in her arms, and smothered his face with kisses.

She sat there, holding him and being held until, at last, the rumblings of hunger brought the wielder to the realization that neither of them had eaten in over twenty-four hours.

"My brave sir, I can't speak for your appetite, but I am famished," she said, getting to her feet and moving toward the hooks that held her pans.

"If you start cooking, I'm not going to complain," Arn said.

He rose to his feet, wobbled, and then steadied. He lifted an arm and sniffed, wrinkling his nose. "But first, I'm going to drag myself down to the stream and wash up. There is no way breakfast is going to smell palatable if it has to compete with this odor."

Carol suddenly realized that she also had not bathed in recent memory. "Gods. I probably smell as bad as you do."

—෴—

By the time they consumed the meal, Arn had recovered from the psychic battles of the previous day. Carol studied him closely.

"So, do I pass the test?" Arn asked, leaning back from his now-empty plate.

"I don't know. You had me so scared."

"Well, you can put your worries to rest. Aside from a nasty hangover, I don't seem to be any the worse for it."

"Do you remember anything?"

"Not really. I remember trying to open my mind, using one of your exercises, and then a sense of drifting. After that I woke up with a mountainous headache."

Carol bit her lip.

"Why? Did I miss something?"

"You very nearly got yourself possessed and practically scared me to death in the process."

"It probably wasn't the most brilliant idea I've ever come up with, but since we are both still here, it wasn't terrible."

"Never do it again."

Arn paused, his face growing more serious. "I've been feeling a growing worry since I awakened. We need to get back to the vale as soon as spring thaw allows us out of here."

A lump formed in her throat. After having shared his dreams, she echoed his worry. Her eyes wandered across their hollow, across the tree-lined meadows, streams, and steaming hot springs, until her gaze settled on the ledge where they had made their home. Her brown eyes misted, but she returned her gaze to Arn's. "I feel it, too."

"I need to say something that you're not going to like," said Arn, "but it needs to be said."

She held her breath.

"I know how much you love your people," said Arn. "And they have always loved you. They don't anymore."

Carol felt as if he had kicked her in the stomach. She did not know what she had expected him to say, but this was not it.

Arn paused, then rose to his feet to gaze out in the direction of Areana's Vale. "They fear you. Worse than that, they have lost respect for you. By the time I arrived, those damned fool priests had convinced everyone that you had lost your mind. Even you feared so. And they were in the process of turning you into a drugged shell of yourself."

With a shock, Carol realized that he was right. Her assumptions about the spell book's organization had set her on the treacherous path that its author had set for her. The good people of Areana's Vale had been right to fear her. She had become obsessed, so sure of her mental prowess that she had refused to accept defeat, even when she needed to stop.

Arn turned back toward Carol, his eyes looking through her, as if seeing something far away. "I believe with all my being that you are destined to be a great leader, but a leader's job is not to be his or her people's friend. It's not even important to be liked. A leader may be feared, but she absolutely must command respect.

"For that reason, we cannot return as if nothing's happened. If you were just to go back to the vale and attempt to return to life as you knew it, there would be mobs of people ready to take action against you. Some would try to hurt you, and others would seek to undermine you at every turn."

The burning in Carol's lungs reminded her that she had not been breathing. Arn's words pulled forth a vision of the choices that lay before her, none of them pleasant. "What would you ask of me?"

"The choice is yours, but I believe that you need to reestablish your old authority and to go beyond that. You will have to make it clear that you are firmly in command of your powers and that those powers have grown beyond the people's wildest imaginings. You will also need to demonstrate that you are in no mood to tolerate opposition.

"Stage a grand entrance that will drop them to their knees in terror. You left there a crazed and broken princess. You must return, dark and terrible in your power, a wielder to be feared and respected. You will wring that respect from them in one fell stroke."

Carol stumbled to her feet, as if the effort of rising could throw off the bands that constricted her chest. Tears flooded her eyes as she motioned for Arn to stay back. She needed to get away from him, away from the terrible images his words brought flooding through her mind. She broke into a run out across the meadow, leaving him standing in place staring after her. Branches clutched at her as she disappeared into the woods on the far side and plunged down a slight incline toward the small pool hidden in the mists. She sank to her knees beside a moss-covered boulder and placed her face in her hands, sobs racking her body.

Thoughts of her childhood and young adult life among these people whom she loved chased one another through her brain. She knew them by name, hundreds and hundreds of families that she had taken the time to get to know. She had taught some of their children to read, had helped make sure the poor were fed and received medical attention above their station when required. She loved them, and they had loved her back. She could not bring herself to accept all of that was just gone.

Yet she heard her father's voice whispering at the back of her mind, telling her that leadership wasn't supposed to be easy. It was a responsibility, a skill that, if practiced correctly, ensured the well-being of those being led. Even though her sadness remained, Carol made the hard decision that her ambition dictated.

—w—

The two ate in silence that evening, brooding. After the meal, Carol informed Arn of her decision. At the first sign of spring, they would leave Misty Hollow and make their way back to the vale. As Arn moved to her side and put his arm around her shoulders, she stared off into the fading twilight.

If her people required darkness to save them, by all the gods, she would bring it.

ACKNOWLEDGMENTS

I want to express my deepest thanks to my lovely wife, Carol, without whose support and loving encouragement this project would never have happened.

I also want to thank Alan and John Ty Werner for the many long evenings spent in my company, brainstorming the history of this world, its many characters, and the story yet to be told.

Many thanks to my wonderful editor, Clarence Haynes, for once again helping me to refine my story.

ABOUT THE AUTHOR

Richard Phillips was born in Roswell, New Mexico, in 1956. He graduated from the United States Military Academy at West Point in 1979 and qualified as an Army Ranger, going on to serve as an officer in the US Army. He earned a master's degree in physics from the Naval Postgraduate School in 1989, completing his thesis work at Los Alamos National Laboratory. After working as a research associate at Lawrence Livermore National Laboratory, he returned to the army to complete his tour of duty.

Today, he lives with his wife, Carol, in Phoenix, where he writes science-fiction thrillers and fantasy—including The Rho Agenda series (*The Second Ship*, *Immune*, and *Wormhole*), The Rho Agenda Inception series (*Once Dead*, *Dead Wrong*, and *Dead Shift*), and The Rho Agenda Assimilation series (*The Kasari Nexus*, *The Altreian Enigma*, and *The Meridian Ascent*). He is also the author of *Mark of Fire*, the first book in the epic Endarian Prophecy fantasy novels.